Praise for *Shatter the Sky*

A New England Book Award Finalist
An Indies Introduce New Voices Selection
An Indies Next Pick
A 2020 Rainbow Book List Selection

"This is a fairytale for people who have never seen themselves
in fairytales before. Anne McCaffrey for the next generation,
and I absolutely devoured it."
—MACKENZI LEE, bestselling author of
The Gentleman's Guide to Vice and Virtue

"Epic storytelling and inclusive world-building. . . .
Come for the dragons; stay for the exhilarating ending that will
have you eagerly awaiting the sequel."
—MELISSA BASHARDOUST, author of *Girls Made of Snow and Glass*

"A wondrous adventure . . . I loved that queerness is
written right into the world without fear or prejudice."
—TESSA GRATTON, author of *Strange Grace*

"Perfect for fans of Tamora Pierce, Renée Ahdieh, and
Cindy Pon, *Shatter the Sky* invites the reader into a world
they will want to visit again and again."
—SAUNDRA MITCHELL, author of *All the Things We Do in the
Dark* and editor of the YA anthologies *All Out* and *All Out Now*

"A captivating debut . . . I was enchanted from the very first page."
—AUDREY COULTHURST, author of *Of Fire and Stars*

"A compelling, emotional, and satisfying read . . .
I wish I'd had books like this to read when I was a teen, and I'm so
glad I get to enjoy this lovely novel now."
—KATE ELLIOTT, author of *Court of Fives* and *Cold Magic*

Shatter the Sky

REBECCA KIM WELLS

SIMON & SCHUSTER BFYR

NEW YORK · LONDON · TORONTO · SYDNEY · NEW DELHI

SIMON & SCHUSTER BFYR

An imprint of Simon & Schuster Children's Publishing Division
1230 Avenue of the Americas, New York, New York 10020

For information about special discounts for bulk purchases, please contact Simon & Schuster Special Sales at 1-866-506-1949 or business@simonandschuster.com.
The Simon & Schuster Speakers Bureau can bring authors to your live event. For more information or to book an event, contact the Simon & Schuster Speakers Bureau at 1-866-248-3049 or visit our website at www.simonspeakers.com.
Also available in a SIMON & SCHUSTER BFYR hardcover edition
Cover design by Chloë Foglia
Interior design by Hilary Zarycky
The text for this book was set in Jenson.
Manufactured in the United States of America
First SIMON & SCHUSTER BFYR paperback edition July 2020
2 4 6 8 10 9 7 5 3 1
The Library of Congress has cataloged the hardcover edition as follows:
Names: Wells, Rebecca Kim, author.
Title: Shatter the sky / Rebecca Kim Wells.
Description: New York : Simon & Schuster Books for Young Readers, 2019. | Summary: Maren, desperate to save her kidnapped girlfriend, plans to steal one of the emperor's dragons and storm the Aurati stronghold, but her success depends on becoming an apprentice to the emperor's mysterious dragon trainer, which proves to be a dangerous venture.
Identifiers: LCCN 2018046224| ISBN 9781534437906 (hardback) | ISBN 9781534437913 (pbk) ISBN 9781534437920 (eBook)
Subjects: | CYAC: Bisexuality—Fiction. | Dragons—Fiction. | Fantasy.
Classification: LCC PZ7.1.W43557 Sh 2019 | DDC [Fic]—dc23
LC record available at https://lccn.loc.gov/2018046224

For Chris and Sarah, the originals

Shatter the Sky

CHAPTER ONE

B reathe. My lungs burned as I pushed myself to go faster up the mountain trail, keeping my eyes fixed on the girl who ran just a few steps ahead of me. Twigs snapped beneath my feet, and my bag thumped against my back with every stride. The scent of pine hung in the air around us, and the muscles in my legs strained as the path steepened. Kaia pulled farther ahead, and I could imagine her laughing at me. She had always been the faster one. *Breathe.* I lifted my gaze just enough to see the crest of the hill, the promise of sky ahead—but instead of following Kaia up and over, I darted off to the left. Navigating through the underbrush, I coasted downhill toward the narrow beach and the water that lay beyond.

The lake of Ilvera was a crystalline blue body nestled into a dip in the side of the mountain that most downmountainers didn't even know existed. As usual, the beach was empty. Most Verrans avoided this place, hating to see the ruins that loomed on the other side of the lake—a cruel reminder of all that had been lost when the tyrant conquered Ilvera. But Kaia and I never minded the solitude.

Giddy triumph caught in my chest as I reached the sand, my steps slowing. I dropped my bag and flopped down on the ground, breathing deeply. The race had seemed like a good idea at the time—something to take our minds off what was coming tonight. But I had dressed for the morning's misty weather, not this unseasonably warm afternoon. I wiped away the sweat beading on my forehead and shaded my eyes as Kaia stumbled to a stop next to me. She bent over, hands on her knees. "No fair! You cheated!"

"So you missed the turn," I said. "That's not my fault."

"You're impossible," she said.

"And what are you going to do about it?" I sat up, shrugging off my jacket.

She paused, considering. "Not a thing, Maren," she said finally, letting her bag fall off her shoulders. She arched an eyebrow. "Not a single thing."

Two boots hit the ground. A tunic and undershirt followed, and after that her trousers, and then she was laughing at me from the lake. I stripped off my clothes and splashed in after her, the frigid water raising gooseflesh on my arms and shocking the air from my lungs. I dove under and surfaced next to Kaia, gasping and laughing at the same time. The sky was clear and the sun bright, and in this instant I felt painfully small and larger than the entire mountain all at once.

Kaia's skin was a deeper brown than mine, though I tanned over the summer months—a trait I'd inherited from my Zefedi father, along with black hair so straight even the wind couldn't curl it. Her hair, on the other hand, was proper Verran: a tumbling mass of rich brown curls when dry. At present it was an unruly mess, streaming water down her back.

I reached out and tugged a curl playfully. Kaia pulled me

close, framing my face with her hands. "I missed you," she said.

"Since yesterday?"

"We were in the kitchens all day, we barely saw each other!"

I laughed, but I couldn't help kissing her. There were a lot of things I couldn't help when it came to Kaia. For a moment we treaded water, close enough to trade breaths in between kisses. Finally I forced myself to move away, slow, like thickened honey.

"I'll miss this next year," she said dreamily.

Next year. I didn't want to think of that, not now. So instead I ducked my head below the water and came up splashing. Kaia mock scowled and returned fire, which led to a brief battle that ended only when I was out of breath, my hands raised in capitulation.

"You surrender?" Her eyes were narrowed in suspicion, hands at the ready.

"I do, I do!"

"Then as the victor, I demand tribute." She tossed her hair back. "A kiss."

Her cheeks were flushed from exertion, her eyes bright and challenging. One thick curl snaked its way over her bare shoulder and dipped below the surface, and I couldn't help my gaze lingering on where her skin met water. Kaia. She looked like a goddess, a legend, one of the dragon mistresses of old. It was times like these that I felt so keenly what everyone else in our village knew to be true: She was meant for greater things.

And for some reason, she had chosen *me*.

I smiled and swam to her, put my arms around her so one hand rested on the small of her back, so I could feel my heart beating against hers, and kissed her.

✦　✦　✦

Not too long afterward we emerged from the lake and flung ourselves onto the sand. We lay side by side as the sun dried us, our faces turned up to the sky. I should have felt peaceful. The lake was our place—it had been this way since we were children. Instead, the dread that had woken me this morning reared its craggy head.

Ilvera had bustled with activity for close to a week in preparation for the Aurati seers' pilgrimage. Most people from our neighboring villages had arrived days ago, and all hands had been put to work. But now there were no more ducks to be dressed, no more buns to be stuffed. Our ceremonial attire was laid out, and the long tables in the dragon hall had been arranged in lines spanning the length of the floor, the Zefedi way. There was nothing left to do but wait.

Most Aurati were Zefedi women who acted as the emperor's watchful eyes, masquerading as administrators woven into the fabric of the empire. But the seers were different creatures, rarely seen outside the pilgrimage. Every seven years they descended from the north and toured the five kingdoms of the empire, doling out prophecies and counting up the emperor's subjects. It was said to be a service, a sign of benevolence from the emperor of Zefed, the Flame of the West.

We in the dragon mountains knew better. Prophecies might help us weather hard winters, but the Aurati's services were just the tyrant's way of keeping control over his kingdoms while he cast his eye across the waters toward his next conquest.

"You're quiet," Kaia said, interrupting my thoughts.

I let out a sigh. "I'm . . . worried. About tonight."

"What's there to be worried about? You were there last time.

We sit. Eat. Stand for a few minutes in front of some old Zefedi crone."

"They're not just some old Zefedi crones. They're *Aurati seers*. What if they decide to—"

"They won't."

"How can you know that? Mother said it happened once to a girl she knew. Even your own mothers have told stories about when their cousin was taken."

Kaia shook her head. "That was a long time ago."

"But it did happen," I said. "What's to stop it from happening again?"

Kaia pushed herself up onto one elbow, her hair falling over her shoulder. "It *won't*," she said firmly. "I won't let them. I swear. No one is getting taken by the seers tonight."

She couldn't know that. "But—"

"No more buts. Don't you trust me?"

I did, but even Kaia—fierce, lionhearted Kaia—could not promise that. Still, there was some measure of comfort to be found in her surety. I nodded.

Her face relaxed, and she smiled. "Now, enough about the seers. Come here."

It was an order I was happy to obey.

Sometime later, I was close to sleep as Kaia charted exploratory routes across my breasts and palmed my stomach, just below the indentation of my belly. The scents of damp sand and lake water were heavy in the air as I closed my eyes, awash in sensation.

"Here, that's the mountain range of Anekta," she murmured as her fingers brushed my hip bone. "We'll cross that and be free and clear until the winter sets in, then we'll turn south to the ocean." Her hand wandered lower, drawing a sigh from my lips.

"Do we have to go?" The words slipped out without thought. If I were fully awake, I would never have allowed myself to say them.

Kaia stilled. "What do you mean, do we have to go?"

"I mean . . ." The question was out—I couldn't take it back now. "Why must you always talk of leaving the mountain? What's so bad about Ilvera?"

She sighed, exasperated, one hand still flat against my skin. "We've been over this. I've always wanted to leave. You know that."

I looked past her, toward the ruins that stood on the opposite shore. Of course I knew—I'd even agreed to go with her next year. And yet . . . "Would you stay?" I whispered. "If I asked you, would you stay?"

"Oh, Maren," she said, and I couldn't bear the tone in her voice. "Don't ask me that. Please."

I tried to keep my expression neutral, even though my stomach suddenly felt queasy. I shouldn't have asked, not when I'd always suspected this answer. There was nothing I could say that would change her mind. If I did not bend, I would lose her.

I swallowed past the lump in my throat. "What about after? Adventuring will grow tiresome eventually. We can come back when . . . when we're ready to settle down."

"Maren, haven't you been paying attention? Why do you think the emperor never installed an Aurat here, when they're falling over each other in other cities? He doesn't care what happens in Ilvera, because soon enough there won't *be* an Ilvera."

My heart stumbled. Had this been true my whole life? Had I been the only fool who hadn't noticed? My mind raced, tallying up the things I'd thought inconsequential. More homegrown foods, lesser-quality cloth, fewer visitors over the years. Young Verrans like my brother Tovin going downmountain. I'd known times were difficult, but bad enough to end us? If that was the case . . .

"Don't you care?" I asked.

Her eyes shone. "I do care," she said. "But I can't change the tide. The best I can do is swim above it. With you."

That had always been her plan. But how could we turn our backs on the mountain, the lake, our families?

Kaia nudged my shoulder. "Please don't be angry with me."

I pressed my lips together and closed my eyes, ignoring her. I wasn't angry. I was terrified.

"Maren, look at me."

I opened my eyes reluctantly and turned my head to meet her gaze. She placed one warm palm against my chest, right below my collarbone.

"I promise everything is going to be fine. Better than fine." She moved closer, and I turned onto my side so that we faced each other, noses almost touching. "Shall I tell you about all the things we'll do when we leave the mountain? All the adventures we'll have in Zefed?" There was a world of enchantment tied up in that word—Zefed—as if the lake and our village and the mountain itself weren't a part of the empire of Zefed to begin with.

She settled her head against the sand and matched her fingertips to mine without waiting for an answer. "It will be spring," she said quietly, "just about this time of year, maybe a little earlier, and I know you'll want to throw the whole village into your pack, but I won't let you. We'll go down the mountain and spend a night at the inn, and then we'll go on to Deletev. From there we'll travel to Gedarin and see the ocean and then go north until we find the ice bears and finally we'll meet the Flame of the West himself and prove ourselves worthy of becoming Talons, and he'll give us dragons of our own—"

I sighed. "He'll give *you* a dragon, maybe. You'll probably save his heir's life or something, and he'll be thrilled to admit you to the dragon guard. But he wouldn't give a dragon to someone like me."

"No interrupting! Besides, he would," Kaia insisted. "If there's any saving of heirs to be done, we'll do it together."

"Even so," I said. "You'll dazzle the entire capital while I applaud from the shadows. Then he'll give you a grand title— Chief Explorer, maybe—and you'll be off across the empire, and every once in a very long while you might write a note—*Wish you were here*—and send it back to me. And I'll be hiding at the palace, faithfully awaiting your return. I could never do what you do, anyway."

Kaia reached out and squeezed my hand. "You don't really think that." The longer I was under her gaze, the more I believed she saw straight through the words I'd said only half in jest. The look she gave me was challenging, daring me to reject her declaration of my worth.

"No," I said, locking away the part of me that had let those words out in the first place. "Of course not."

"Good," she said. "Because you'll be brilliant too. You just don't know it yet."

I refrained from stating just how much I didn't know anything of the sort, because it didn't matter. Just as this talk of dragons didn't really matter, for everyone knew the emperor of Zefed would never grant a dragon to a girl from Ilvera. As long as Kaia and I were together, we would be happy. It didn't matter that she would leave without me if she had to, because I knew I could never leave her. We *were* going to be together. Even if it cost me the mountain and everything I'd ever known.

Kaia turned so that her back was to me and pulled my arm over her waist. I nuzzled my face against her neck, inhaling the distinct salt-sweet honeyed scent of her skin. Under the summer sun, we fell asleep.

The sky was purpling when I woke. We were clearly late. I shook Kaia awake, and we brushed sand off our bodies as best we could before scrambling into our trousers and shirts. We shoved our feet into our boots and trotted briskly up the beach and down the trail that my grandmother had said was once a wide road of polished white stone.

"Do you think they've arrived?" I said.

"Not yet," Kaia replied, ducking around a tangle of thistleweed. "We would have heard the horns for sure, and—"

A deep, somber note sounded in the distance, reverberating through my chest. Kaia and I looked at each other, the alarm in her eyes mirroring the fear that quickened my pulse. The Aurati seers were here.

CHAPTER TWO

Our dragon hall was the largest building the first tyrant
had left intact after conquering our mountain. It could
house all four villages of Ilvera now that so many had
gone downmountain, and it was already crowded as
Kaia and I entered through the carved stone doors. Not every
Verran was required to attend the feast before the Telling, but
most did. No one wanted to risk standing out to the Aurati as
someone who hadn't celebrated their coming.

My parents stood together, Mother in her festival dress,
purple with copper trimmings. "There you are!" She drew me
into a hug, and I could feel the tension in her body. "You're late,"
she whispered in my ear.

"I'm sorry," I said. I'd had to stop at home to wash and
change. My own dress was twilight blue, with gold ribbing
around its low collar and draped sleeves. It was impractically
long—too long to run in without holding the skirts up by my
sides—but I loved it nonetheless.

Mother nodded, though her expression said I was in for a
scolding once the Aurati had left. "Remember," she said, "don't
draw their attention."

"Such a worrier," Father teased gently. "Everything will be

fine. Just like the last Telling, and the one before that." He smiled at Kaia, who squeezed my hand one last time before walking to meet her mothers.

At that moment a hush fell over the hall, and we turned to look toward the doors. The Aurati. They were too far away to see clearly, but the crowd parted like water before them. I shivered, the momentary happiness of wearing fine things dissolving in an instant.

The possibility that the emperor might one day send his dragons to finish what his many-times-grandfather had started by burning Ilvera to the ground was a tangible danger we could turn over in our minds. The threat represented by the Aurati seers was more sinister, harder to grasp. Seeing the future was the least of their rumored abilities. If you listened to the stories, they could run for days, faster than any human, without tiring. They could cut down a man with one flash of a blade or a single prick of their poison-tipped tails. If you were fortunate enough to learn a seer's true name, you could speak it into a pool of clear water during the night of a new moon and see the future yourself—and change it. And still others claimed that instead it would call a curse down upon your family forever.

The Verran song of welcome broke the stillness and spread throughout the hall. I joined in, though the act felt wrong. Ilvera was a place of music; we sang in joy and sorrow, in supplication and in striving. But the closer the Aurati came, the more the words I sang felt tainted. Performative.

There were three seers, each wearing the dark green cloak that marked them as the Aurati elite. Their hoods were down, faces bare, but they did not speak or smile. Up close they seemed human enough, though I supposed their loose clothing could mask any number of grotesqueries underneath. Two stood almost as tall as Father, but it was the shorter one in the middle who drew my eye. The way she walked made her look almost like a snake, its head wavering, ready to strike. Behind them walked Elder Strata, the head of the Verran council, her expression stoic.

My voice faltered as the Aurati drew even with us, Mother's warning ringing in my ears. *The Aurati take girls.* This was one fact no one disputed. It didn't happen every pilgrimage, nor every other. But after the feast, during the Telling, they would sometimes claim a girl. And that girl, once taken, was never seen again. Anyone who had ever stood between the Aurati and their chosen had been cut down, their house reduced to ash and smoke as a warning to the rest of Ilvera.

I averted my gaze until they passed by, my heart thudding in my chest.

The Aurati reached the front of the hall, where a table had been set on the speaker's mound. Elder Strata ushered them to their seats and turned to face us. She raised her hands and cleared her throat. "Let us welcome the illustrious emissaries of the emperor of Zefed, the Flame of the West. Let us receive their wisdom with gratitude. Let us rejoice, for winter has come and gone, and we are the stronger for it."

She paused. From where I stood I couldn't read the expression on her face. Then she drew herself up to her full height and clapped her hands, signaling the start of the feast.

Taking care to avoid tripping over the children running about, I followed my parents to the table near the front of the hall reserved for council members and their families. Close to half of the council was already seated when we arrived, and Mother took her place, with Father and me beside her.

The feast that had taken so long to prepare wasn't as bountiful as those I remembered from the past—no swans this year, or the distinctive mulled wine that was only brewed in the kingdom of Kyseal. Our village saved and traded for months to bring those delicacies up the mountain, and this year it was clear we'd fallen short. But we did have ducks paired with cloves and bright oranges to honor Zefed, and yams, and delicate cress broth to spoon over the stuffed buns that Kaia and I had spent hours on yesterday.

The sight of the feast turned my stomach. Seven years ago I'd been too young to understand all that was happening, and I'd eaten so much candied ginger I'd been sick. Not so today. I put food onto my plate for the sake of appearances and looked about the hall.

Almost everyone was inside now, and conversation filled the space. The best cuts of meat and freshest fruit had been served to the Aurati, though their stony faces made it impossible to tell if they appreciated the honor. I didn't like them in our dragon hall. Their green cloaks were a blemish against the silvery domed ceiling and blue tiled floor.

I turned away and spotted Kaia sitting at a table across the way, leaning against her mother Thileva's shoulder. I waved, and they both smiled back.

Mother was deep in conversation with Elder Strata, her voice hushed.

"The council has already spoken on the matter. As I said

before, no good will come of it," Strata said tiredly.

"But Ilvera is weakening," Mother said. "Harvests are smaller, the things we send down to Zefed no longer turn the same profits, and our children bleed away down the mountain. The only industry here is that gods-blasted pit of slime." Her mouth twisted as she said the words—no Verran spoke about the dragon fortress at the foot of the mountain without contempt. "We need a new trade. If the emperor would only help us begin, we could make our way. But without *something* new, I fear we will wither away completely. The Aurati are his eyes and ears. They can carry our request to the Flame."

Elder Strata studied her plate intently. "You seem to believe that these are problems the emperor would remedy, if he were aware of them. But I am certain he already knows—and that this is exactly what he intends."

Silence fell over the table, and I realized that more people had been listening than I'd thought. Someone hissed that we'd best stay quiet, lest the Aurati conclude our talk was threatening enough to mention to the emperor. I looked down to find I was clenching my spoon so hard that my knuckles had whitened. I set it down carefully. So Kaia had been right. And this whole time I'd been oblivious to it all.

Father was determinedly cutting his duck into tiny pieces. Mother raised her chin but made no reply. Elder Strata nodded once. Then she pushed back from the table and swept toward the Aurati. She ascended the speaker's mound and turned to face the hall. Raising her hands, she clapped three times. It was a mark of how tense we were that silence immediately followed.

"By the grace of the Flame of the West, the Telling will now begin," she cried, her words echoing through the hall. The three Aurati stood from their seats and moved in front of the table, facing us.

The council members rose first. Everyone else followed their lead, and we formed a snaking line leading up to the mound. Each family would now approach the Aurati to be counted for the census of Zefed. Not all families would receive a prophecy, but those who did would hold the words dear. Everyone knew an Aurati prophecy came true, even if they were sometimes difficult to decipher or it took years for them to come to pass.

The only good thing about being near the front of the line was that it would be over quickly. Still, I could feel my palms growing damp as we waited. My hazy memories brought forth images of people kneeling before the Aurati, whispered pronouncements, tears—and the occasional smile. No girls had been taken last time. Kaia had been right about Ilvera; surely she was right about this, too. There was nothing to fear. Nothing except inadvertently drawing out the Aurati's wrath.

Father's hand was on my elbow as we moved forward, his other arm around Mother's shoulder. Kaia bobbed up beside us, giving me a hug. "Here," she said, opening her hand to reveal a blue button flower.

"Where did you get this?" I asked. The delicate sugar confections were flavored with infused oils and dissolved on the tongue. They were one of my favorite sweets, but they were hard to make and even harder to come by in Ilvera.

"From a trader. Here, eat it before it melts."

I popped it into my mouth, savoring the burst of ripe orange as the flower disintegrated. "Thank you," I said, giving her a quick kiss.

"It's going to be fine. You're almost done." She smiled, nodding to the front.

She had distracted me—while we'd talked, three families had already gone before the Aurati, and suddenly it was my turn. Kaia squeezed my hand and returned to her place in line with her mothers. The Aurati looked down from the speaker's mound as we approached.

The Aurat on the right frowned. Her cape was fastened securely around her neck even in the heat, and she held a long scroll of paper, the finest I'd ever seen. "Names?"

"Rashida and Ferrik Vilna," Mother said. "And our daughter, Maren."

"Rashida the council member?"

"Yes. My term ends in two years," Mother replied.

The Aurat perused her scroll. "You have a son, do you not?"

Father straightened up to his full height. "Tovin. He has gone downmountain."

The Aurat raised an eyebrow. "You're the one from Oskiath?" Father nodded shortly, though I thought the question unnecessary. It was obvious Old Zefedi blood ran in his veins, from his straight black hair and lighter brown complexion to his tall stature and the troth rings that no Verran wore. The Aurat marked something on her scroll before looking to her companion.

The shorter seer extended her hand to my mother. "Come."

Mother stepped up to the speaker's mound. The Aurat bent down and placed one hand on her forehead, one at her wrist. Her lips moved, but I couldn't hear what was said as their gazes met and held. One, two, three breaths—and then the Aurat released her, turning to Father. She repeated the ritual, though she didn't have to bend nearly so far down.

I stepped up as Father retreated. I was starkly aware of the weight of Ilvera's collective gaze. The Aurat seized my wrist and put her other hand to my forehead, fingers featherlight on my skin. It was a surprisingly delicate touch.

"Maren." Her voice was a whisper. "Tell me what you did this morning." Her eyes were so dark they were almost black. I hesitated. For my life I could not think of what could be dangerous about answering this question.

The Aurat cleared her throat, clearly impatient.

"I went for a walk. Collected berries." There. That was innocuous enough.

"And?"

I fought to keep the flush from my cheeks. The lake, and the time Kaia and I had spent there—that wasn't for them. "And then I came home to the feast."

I didn't dare blink, but the Aurat seemed satisfied. She turned to glance at her second companion, the one who hadn't spoken yet, before returning her attention to me. "Are you happy here?" she asked, her voice low. If I hadn't known better, I might have mistaken her tone for concern. But what did the Aurati care if I was happy?

I frowned. "Why would I not be?"

The Aurat nodded, releasing her hold on me. Her companion looked down at her scroll. "Fire. That is what the Aurati see written in your future."

No prophecy had fallen my way during the last Aurati

pilgrimage, and I had been too young to receive one the time before. But they couldn't all be so vague, could they? In any case, I knew there would be no further clarification. I made to step back from the mound.

"You are not dismissed."

The words cut through the air like a knife. I froze in place.

The tallest Aurat pointed to the side of the hall. "You will stand there until you are called."

Mother gasped. Frightened murmurs broke out across the dragon hall. I moved woodenly, my mind racing. The three families that had gone before us hadn't been singled out like this. They had merely been counted and sent on their way. But none of those families had girls.

Dread made the time slow to a crawl. My parents stood at a distance, their hands tightly clasped. It was almost a relief when a second girl was sent to stand at my side, for at least I was no longer alone. I waited as the hall gradually emptied. Five, seven, thirteen of us girls told to wait. Then it was Kaia's turn. She came to stand beside me, and I took her hand as she rested her head on my shoulder.

"What was your prophecy?" she whispered.

"Fire."

"That's all?"

I shrugged. "What about you?"

Kaia shook her head. No prophecy for her, then.

Her hair was falling out of its knot, and I brushed it behind her ear. "The tie broke," she said. "I didn't have time to go back for another."

"Here." I took out one of my silver clasps and passed it to her.

She smiled, and her gaze flickered to the front of the hall. "Everything's going to be all right, you know. Better than all right."

"Promise?"

Kaia straightened, putting her hands on my shoulders. "Maren. I promise."

Her words should not have comforted me as much as they did. But that was Kaia—her courage unyielding, her confidence contagious. I leaned into her embrace.

As the footsteps of the last family leaving the hall faded away, all three Aurati stepped down from the speaker's mound and walked toward us. I hadn't thought the dragon hall could feel small, but with the Aurati here, it did. The third Aurat frightened me the most now. She was pacing up and down our line like a wolf stalking its prey. I squeezed Kaia's hand as the Aurat passed. I didn't dare glance over at Mother or Father or any of the other parents of us chosen ones, knowing my own fear would be reflected on their faces.

The Aurat turned and made her way slowly back along the line. She stopped before us, her eyes fixed on Kaia.

I gripped Kaia's hand tighter still.

"Kaia," the Aurat said. "Daughter of Mena and Thileva. You will accompany us back to Lumina."

The other girls immediately fell back, leaving a semicircle of space around us. Kaia was speechless. It was the first time I had ever seen her so struck. But words clawed their way up my throat and out of my mouth before I could snatch them back. "No! You can't take her!"

Faster than I'd ever seen someone move, the Aurat reached

out and struck me across the face. I cried out, my hand covering my burning cheek.

"It is not your place to question the Aurati. You are dismissed." She turned to Kaia. "Come."

"I won't!" Kaia cried, pulling me back to her. I locked my arms around her waist, my entire body shaking.

All three Aurati raised their hands. The air stilled, as though some great beast were holding its breath. Then the lights in the dragon hall flickered, and went out.

Incomprehensible cries filled the air and suddenly there were hands on my arms, tugging and trying to pry up my fingers one by one. I felt Kaia kick out against our assailants. There was cover in the dark, if we could only—another sharp yank on my waist, pulling me backward, off my feet, and my grip broke.

"No! Kaia!"

"Maren!" Her fingernails dug into my skin, scratching as I was wrenched away.

I struggled, dragging my feet on the floor, but the arms around me were like iron and I could not get free.

"Kaia!"

"Maren!" This time Kaia's voice sounded farther away. "Maren, I'll come back to you. Whatever it takes, I'll—" Her words were cut off by the thunderous boom of doors slamming shut. The sound echoed throughout the hall, shocking me into silence. The lights flickered back on. The grip on me loosened, and I sank to the ground, the cold tile kissing my knees.

She was gone. Kaia was gone.

I began to sob, pressing my fingers against the scratches on my arms where Kaia had tried to hold me. I wished they would never fade. I wished I had been braver, done something *more*. I wished—more than anything, I wished that we were still lying under the sun at the lake, our only concern getting home before it was too dark to see.

CHAPTER THREE

The first time I see her I am five, and she sits higher up in a tree than I've ever seen anyone sit, shrieking with laughter as our minders try to coax her down.

The first time I notice her we are ten, and we've been put to work grinding cinnamon for a feast. The bowl wobbles and falls, cinnamon coating her arm. Instead of blushing and ducking her head, she touches the tip of her tongue to her forearm and sits back, mouth twisting.

"Not very good by itself," she comments to no one in particular, and I can't say why, but I take it upon myself to prove her wrong.

Moments later I'm coughing up the spice clogging my throat. She laughs at me, but it's not a laugh of malice. It's pure delight. She offers me a bowl of coarse brown sugar, and we pilfer some together, giggling at our daring, and from that moment on we are inseparable.

"Maren." I blinked, the sound of Father's voice pulling me out of the past. I looked up into his concerned face. He sat beside me at the table, not commenting on the bowl of food that had gone untouched in front of me.

"Have I ever told you the story of how I met the most beautiful woman in the world?" he asked, drawing me into a hug.

Of course he had. It had been my favorite bedtime tale

growing up—how my mother, a girl of the dragon mountain, had bewitched him so completely he gave up everything he had to follow her back to Ilvera. But today I couldn't go through the familiar motions: a smile and a shake of my head, saying that I had *never* heard such a story in my life.

When I didn't respond, Father pressed a kiss to the top of my head. "Well, let me see," he said. He turned the troth ring on his small finger around—that was the one he wore for Mother. "When I left Oskiath and traveled the other four kingdoms of Zefed, I saw many strange and wondrous things, but nothing that quenched the yearning in my heart for something *more*. Not until I got to Deletev."

"Not quite Deletev," I corrected, leaning my head against his shoulder.

"That's right. The road outside Deletev. And it was on that road that I came across a girl having a bit of trouble involving a broken cart full of starfruit. I stopped to see if I could help, and at first she told me to go away."

I smiled. Just a little.

"But I stayed, and once we determined the axle was broken, she looked down her nose at me and said she *supposed* I could help, but one wrong move and she'd cut off my fingers before I could blink.

"I agreed to her terms, of course. You don't meet a girl like that every day. So we split the fruit between our bags and started the journey up the mountain. It's a long three days uphill from Deletev to Ilvera. By the end of it I was sure that Rashida was the most beautiful woman in the world. Not only that, I knew she was among the most tenacious—when we arrived, I discovered she'd been stealing starfruit out of my bag and moving it to her own every night. That was it for me. With her, I felt at last like I was home."

He didn't mention the trials he'd had to face to convince the Verran council to allow him—an outsider with Old Zefedi blood—to stay in Ilvera, but that was a different story. I sighed, pulling away from him. "I don't see why you're telling me this *now*."

"Maren," he said, taking my hand between his own, "losing Kaia was difficult. She was special—your home, like your mother is to me."

I yanked my hand away sharply. "*Is* special. Is *radiant*." She had been the only one for me since we were ten—no other person in Ilvera had ever held my attention before or since.

"Yes, Maren. And your light burns just as bright, in your own way. You are seventeen years old. Tomorrow will come, and the next day, and I will not have you lose them all to darkness."

"But she promised that nothing bad would happen. She *promised*."

Father closed his eyes. "I know. But listen to me. This is more important than a broken promise."

"What is?"

"*You*," Father said. I was surprised by the heat in his voice. He squeezed my hand. "You have a future. You can do anything, daughter mine. And today what you're going to do is go outside for a walk. In the forest."

"I can't."

"You can. You love the forest."

"I love her," I said, hot tears pricking the edges of my eyes, "and I didn't tell her one last time, when they came, and—" It was too much. My face twisted, and I broke, tears spilling down my cheeks anew. She was gone. She was gone forever.

I'll come back to you. But no one taken had ever returned.

"Oh, my child. She knows." Father's Zefedi accent was stronger than usual as his voice filled with emotion. For a long time he held me as I cried.

I lingered as long as I could while changing into a presentable outfit, but when I had finished, Father was there with a wrapped parcel of steamed buns and an encouraging smile that swept me out the door. At the edge of the forest I paused under the first hanging branches. With Kaia, the world had seemed navigable. By myself, it was unimaginable. I considered turning back, but I knew I would not be able to meet my father's eyes if I returned so soon.

I could do this. I *would* do this, if only this.

One foot in front of the other. There was the tree where we'd leaned the morning before the Aurati had come. If I closed my eyes, I could still feel Kaia's lips against mine, our fingers intertwined as we'd kissed. There was the fork in the trail that led to the brambleberry bushes and the place where Kaia had traced a circle on my palm with her finger and whispered her dreams of adventures outside of Ilvera for the very first time. There, the first fight we'd had—the first time I'd asked her not to leave our village, before I'd realized that on this subject, she was unshakable. Memory washed through me so viscerally it hurt, but now that I had started this walk, I felt I had to see it through.

I counted my breaths, trying to distract myself from the building pressure in my chest. If I started sobbing, I was afraid that I wouldn't be able to stop.

Up and up and up I climbed, the summer clouds giving way to full afternoon sun too bright for my thoughts. I could not go down to the beach. Instead I circled the lake slowly, keeping a generous buffer of forest between the water and myself as I made my way around to the other side: the dragon ruins of Ilvera.

The first humans to climb the mountain had been Lirusan explorers who bonded with the dragons native to this region, creating a society neither human nor dragon, but somewhere in between. This became Ilvera, one of four great clans, each settled on their own mountain peak. But when the first emperor of Zefed had waged war on us, he'd quickly whittled them down to one. And when he could not defeat Ilvera through battle outright, he'd stolen our dragons, tearing out the mountain's beating heart.

Ilvera was claimed by the empire, and our lands were swept up into the kingdom of Eronne, though only the foolhardy or very powerful would dare call us Zefedi to our faces. Zefed was the outsider, the invader, the tyrant. We were Verran only, and would always be so. My ancestors had rebuilt our clan, but even now, generations later, our people let these ruins be. For this was the old seat of Ilvera's power, the bones of where the dragons themselves had dwelt. A memorial to all that we'd lost.

Even at a fraction of their original size, the ruins made me marvel at how many people must once have lived here—and how many dragons. Most buildings had been destroyed during the invasion, but here and there were intact foundations, even a stubborn wall or two of white stone. My favorite place was the corner of what I could only imagine had been some grand dragon lair, as the remaining pillars stretched at least ten times my height into the air. There was a lonely staircase here that hugged the wall, climbing to nowhere.

I picked my way through the rubble and lay down across the bottom stair, stretching out my legs. It was hot enough that I was sweating, but I didn't mind the warmth of the stone against my back. I hated to admit that Father was right, but I did prefer being out here to lying curled up on my bed in a dank darkness that only amplified what I was feeling inside. I sighed, put my hat over my face, and closed my eyes.

I run, my footsteps echoing down the hall. There is a room ahead of me with doors—eight, all closed. Screams rend the air—Kaia! I have to find her. I choose at random, fling open the door. Behind it stand three Aurati, naked blades in their hands, and I slam the door shut. The second door hides a lion, the third only a stone on the ground. The fourth is locked—I slam my shoulder against it, once, twice, before it finally gives way. I stumble into a black cavern that glows like coals in a dying fire, and I sense there is something monstrous there in the shadows, but I cannot see it.

I started upright, disoriented, heart pounding. It took a moment to remember where I was, to sink back into my body. The dream hadn't been a nightmare, not exactly. But it had been overwhelming, and it lingered like a cobweb in my mind as I rubbed my eyes. The adrenaline was still racing through me, and I got to my feet, dizzy and restless. I stretched my arms above my head and shook out my legs, looking up at the sky. It was late afternoon now. Father would be pleased I'd stayed out so long.

Before heading back, I climbed the staircase, tracing the carved patterns and claw marks that still showed on the wall. What must it have been like, humans and dragons living side by side? I would have given almost anything to see Ilvera as it once had been.

At the peak of the staircase I could look out all the way down the mountain to the fortress that sat at its base. The black complex was massive—almost large enough to be its own village. My lip curled with distaste.

After the emperor of Zefed had stolen our dragons, he had wanted to remove them completely from the influence of the mountain. So he sent them across the plains to the west, back to his homeland. He would have succeeded, had it not been for what happened next: The dragons began to die. No one knew exactly how many kits died under unfamiliar skies during this time, but it was enough to force the tyrant to bring them back to our mountain. Now, while full grown dragons were free to roam with their masters, the emperor's Talons, the kits were raised here.

Given our history with dragons and wary of an uprising, the emperor forbade Verrans from working at the fortress—not that any of us would stoop so low. So the complex remained a blight on the face of Ilvera, a place that bragged only of what we had lost.

I squared my shoulders. The emperor had been right to fear us. If the stories were to be believed, our ancestors flew on the backs of dragons and breathed fire themselves. How they would scorn me now. I was just a frightened girl with a broken heart, and no hope for a future.

A fresh wind blew across my face, and the sunburned stone warmed the palms of my hands, and as I looked down the mountain, a thought bloomed in me. A dangerous thought.

I am a dragon girl without a dragon. But what if I got one? What could I do then?

CHAPTER FOUR

The part of me that knew the thought was absurd—the part that would have dismissed it as a wisp of daydream—was silent. In its place was a strange fire that grew bolder every second that passed. I grabbed my pack and left the ruins at a trot, the sun just beginning its descent toward the mountain. Father had been right—I could not allow myself to wallow in darkness. But that didn't mean leaving Kaia to fade into memory. I could see it now. With a dragon, I would hold the same strength that fueled the tyrant's army. Whatever power the Aurati possessed would be no match for it. If I had a dragon, I could storm their stronghold. I could steal Kaia back.

It was an impossible idea, and yet now that it had presented itself, it felt inescapable. Which led to the next, unavoidable question: How could I possibly get my hands on a dragon? I didn't know as much about our history as most of Ilvera's elders, but I knew there was no way I could take an adult dragon. For one thing, the adults were rarely brought back to the mountain. For another, even if one did appear, it would already be bonded to a Talon. By all accounts, that bond was unbreakable. So if I wanted a dragon, it would have to be a young one that was not yet bonded.

I slowed to a walk. The fortress. If I wanted a dragon, I would have to get inside. It was the only way.

An ache had settled just behind my eyes, and I rubbed at my temples. The thought was simple, but making it into reality . . . I felt dizzy, exhaustion beckoning me to sleep. At the same time, the despair that had swallowed me last night had finally been beaten back. There was rage in its place, a heat that burned in my chest and demanded action, and I would not let it go. I was going to get Kaia back, no matter what it took.

By the time I was home, I'd prepared my strategy. Father would easily swallow the lie I was about to tell. It was Mother who would be harder to convince. She was back from her council meeting when I arrived, lying on the ground outside the house with her head resting against a large flat stone. She turned her head as I approached, eyes shaded by a hand.

"Finally! I was beginning to think you'd gotten lost."

A joke. No daughter of Ilvera would ever be lost on this mountain. I shrugged.

"And how was your walk?"

"Fine," I said.

"Just fine?" she said, her voice suspiciously nonchalant. She sat up. Her long brown hair was still plaited and swept up in the council braids, making her look even more commanding than usual.

The best way to catch my mother's attention was to act indifferent. Now she watched me the way a stellar hawk watched an unsuspecting rabbit—exactly the way I'd hoped she would.

"Well . . . there is something." I sat down across from her. "Promise you won't be mad?"

"Of course."

I took a deep breath. "I was thinking of going downmountain."

Whatever she'd been expecting, it wasn't this. She tried to mask her surprise, but I could still see it in the way her eyebrows lifted, just slightly. "Downmountain? Really?"

I looked down at my hands. "I love Ilvera. So much. But Kaia's gone, and it's hard to be here right now. Maybe I need to be someplace new. Somewhere she hasn't been. Just for a while."

Mother frowned. "Maren, this seems drastic."

Father leaned his head out of our front window. "What's drastic?"

"I want to go downmountain," I said. "Not for forever, just a little while, Father. I feel . . . restless."

He looked at Mother. "Come inside, both of you. Talk's better with food, and supper's ready."

I followed Mother inside. Supper was a chicken soup with fresh bread and pickled vegetables spiced with peppers so hot my nose watered as I entered the kitchen. Father's gaze dropped instantly to my full bag, and I realized that I'd completely forgotten the food he'd given me.

"Not hungry?"

"I forgot," I said. I sat down at the table, on edge. At the ruins I had felt vibrant and alive. Being home again reminded me only of how I'd woken up this morning. I couldn't go back to feeling that way.

Mother sat down next to me, arms crossed. Father passed full bowls across the table. I knew what they were thinking about. Tovin had left the mountain too, and hadn't been back since. But that had been only two years ago—not such a long time to be gone, considering how far he had traveled. We'd received letters from so many places.

"I think you going downmountain is a fine idea," Father said finally.

Mother glared. "Ferrik!"

"Why not?"

"Don't you think it's a little soon for her to make these kinds of decisions?"

"In Oskiath people leave their homes for apprenticeships when they're much younger than me. Don't they, Father?" I said, as indignant as if I truly did mean to go downmountain and find an innocent way to occupy myself for a season or two.

"Well, this isn't exactly Oskiath, is it?" Mother snapped.

"What's wrong with wanting to see something besides this mountain for the rest of my life?" I argued back. I was almost crying now, though I couldn't say why.

Father moved, placed an arm around my shoulder. "There's nothing wrong with it," he said gently.

"No," Mother said, her voice strained. "I just never thought it was something you truly wanted. You were never like Tovin."

"We were always going to leave someday. You knew that."

The droop in her shoulders told me that despite knowing the plans Kaia and I had made, she had hoped I wouldn't go. And I couldn't even fault her. Before Kaia, I would never have willingly left the mountain.

"Best to leave this be for now, little one," Father said. "Your mother and I need to speak about it."

I knew when to make a strategic retreat. The rest of the

meal was quiet, each of us occupied by stormy thoughts.

Long after most lanterns had been dimmed for the night, light still shone under the door of my parents' room. In the morning they would present a united front, no matter the decision. If I wanted to know more of what they thought individually, this was the only time to find out. After going through the motions of preparing for sleep, I got out of bed and crept over to my parents' room.

"She's too young," I heard Mother say.

"You know that's not true," Father replied.

"She won't be safe."

"Staying here does not guarantee safety. She's almost grown. She needs more than Ilvera can offer."

"But she's *mine*," Mother said, her voice breaking. "She's my daughter, a true Verran. This mountain is meant for her."

A pause. "Zefed is changing. So is Ilvera. A season spent away will benefit the mountain, when she returns."

"And what if she doesn't?"

"Rashida, she isn't happy. Even if she meant not to return, you could not hold her here in a cage. Not even to keep her safe. It would crush her."

There was a strange, muffled sound, and an ache bloomed in my chest as I realized what it was. My mother was crying. I backed away from the door as Father began to sing, a Zefedi lullaby about a pair of river otters building a den. I'd heard enough. To linger was wrong, an intrusion into something I had no place seeing.

They were waiting in the kitchen in the morning. I did my best to look apprehensive, even knowing what I'd overheard.

"We're in agreement," Father said. "You may go down-mountain."

"Thank you!" I felt a rush of relief. "Thank you, thank you!"

Mother smiled. There was no sign of tears in her eyes, though she was quiet and slow to move. "Your father has friends in Deletev. He'll write a letter of introduction for you to carry."

Deletev. I couldn't go there. It was so close they might come down to check up on me. I bit my lip. "I wasn't thinking of Deletev," I said. "Maybe . . . Oskiath?"

Oskiath was the northernmost kingdom in Zefed and had the advantages of being both far away and Father's homeland.

"Oskiath?" My parents exchanged a glance. "That doesn't have anything to do with the Aurati, does it?" said Mother hesitantly.

I blinked, surprised. Lumina, the Aurati stronghold, was in the north, but its proximity to Oskiath hadn't even occurred to me when I'd tossed out the name. "No," I said, a little dismayed at my oversight. "That's not it at all." Though I *would* have to pass through Oskiath to get to it—to Kaia.

"Are you sure?" Father said. "It's a long way to go."

I drew on everything Father had told me about the kingdom where he had been born. "It would be an adventure. I could walk the Bridge of Ankarin and eat winter peaches and see the ice bears," I said, citing the mystical creatures that had featured in many of Father's childhood stories. "And maybe I could meet Cousin Gemed?"

Father's shoulders tensed. "You'll see ice bears, if you're there through the winter. But that pile of scorched dirt stopped being my cousin when he started working *there*." Like a Verran, he did not name the dragon fortress in speech, but it was clear what he was talking about. "I can address you to someone else. Perhaps Katelin. She was a friend to my mother and lives in Belat."

I looked down and let my hair fall over my face, hoping to disguise my excitement. Gemed and Father had grown up together in Oskiath, but they hadn't spoken since Gemed took a job at the fortress. Father had complained loudly about it when he'd heard—but that had been years ago. I hadn't been sure he was still there, or even alive. Now at least I'd have one potential contact at the fortress.

When I trusted myself to be able to keep my expression straight, I looked up again. "I don't understand why he would work there."

"Working with the dragons is considered an honor among the Zefedi people. It's not difficult to understand why he would jump at the opportunity."

"But he was your family," I said.

Father shrugged. "When I knew him, he had little interest in that path. But time can change many things."

Mother waved a hand dismissively. "Enough about that. You have a journey to prepare for."

I smiled at her. "Thank you, so much."

"You're getting too old to ask for permission anyway," she said, smiling ruefully.

Easy. That was the word that kept ringing through my head after I left the kitchen table. It had been easy to get my parents to agree to what I'd asked—were they so worried about me that they would have agreed to anything I proposed? I suddenly felt guilty for taking advantage of their concern for me, but I brushed the feeling aside. Instead, I thought about how I might be able to convince Cousin Gemed to help me into the fortress, despite the falling-out he'd had with Father.

The first step would be to get close to the fortress entrance without being turned away or killed outright. I was helped by the fact that I took after my father in physical appearance much more than my mother. Most differences in my build and facial features I could credit to a Lirusan grandmother. There was no reason for anyone to suspect Verran ancestry—as long as I played the part right. All I needed now was some Zefedi clothing. And I knew exactly where I could get some.

Mena opened the door when I knocked. "Maren," she said. "Come in."

I stepped over the threshold, and she immediately enveloped me in a tight embrace.

"Would you like some tea? I'm sorry Thileva won't be able to visit with you. She's . . . not up to seeing people just now." Mena stepped back and wiped at her eyes, then turned to bustle around the kitchen in search of a suitable cup.

I didn't need to imagine how Thileva was feeling. I shifted uncomfortably from foot to foot. Since I'd decided on my path, I'd been seized by a growing certainty about what I meant to do. I was so determined that I was almost afraid to linger too long on anything outside of this quest, for fear that my newfound resolve would splinter apart. All that mattered was getting the dragon that would enable me to save Kaia, and everything I did had to be in pursuit of that aim.

"I'm sorry," I said.

Mena poured hot tea into a cup. "Everyone is, these days. Strata came to extend the sympathies of the council—sympathies, after we begged them to help get her back. 'Nothing to be done,'" she mocked Strata, pursing her lips in disgust. "Spineless, that's what she is."

She sighed. "I shouldn't be talking this way. But it's been difficult, not just because she was our daughter. That girl could have done anything. I wouldn't have been surprised to hear she tamed a great whale, or treated with the emperor himself. She was better than this place. Better than all of us. But now, shackled to the Aurati? What a *waste*."

"Mena," I said, eager to be finished with this conversation. "I don't mean to overstep, but I was wondering . . ."

"What?"

"We didn't get to say a true good-bye. I was hoping you might let me sit in her room."

Mena blinked, her eyes wet. "Of course. Take all the time you need."

I nodded.

Kaia's room was at the front of the house, with a window that caught the sun in the morning. Bed against one wall, a large trunk at its foot with clothing splayed haphazardly across the top. A small bronze mirror lay in the corner, clasp open.

Heartache struck me like a blow, and I sank to my knees. The room still smelled like her—a lick of salt, a spoon of honey, something else I couldn't describe but was intangibly *her*. She might have just stepped out for a walk. What were the Aurati doing to her? Had she tried to escape? What use could the Aurati possibly have for someone who didn't want to join their ranks?

I pressed my face against the bedclothes, squeezing my eyes shut. I would not cry. I had no time for tears; I was here for a purpose. I was going to get her back. Everything was going to be fine.

I failed. There, surrounded by reminders of Kaia, I cried.

Eventually my tears subsided into sniffly hiccups, and I sat back on my heels. I pushed the clothing off the trunk and lifted the lid. Here were Kaia's treasured possessions. The vial of star anise oil gifted to her by her grandfather. A carved dragon figurine small enough to fit in my palm and a companion ice bear. A woven shawl from Kyseal that contained all the colors of a sunset. The dried bouquet of leaves I'd collected for her just as the summer was fading last year, when I'd promised to travel with her away from Ilvera. I handled these carefully as I lifted them out of the box, hunting for the bag I knew would be near the bottom.

Traders from Gedarin had come up the mountain two years ago—unusual, considering the difficulty of the journey. I'd been under the influence of a head cold, but Kaia's enthusiasm buoyed me out of it as we wandered through the makeshift market they'd set up. She'd gushed over the carved wooden figurines and exclaimed over the fashions, and we'd eaten far too many stuffed peppers, until my father had called me in for the night. I'd snuck away to purchase the dragon for her birthday, and she'd bought a few outfits in the Zefedi style, all loose flowing lines and earth tones. I scrunched up my nose. Everyday Zefedi clothing was boring, but I was thankful in this moment that Kaia had purchased them.

There were two Zefedi tunics, a pair of long trousers, and

a dress in the trunk. I bundled them down as tightly as I could and shoved them into my pack. The dragon figurine caught my eye once more as I reached up to close the trunk—I snatched it and stashed it away as well.

I didn't look back as I left her room.

CHAPTER FIVE

Rough stones underfoot, pounding heart. I waited until they were all asleep—I've discovered Aurati are women like anyone else, no claws beneath their cloaks, no poison-tipped tails—and I cut the cords that bound my wrists with the knife I hid under my sleeve. Now I run, hair whipping in the wind. I'm a Verran girl, and this is a forest like any other. First I'll find the river, then follow it home—to Maren. Whatever it takes.

A branch cuts across my cheek and I slip, my ankle turning on the uneven stones. I fall hard. Something strikes me in the ribs and I gasp for breath. Someone yanks me upright, cold laughter filling the air. I can hear the sound of rushing water, but now there are new cords pulled tight around my wrists. We march back to the camp, my ankle throbbing with pain. They knew I would try this. They let me try anyway, knowing they could catch me. The knowledge beats into me with every step. I've lost, and for the first time, I am truly afraid.

The morning I was to leave for Oskiath I woke with a pit in my stomach. My eyes were heavy from lack of sleep—my nightmare had felt so real. I had *been* Kaia, had felt her heart beat like it was my own . . . but that wasn't possible. I tried to shake it off as I rechecked my bag. Enough coin to put me on a wagon going north, clothing to keep me warm, a sleeping mat—I forced my hands to still. I'd packed and unpacked enough over the last few days to know the contents by heart. It was time.

Mother was cooking this morning—a rare occasion. She turned around as I entered and set a stack of golden honey cakes on my plate, drizzled with the remains of the blackberry syrup from last summer. Her eyes were red, but she still made a credible effort at a smile as she sat down next to me. I was quiet too, the remnants of the dream still clinging to my thoughts as I ate.

"It's silly," she said after a while. "But every time your father goes on a trip, I fear he won't return. It's been this way since Tovin went downmountain. And now you . . ."

I was surprised. This was a different side of my mother, who was normally brash and quick to speak, even quicker to anger. Now she sighed and put an arm around my shoulder.

"I wish you wouldn't go, but I know I can't stop you."

I wanted to say something reassuring, to tell her I would come back, even though I knew that was far from certain. Instead I said, "I had a dream about her."

"About Kaia?"

I nodded. "She was afraid. She tried to run from the Aurati, but they caught her. It felt so *real*. Like . . . like I *was* her."

Mother tilted her head, looking at me intently. "Have you had dreams like this before? Dreams that felt real in the same way?"

I bit my lip. "Right before I decided to leave. I had a dream that I came to a room with many doors. I was looking for Kaia, but when I opened one of the doors, I found something else—a monster, I think." I frowned. "That never happened, though. My dream about Kaia last night, it seemed like it was really happening."

Her expression shifted. Just slightly, as though something had fallen into place.

"What is it?" I asked.

"Maren, I—can't be sure." She folded her hands in front of her on the table. "What you're describing *sounds* like a dragon dream. But that would be impossible."

"Why?"

"In the time before, some Verrans walked the sleep of dragons. Through dreaming they shared the dragons' visions. I understand being chosen like this was a sign of immense favor."

Of course that was impossible. I could not be having dragon dreams when there was no dragon nearby whose sleep I might walk. The tyrant had taken them all. And yet . . .

"What sort of visions?" I asked.

"Dragons are believed to dream truly. Perhaps your dream showed things that have actually happened. Or will happen in the future. Anyway, the stories are vague when it comes to the whats and wherefores. Maybe the vision was meant as some sort of message for you. Or maybe it was just a dream."

I waited, but she didn't say anything else. "What should I do?"

"You shouldn't disregard them. Take heed. I wish I knew more to tell you." She looked down at her hands. "But enough about that. Listen to me now. Your father may tell you things about how the people are downmountain. What to expect. And you listen to him well, but you have to know. Ferrik is ours, yours and mine. But he is also one of *them*. When he leaves Ilvera, he can still move as a man of Zefed. His experiences cannot be a guide for your own."

I shrugged off her warning. "I'll be fine, Mother. Tovin was fine."

"And I told Tovin the same thing." She squeezed me in a tight hug. "I just want you to be *careful*. Use your father's name—go by ben Gao, not Vilna. Find the people he suggests, and keep to yourself. Don't start trouble."

"I won't."

"Promise me."

"I promise," I said.

She nodded sharply. "Good. Then go wash up. You have to be presentable."

Presentable? It was a three-day journey to the base of the mountain. Anything presentable now would be travel-mucked long before its end. But I finished breakfast and washed my face anyway, then brushed out my hair and braided it neatly.

Father met us at the door. "Time to go."

"How far are you coming?" I said.

"Just to the bridge."

I smiled. The road to Deletev paralleled the Serpent, the river that flowed down from the lakes to the base of the mountain. We would reach the bridge that crossed it late in the afternoon—more than a safe distance before I would deviate from the path my parents had laid out. For now I would be glad of my father's company.

Mother framed my face with her hands. "My dragon daughter." She hummed a short melody, the first refrain of a safe-traveling song. Father and I joined in, and for a moment we all stood, a wobbly musical huddle in the doorway. Finally Mother sniffed and stepped back. "You are the daughter of my heart," she said. "Remember that."

"I love you," I said.

One more hug all around and then we were out, the road before us.

I had to squint against the morning light. It made everything too bright, too hot. The ache that had settled in my chest flared as we passed through Ilvera proper, heading toward the forest trails I'd walked so many times before. I loved this place— the houses built against the insides of the old halls, nestled together like birds in a storm. The sweeping gardens, the communal songs that woke the village in the morning and soothed us to sleep at night. Now I was leaving it, everything I had never wanted to bid farewell to, for a reckless, dangerous chance. A single stray hope so ludicrous it was almost laughable.

We walked on. The season was in our favor, as rain or snow would have forced us to carry more equipment than we did now. But my pack grew heavier just the same, the straps digging deeper into my shoulders with each passing hour. My thoughts began to wander. What if I could not take a dragon? What if I slipped up and revealed myself as an imposter? What if I couldn't even make it into the fortress to begin with?

"You look so worried. Try not to be," Father said.

I looked up. It was the first he'd spoken since we'd left. "How can I *not* worry?" I said.

"It's true there will be much that exists outside your control. But that's what this journey is for: to discover Zefed. And yourself."

"I just don't want to be unprepared."

"Sometimes you can't help but be unprepared."

I didn't have anything to say to that, so I only nodded.

It was close to midday when Father stopped at the edge of a rocky outcropping. "There," he said, raising a hand to point.

From this height I could see the Serpent split halfway down the mountain. The first half, the one we were following, meandered gently down the mountainside. Its other half swerved and carved a steep trail across the rock before breaking again over an outcrop into two waterfalls that descended like a parted curtain on either side of the mountain face. A peninsula of land jutted out from the mountain between them, enclosed by high man-made walls.

Inside the walls, I could see the tops of trees near the mountain and a large stone courtyard farther away from the falls. A tall, freestanding structure sat in the center of that courtyard, its black stone towers sharpened to fine points that pierced the sky. The fortress itself. I couldn't stop the involuntary shiver that ran across my skin, and I turned away, not yet ready to face it. Father wrapped me in a one-armed hug as we retreated from the outcropping. "It's an evil place," he said softly. "I'm thankful we're well away from it."

I was thankful when the path curved back into the forest and the trees blocked the view once more.

"What do you think happened to Gemed? You said he wasn't the sort for . . . that kind of work."

Father huffed. "*Maren.*"

"I want to know. Truly. He was your cousin."

"That was a long time ago."

"*Father.*"

"All right, all right." He shook his head. "Gemed—he always had a flair for the dramatic. He never talked of the fortress, but he loved the dragons. Every time a Talon came through our town, he was a burr in their side. Chafed him a bit, that his family wasn't high enough to be considered for the dragon guard. That could be why."

To be closer to the dragons. The thought that I had something in common with a man who would serve the tyrant's regime willingly was nauseating. But perhaps that was something I could take advantage of.

"What about his family?"

"His parents wouldn't have minded. He doesn't have a heartmate of his own, at least not the last I heard." His expression turned even more somber. "Let's leave this behind, youngling. It's no talk for lifting spirits."

When the sun reached its highest point in the sky, we stopped to eat near the Serpent. It was a comfort to have the water at our side as we ate the buns and brambleberry cake Father had packed. I flopped backward onto the blanket we'd spread out. The shade under the trees was a welcome respite from the heat. After tying together his pack, Father stretched out beside me, resting his head on his hands.

"All right?" he asked quietly.

"Just sore. It's nothing."

"You know, you don't have to do this, Maren."

"What do you mean?" I sat up, crossing my arms. "I *want* to."

"It was difficult for your mother to let you go. For me, as well. I know you may have felt pressured to make a change. But

I wanted to say this too. You don't need to leave home to prove a point."

Suddenly I found it difficult to swallow. I wished I'd spoken more to them before I left. I wanted—I wanted them to know what I was truly doing. But if I told Father now, I would never take another step. Mother was the firebrand of the two of them, but if Father knew that I intended to steal a dragon from the emperor of Zefed, I would never leave our house unescorted again.

"I need this," I said, allowing my voice to crack. "Since Kaia was taken, I just—I can't stay in Ilvera. Not right now."

"I know. We're just . . . worried."

Worried. As if he could even begin to understand. I knew most of our village had assumed Kaia and I would part ways eventually. She was meant for greater things than one mountain, one girl. But for me it had been Kaia without thought, without question. Once she was in my life, I'd never considered a world without her at the center. Now that she was gone, the only thing that even began to fill that emptiness was the task I'd put myself to.

"I'm not changing my mind." I stood up. "Let's go."

I was grateful that he did not try to break the silence that fell into the space between us. It surprised me how quickly we settled into a rhythm. Father and I hadn't walked this way in some time. In fact, now that I thought about it, I couldn't remember the last time it had been only the two of us walking together. For years it had been Kaia and me, and rarely anyone else. Gradually, my black mood began to improve.

An hour or so later we stopped again by the Serpent to drink, and I wiped sweat from my forehead. Early summer still, but it was already clear that this would be a dragon year in truth. The heat beat down upon us even through the trees, and as evening approached, I was more than ready to drop my pack and collapse.

Father had given me various pieces of advice for traveling throughout Zefed, the first of which was: Don't refer to the downmountainers as Zefedi, as most Verrans did. Doing so would mark me as an outsider, something to be avoided these days. Instead, I should say I was from Eronne, and identify others by their kingdom of origin as well. It's a difficult time in Zefed, he'd said, and better to keep your head down than get entangled in a conflict you don't understand.

When the bridge came into view at last, Father pulled me into his arms. "I'm going to miss you."

"Me too," I whispered, a lump forming in my throat. I hugged him tightly.

"When you get to Deletev, go to the Braided Coil. When you get there, ask for Harik and give him my papers. He'll help you find safe passage to Oskiath."

I nodded.

He had to know that the longer he stayed the less likely I was to continue on. So he stepped back and smiled and ruffled my hair. "Well, be on with you," he said gruffly. "No time like the present."

"Right," I said.

I watched as he started back up the trail and waited until he was out of sight. I blinked hard against the tears that gathered at the corners of my eyes. Several shaky breaths shuddered through me.

And then I turned and walked on.

I camped early, telling myself that it was because I wanted a good start in the morning. In truth, my back ached, and my feet were swollen and red. After laying out my mat and settling upon it, I reached into my pack and closed my fingers around the carved dragon I'd taken from Kaia's room.

I felt slightly guilty about taking it without Mena's permission but tried as best I could to banish the thought. The dragon felt like I was holding a piece of my bond with Kaia in my hand. I couldn't have left it. *Whatever it takes.*

In the morning I felt as though I hadn't slept at all. At least no nightmares had visited me—they were disquieting, even if they were some sign of favor. I walked down to the stream and waded straight in, the cold water shocking me into a semblance of waking. After washing, I squelched back onto solid ground. In this heat I would be dry soon enough.

Now I was glad to be alone. Even in my father's careful presence, every attention I was paid had felt like a weapon probing against the shell I'd put up.

The day passed quickly, and I began to doze off shortly after making camp that night, my exhaustion flattening any compulsion I might have had to think too long on what was to come. This was just as well, for tomorrow I would reach the base of the mountain.

CHAPTER SIX

I n anticipation of arriving at the fortress, I changed into my
Zefedi clothing. The trousers were slightly too short and the
tunic hung loose, but it was good enough, I hoped. I belted
on the hunting knife that Mother had insisted I carry—if I
needed it, it would be of little help stuffed away. Then I brought
out a small leather pouch from my pack. I upended it over my
palm. Out fell a simple silver ring, tarnished slightly by time and
inattention.

Father had made it for me during one of his trips downmountain when I was a child—a troth ring. The Zefedi wore
them to represent their bonds, each placement signifying a
different important relationship. This one was for family, and
I slipped it over the pointer finger on my right hand. If I had
grown up in Zefed, I would have made one of my own to go
over the smallest finger on my left hand, for my bond with Kaia.
Every child of Zefed was taught how at the age of fourteen. The
act of making a troth ring signified the Zefedi coming of age,
when one was considered old enough to take responsibility for
their own promises, debts, and relationships. We didn't have
the tools in Ilvera, so I'd only learned the theory of it, not the
practice.

I tied my Verran clothing in a knot and buried it in the soft earth under the tree that had hosted me for the night. In truth I should have burned it, leaving no trace even for the keenest of searchers, but I couldn't bring myself to destroy it. Then I pulled the pack over my shoulders and stood upright, taking a deep breath. Everything I'd done up until now could be undone with little effort. I could turn around and walk back up the mountain. My parents would welcome me with relief.

This would no longer be the case once I arrived at the wayfarers' inn. The inn at the base of the mountain served as the last stopping point for travelers on their way to the fortress. As a result, most Verrans avoided it despite its convenient location. But I needed a place to settle myself before I arrived, and witnesses who would be able to corroborate at least part of my journey. The inn would provide both.

I kept my distance at first, circling the building, so that by the time I made my final approach it appeared as if I had traveled from Deletev. The inn was large and simply built, constructed for endurance rather than aesthetics. I slowed the closer I got, running through my list in my head. *Clothing. Point of origin. Troth ring. Backstory. I was traveling to the fortress to visit an uncle and inquire about work.* I'd already decided not to change my name. Father had named me for his grandmother, and Maren was a common enough name in Zefed not to draw particular notice on its own.

Still, I was second-guessing myself right up to the door, and was so nervous that when it opened, I almost let slip the traveler's song out of habit.

Instead I put three fingers to my forehead and bowed my

head to greet the innkeeper in the Zefedi way. "Do you have a room available for the night?" I asked in Zefedi, doing my best to imitate Father's accent.

"Three feathers," she said, barely glancing at me. "Supper included."

I dug in my pocket and pulled out the coins I'd separated from my purse this morning. Father had warned me about how expensive things were likely to be. I'd set aside five feathers for the inn, knowing it was probably too much, but I hadn't wanted the vulnerability of scrounging around in my pack after coming up short.

I dropped the feathers into the innkeeper's hand. She bit down on each in turn and, satisfied, waved me through.

There were only a few people downstairs, as it was early in the day. The innkeeper sorted through a key ring on her belt and selected one. "Here," she said. "That's the third room on the right, second floor. Supper's served after the sun sets."

"Thank you," I said. She shrugged and retreated to a table near the door. Were all Zefedi so inhospitable? At least her directions were clear, once I'd crossed the room and found the stairway. My key turned easily in the lock, and the door opened onto a small room furnished with a bed and a standing washbasin with a chair and a mirror. I locked the door behind me, then let out a deep breath of pent-up tension.

So far, a success. The innkeeper hadn't remarked on anything out of the ordinary about my appearance. No one had looked at me askance. The room seemed secure enough.

I emptied my pack onto the bed and sorted out its contents. Clothing and bedroll to one side. A water skin and a knotted cloth containing the remnants of my travel rations. The purse, the carved dragon, my one remaining silver hair clasp. A map of the five kingdoms of Zefed and the letters of introduction that Father had written for me. I took them out now and unfolded them.

I'd read both already. In one Father addressed himself to a general audience, stating my identity and reason for travel to Oskiath. The other was a list of people, including locations and their relation to Father, who I could presumably trust and approach for help. It was Father's intention that I seek out Katelin in Belat.

I refolded the list and stowed it away. They were names I wouldn't use. The letter I kept out. I would need it tomorrow.

Having reassured myself that everything was accounted for and that to any reasonable eye I looked like exactly who I claimed to be, I packed it all up again. Now there was nothing to do but wait.

My stomach was growling fiercely by the time the sun set. I'd debated whether to go down for supper—it would be an opportunity for my facade to slip—but decided eventually that it would be more suspicious for an exhausted traveler *not* to take full advantage of a hearty meal. So when the smells of food cooking wafted upstairs, I locked the door to my room and went downstairs.

The main dining room was much more crowded than when I'd arrived, and I entered hesitantly. Something seemed off to me, and I swept my gaze around the room for the source of my unease. When the answer came to me, I almost laughed in relief.

I wasn't tall. That was it.

I was accustomed to being the tallest in any given company except my father's. But here my height was unremarkable, and there were as many people taller than me in this room as there were shorter. Similarly, my skin—the light brown Mother had once described as sunlight on river clay, unusual enough to be remarkable in Ilvera—was the same color as that of several others. Here I was perfectly average.

Smiling at this unexpected shift in perspective, I joined the line for supper, a sweet vegetable and chicken curry over red-grain rice—a rarity in Ilvera. Other differences struck me as I waited. The men wore their hair almost as long as the women, though they all tied it back, out of their faces. The plaits the women wore were similar enough to mine, except for the small braids some had styled that tucked behind their ears. I resisted the urge to touch my own hair. Most in the room had knives strapped to their belts as casually as I might have carried a water skin. Was that the way of all Zefedi, or only of wary travelers? I couldn't be sure.

After taking my bowl and spoon, I sat at a table in the corner, hoping to eat undisturbed and retreat to my room. It became apparent that this was not to be the case as a late party arrived at the inn, crowding into every available seat. My solitary table was overrun by a group of five young people still wearing their traveling clothes and smelling like sweat and dirt. I looked down, hoping that my concentration on my food would be enough to deter them from trying to make conversation with me. They all spoke Zefedi—not surprising, as it was the official language of the empire. Like Verran, the Lirusan and Celet languages had been driven out of most public spaces. But we on the mountain benefited from our isolation—in Ilvera, we only spoke Zefedi when outsiders were present. It was more difficult for down-mountainers to retain the language of their ancestors.

"I can't wait for tomorrow," said the boy sitting next to me. "A proper bath, finally!"

"You mean the day *after* tomorrow," countered a black-haired girl sitting across the table, who was unquestionably the leader of the bunch. Three small braids fell from her forehead and were tucked over her left ear. Her face was strikingly angular, with edges that softened when she smiled. "The fortress doesn't let anyone stay there overnight who isn't authorized. We'll come back this way after the delivery, but the closest bathhouses are in Deletev."

My ears pricked up. They were delivering goods to the fortress?

"We should have stopped in Deletev on the way here, like always," the boy grumbled.

The look that passed around the table told me that this complaint had been aired before.

"Not this time," the girl said firmly. She turned and caught my eye before I could look away. "Hello there," she said, looking at me with interest.

Would I draw less attention by leaving or by staying? "Hello," I said hesitantly.

"Sorry, we took over your table without even asking! I'm Vienne," she said, bowing slightly in her seat. She introduced her companions, whose names I knew I wouldn't be able to remember.

"I'm Maren," I said.

"Where are you traveling from?"

"Oskiath," I said, pleased by how smoothly the lie rolled off my tongue.

"So far!" Vienne went on to say she had visited Oskiath as a child, but most of the group were from Eronne or Gedarin. They were transporting supplies from the coast of Gedarin to the fortress. Left unsaid was the unusual hurry they were in, though it was apparent in their tone and the looks they exchanged.

"Is it true, what they're saying about Ruzi?" asked the boy sitting next to me.

One of his companions interrupted. "I heard the new small king has lost control, and they're completely reliant on Kyseal and Oskiath."

"I heard people are fleeing the kingdom!"

"I heard the emperor's purging the place, ever since the prophecies . . ."

Panic rose up in me. When the Flame of the West had defeated the Lirusan and Celet peoples and stolen their land to found the Zefedi empire, he split it into five kingdoms. He chose Gedarin for his own court and elevated four trusted generals to rule over the rest—they became the small kings of Zefed. Of the kingdoms, I knew the most about Oskiath and Eronne, the kingdom that had claimed Ilvera after the dragons had been stolen. I didn't know anything about Ruzi. Why hadn't my parents told me there was unrest on such a large scale? Perhaps they hadn't known, but that didn't help me now. "It's hard to say," I said carefully. "None of my family knows exactly what word is to be trusted."

"But you must have seen *something*. What about their lost prince, have you heard anything about him?"

"I—"

"Oh, leave her alone," Vienne said. "Besides, we're not on the road anymore. You can't be sure who's listening." She tilted her head toward the rest of the room.

I flashed her a grateful smile. As the talk at the table turned to what they would do once they arrived in Deletev, Vienne leaned in toward me.

"You'll have to forgive my friends," she said. "They've been traveling too long, they don't remember how to talk in polite company." Under the dust of travel I detected another scent that clung to her skin: a citrusy, spicy perfume.

I laughed. "It's no trouble. Though I'm a poor excuse for polite company."

"I wouldn't say that." Our eyes met and held, and she winked. I blushed, looking away, and was grateful when she was pulled into the others' conversation. Under the table my hands were shaking, and I pressed my palms against my thighs until they calmed enough to hold my spoon again.

At the end of the meal, I bid the table good night and went upstairs.

"Maren!" I turned, my key already in the lock, to see Vienne standing at the top of the stairs, a bottle of wine in hand. I tensed.

"Vienne," I said cautiously. Had I made a mistake already, perhaps slipped back to speaking Verran without realizing?

"I wanted to say I liked meeting you, and . . . to wish you good night," she said, walking toward me. Lantern light glinted off the pendant resting in the hollow of her throat, and my heart thumped in my chest. I was suddenly all too aware that we were alone in the hallway.

A nervous laugh escaped me. "Oh. Well—good night."

She held up the bottle. "I also was wondering if you'd like some company."

Heat flooded my body as I realized what she was asking. I forced myself to look her in the eye. "I'm not—you're beautiful—but I—I have someone," I stammered.

"Oh," she said not unkindly, tilting her head. "I didn't realize." Her gaze dropped to my left hand.

My heart fell. She was looking for a troth ring that wasn't there. "*Had* someone," I corrected. "We parted ways. Recently. I'm sorry—I'm still not used to it."

She grinned. "And you're certain that wouldn't be helped by a good glass of wine and a good—"

"You flatter me," I said, cutting her off. If my cheeks had been red before, they were flaming now. "But I'm sorry. I can't."

"Very well." She was taller than me and had to lean down to press a kiss against my cheek just on the outside of my mouth. "My room is at the end of the hall to the right, if you change your mind."

She turned and walked away, and I hurried to enter my room and lock the door behind me. The corner of my mouth was still tingling as I flung myself across the bed, flushed and unhappy. I shouldn't have let her kiss me. Shouldn't have admired the curve of her neck, however briefly. Vienne's striking features and her attentions were enough to turn any girl's head, but mine should not have moved. I felt like my chest had been cracked open, and my heart was threatening to spill out. The person who should have been making such overtures to me was far, far away, and I didn't even have a troth ring to signify her importance.

I took in a deep breath and held it, willing my mind to clear.

I would put this behind me. I could not waste my time in tears, if I was to get Kaia back. And I would. I must.

In the morning, I watched from my window until I saw Vienne and her company leave the inn, and gave them a head start before departing. Today I'd fashioned my hair after Vienne's, though it had taken me some time to arrange the small braids properly. They still felt strange, a slight imbalance toward my left side.

It was midday when I reached the fortress. I could smell it before I saw it. Acrid, burnt air filled my nostrils, betraying the presence of dragons. The trees thinned and then fell away entirely, leaving a barren expanse of land that stretched ahead of me. All the better to see who was coming, I supposed. I crested the last hill and stopped, shocked into stillness.

The fortress was even more imposing than it had looked from higher up the mountain. Up close I could now see that the outer walls were wide enough to accommodate watchtowers and a walkway above. The peninsula was surrounded by the river formed by the two waterfalls, and the only way across seemed to be a drawbridge that divided in the center and required someone on each side of the torrent to lower their half. I was prepared to bluff my way into the fortress, but I had no plan for when it was time to escape. Was I going to my doom, here and now?

Courage, I told myself. *Whatever it takes. Kaia wouldn't give up.*

I tucked the dragon figurine into my pocket and brushed my fingers against my father's letter of introduction. Then I started down the hill.

As I approached, I could see the drawbridge was down and the last of the carts from Vienne's delivery were entering through the gate. Two guards remained stationed in front of the towers just before the drawbridge. I swallowed hard and drew myself upright. I'd gathered some dust over the course of the morning, but now I tried to walk like my mother, with easy authority.

My heart raced as I walked up to the guards. I could do this. I *must* do this. When they looked over at me, I touched my forehead and bowed. "I'm here to see my uncle. I was told he works here."

One of them scratched at his neck. "And who's your uncle, then?"

"Gemed of Oskiath."

The guards snorted in disbelief. "Gemed? The cook has a family?"

I tried not to let any sign of relief show on my face. "He's my father's cousin," I said. "They haven't spoken in a long time, but he'll see me. Tell him that Ferrik ben Gao's daughter is here."

The guards exchanged a look, and the older one nodded. The other ducked inside one of the towers and spoke to a young man seated there, too quietly for me to hear. Then the runner took off across the drawbridge and into the fortress, dodging around the delivery carts.

The other guard waved me to the side, where I put my hands in my pockets and tried to look bored and nonthreatening. Minutes crawled by. My nose itched, but I resisted the urge to scratch it.

"Greetings!"

The person who came striding across the bridge to me wasn't someone I would have paired with my father in any circumstance. He was short and thin, and his pinched face looked a little like a rat's, but it smoothed into delighted surprise as he took my hand and held me at arm's length. "Cousin-daughter! What an unexpected visit!"

With a nod at the guards, he led me away from the guard tower, off to the side of the road. Once out of earshot, the mask of friendliness dropped from his face. "Who are you?" he growled.

"I—I'm Ferrik ben Gao's daughter," I stammered. "He said you were a cousin of his."

"I heard he took up with one of them Verran folk."

"My mother," I said. "My name is Maren."

He looked me up and down cursorily. "You don't look much like a girl from the mountain. Don't talk like one, either."

I frowned at the insult—as if Zefedi was such a difficult language to learn. Every Verran spoke enough to get by, and my father had made sure I was fluent. "They say I take after my father, mostly."

"Hmph. Let's say you're telling the truth—what's a Verran brat doing here, looking for me?"

I bit my lip. I hadn't prepared for this moment nearly enough. "I'm looking for work," I said. At Gemed's incredulous expression I barreled on. "There's not much to be had up the mountain. Father said that I might come here, that you could get me a position. I don't need much. And I can work hard."

Gemed spat on the ground. "That's a crimson lie. I haven't spoken to Ferrik in years, and if you really were his daughter you'd know it's because he considers me lower than scum now that he lives atop his precious mountain. He would never send his daughter here, to me. Go try your story on someone else."

"All right, all right!" I said. "He didn't send me to you. He doesn't know I'm here at all, and you're right, he would never approve. But Ferrik ben Gao *is* my father." I pulled the letter of introduction out of my pocket and passed it to him, hoping he wouldn't notice the way my hand shook.

Gemed took the letter and glanced over it, his expression darkening as he read. "It's a passable imitation of a man's writing," he grunted, passing it back to me. "Says you're on your way to Oskiath. So what are you doing here?"

I had to put a grain of truth in my story, though it cost me to say it. "Ilvera is dying. Father won't leave, but I can't stay in a place that won't even acknowledge that it's part of the empire." I forced my nose to wrinkle in disgust. "I'm Zefedi-born. I want to see Zefed, and I want to see the dragons. I thought you would understand."

"You and every other Zefedi brat. So go to Deletev and pay for a pit fight."

"*Please*," I said. "I'm not here to cause trouble. I've just always wanted to see them. And not fighting, either. The guards said you were the fortress cook, didn't they? I can cook."

"So could a donkey if you teach it right. Anyone can slice rock tubers."

"Then let me. I can fetch water or wash dishes. Anything anyone else doesn't want to do, I'll do it. Please, I've dreamed about seeing them for so long."

"There are already people who do all those things," Gemed said. He looked back at the gate. "Besides, this isn't a good place for a girl from Ilvera. Go home. Or to Oskiath. Wherever you want, as long as it's not here."

He was leaving. I couldn't fail now, not after coming this far. No. I needed a new plan. *Think. What would Kaia do?*

I caught his arm as he turned away. "You're right," I said, a surge of adrenaline running through me. "A Verran girl wouldn't be welcomed here—and neither would someone with a family up the Verran mountain."

Gemed's body stiffened. He turned back, glaring at me. "What are you playing at?"

No turning back now. "What do you think would happen if I told them you were my father? That you're well acquainted with Ilvera, in fact? That your true loyalties might not lie with the emperor? You'd be thrown out in disgrace, if not killed outright."

He snorted. "They wouldn't believe you."

"Why wouldn't they? I look Zefedi enough, don't you think?" I said, growing more confident as I spoke. "And I could tell them so many things about you. Your family back in Oskiath. Your apprenticeships, your friends. I know about the time you ran down a deer with my father. I know how you got the scar on your right leg."

"He told you so much?" he said quietly. There was a hint of pain in his voice now—possibly regret. I seized the opportunity.

"My father said you were like me, when you were younger. Always talking about the dragons. And I really am looking for work."

"Here, at the dragon fortress."

I nodded, staring him down. I would not be the one to break eye contact first. "Please."

Finally, he looked away. "On any other day my answer would be no." My heart leaped, and he shook his head. "Don't think yourself lucky. We're in need of a food taster. We've gone through two in the last month. You want a position so badly you'll try blackmail. Do you want it badly enough to court death?"

I didn't know what to think, except that if I did not make

this choice quickly, it would be made for me. Gemed was no friend to my father. That was obvious, considering how he offered such a position so cavalierly.

And yet . . . he had come when I gave my father's name, hadn't he?

I took a deep breath. "I'll do it."

Gemed's face twisted, and for a fleeting moment I thought I saw another person under the facade—someone who had hoped I wouldn't take him up on his offer.

The moment passed. "Well, then. Anything on you that might contradict the story you're telling?"

I frowned. "Just the letter."

"Then you'll want to dispose of it. Now is best." He turned back to the gate. "Well, come on then. Don't say anything foolish. In fact, best not to say anything at all, if you can help it."

He lifted a hand in acknowledgment to the guards as we passed the guard tower. "Needs work," he grunted, jerking his head in my direction. "I'll see Kellyn about a post in the kitchen."

He continued past them without looking to see if I would follow.

Halfway across the bridge, I paused and glanced behind me. The guards had gone back to facing the forest, so I crumpled my father's papers into a ball and dropped it over the side, watching as the water swept it away. As I passed under the main archway of the fortress, I looked up at the raised iron gate—sharp-fanged jaws ready to snap shut. My palms were sweating, my heart pounding. I was struck suddenly by the thought that I was going to my death. And yet I walked on, into the prison that housed the dragons of Ilvera.

CHAPTER SEVEN

I
nside the fortress, the courtyard was still crowded and busy as the delivery was unloaded. I ran after Gemed through the commotion, keeping my eyes on his fast-retreating back. Even so, there was no missing the scorch marks on the inside of the thick stone walls, or the grooves so long and deep that I imagined claws larger than my head raking down the stone. I shivered, then steeled myself. *That* was the creature that could defeat the Aurati. And I would master one of them.

Gemed turned left, and I followed, barely avoiding a collision with a man walking briskly in the other direction.

"Keep up!" Gemed said sharply. I scrambled after him. We passed into the fortress proper, which opened onto a vast gathering hall full of tables and chairs—another place known to showcase dragons, it seemed, as there were more scorch and claw marks on the walls here. Our footsteps echoed through the hall and up one flight of stairs, then another turn, and another, each coming so quickly that I could not miss a step, or else be left behind. Even half trotting it was difficult to keep pace with him.

Finally, Gemed halted beside a guarded door in a hallway that looked exactly like all the others. "Every person who seeks work at the fortress must be approved by Kellyn," he said. "I can't help you with this."

He looked to one of the guards. "Is she in?" The guard nodded and knocked on the door. Hearing a muffled answer from within, he pushed it open.

The room was modest in size. A wooden desk took up half the floor, which was covered by a thick brown carpet. And behind that desk, framed by a small window opposite the door, sat an Aurat.

My chest seized before reason could calm it. Of course Kellyn would be an Aurat. The emperor of Zefed would trust no one else to ensure that his dragons were raised to meet his every requirement. I concentrated on relaxing my stance. Kellyn was no seer—she wore the blue cords of a scribe. She could not see inside me, so all I had to do was sell my story.

"My cousin's daughter needs work," Gemed explained. "Given the recent problems, I brought her to you first."

"Of course," she said, indicating the chair in front of the desk. "Please, sit."

I bowed and sat. For a moment we regarded each other. Kellyn was a plump woman of middling age with warm brown skin and the prominent cheekbones and jawline that suggested Celet heritage. Her dark hair was worn loose, and her face was open and inviting. In other words, the opposite of how I'd always pictured Aurati.

"What's your name?"

"Maren ben Gao."

"Where have you come from?"

"Oskiath, eastern provinces," I said. "My family owns a farm, but I've no interest in it. My father said Gemed might help."

"I see." She sat straighter. "But why here? Your father doesn't have friends in other places?"

I took a breath, trying to channel Kaia. "That's my fault. He's tried, but most of his friends' vocations are so . . . boring. I wanted something *more*."

Kellyn frowned. "Your pack. Put it on the desk."

I did what she asked without hesitation. She untied the top and searched it with ruthless efficiency. Clothing, coin, my hair clasp, the carved dragon—all piled neatly to one side as she dug her fingers into every pocket, every seam. After the pack was empty, she looked at me again. "Pockets," she said. "Empty them."

I made a show of going through my jacket pockets one by one.

Kellyn sat back, looking almost disappointed that her search had turned up nothing suspicious. "You truly need someone in the kitchens?" she asked Gemed.

He shrugged. "We've been shorthanded since last week, and you know the lord needs a new food taster."

She nodded. "Please step outside, Gemed."

I sat as straight as I could as the door closed behind him. Kellyn opened a desk drawer and withdrew a vial about the size of her thumb.

"Do you know what this is?" she said.

I shook my head.

There was an empty glass on the desk. She poured water into it and added three drops from the vial. Then she picked up the glass and circled the desk, coming to stand just before me. "Drink," she said.

"What is it?"

"It won't hurt you," she said. "Drink."

I could protest, perhaps. But if I did, I would surely be turned away. I took the glass, feeling the weight of it in my hand. Then I brought it to my lips and drank.

The water was cold. Whatever Kellyn had put in the glass added little besides a slight metallic taste that lingered on my tongue after I swallowed. I emptied the glass and set it back on the desk.

I took a breath. And then suddenly I felt like I was underwater, removed from the rest of the world. I turned my head, trying to focus on Kellyn's face, which had blurred before me. She leaned down and snapped her fingers in front of my eyes.

"Tell me your name."

"Maren," I said. The word slipped out without thought. Whatever I'd drunk must have had the effect of loosening tongues, lowering inhibitions. My heart beat loudly in my ears. I tried to slow my breathing, my thoughts. Whatever she asked me next, I could not allow myself to answer quickly. But I could not lie, either.

"Why have you come to the fortress?"

I took a breath. "Dragons. I wanted . . . to see them." That wasn't so unusual, was it?

"Do you mean harm to the dragons?"

Easily answered. "No," I said.

"Do you mean harm to the emperor?"

My hand rested on my thigh. I pressed down until I could feel the pressure on my skin. "No."

"No?"

More firmly now. "No," I said. It wasn't a lie. I meant harm to the Aurati, not the emperor. A fine line, but a real one.

Kellyn leveled such a look at me that I leaned slightly away from her, as though that would be enough to escape. "You do know that if you are found to be lying, the consequences will fall on both you and your uncle."

Whatever it takes. I swallowed. "I understand," I said.

The effects of the drugged water were wearing off. The room was sliding back into focus, though I could feel that my palms were clammy. Everything felt strangely bright—Kellyn's cords, the edge of a blade mounted on the wall, the sharpness in her voice as she called Gemed back into the room.

"You vouch for your cousin's child?"

He cleared his throat. "I do." He sounded so gruffly sincere I almost believed him myself.

"Then you're responsible for her—on a trial basis." She produced paper and quill and slashed a signature across the bottom of the page, then handed the paper to me. "Any one of the guards may ask to see this, so you'd do well to keep it with you at all times. Gemed will tell you where you're needed. You seem like a smart girl, so I'm sure you already know to stay out of places you're not meant to be." She glanced down at her desk. "You can take your things now."

"I've got to get to the kitchens," Gemed said, opening the door. "Let's go."

I pocketed the paper Kellyn had given me and swept my things back into my pack, feeling wobbly. "Thank you," I said just as the door closed behind us.

Gemed merely grunted in response.

The kitchen was on the ground floor of the fortress. It was spacious and well kept, though empty of people. We'd arrived during what seemed to be a late-afternoon lull, when I would have expected supper preparations to be underway.

"Kitchen," Gemed said. "I run it, you work here. You can put your things in the room yonder." He indicated a hallway at the other end of the kitchen. Then he turned away and busied himself at the long table that spanned most of the room.

"Is that all?" I asked.

Gemed answered without turning. "You'll leave here sooner rather than later, make no mistake. Most people who come to the fortress do."

I raised my chin. "Not me."

"Yes, well. Maybe you'll last the week. Since there's dragon in your blood and all."

It was a dismissive afterthought, but I clung to it, as if the blood that ran in my veins was all I needed to carry me through what was to come.

The dormitory at the end of the hall housed dozens of bunks lined up against the walls. I chose an empty one in the corner, tucking my bag on the floor below the bed frame before returning to the kitchen.

"Is there something I should do?" I asked. Truth be told, I wasn't looking forward to the work. The kitchen had always been my father's sphere of influence, and while I was a competent cook, I wasn't what anyone would call inspired when it came to food preparation.

Gemed looked up. "I'm too busy to teach you your right hand from your left at the moment. Come back later."

"Can I go outside?" I said.

"Doesn't matter to me."

"What are the rules?" I feared breaking them inadvertently and being forced to leave more than I feared looking foolish for asking.

Gemed snorted. "What does a ben Gao daughter care for rules? Rules of the fortress are easy. Keep your head down and your mouth shut. Don't poke your nose into places where it's liable to be cut off. Don't mention where you really come from, if you want to keep your head."

I wanted to ask more, but it was clear that Gemed's patience had reached its limit.

Back in the main hallway, I took the identification paper from my pocket and smoothed it out, tracing the lines Kellyn had written. Then I leaned back against the wall and breathed a sigh of relief. I had done it. I was here, in the dragon fortress.

But this was only the first phase of my plan. I still had to find the dragons. To tame one. To steal it. And what better opportunity to explore than now, when I was new and could say I was lost if discovered somewhere I wasn't supposed to be?

I peeked inside the grand hall, but something about the space intimidated me. It was like an unexpected clearing in the forest—inviting, but far more dangerous than sticking to the trees. I stayed my course, keeping track of my turns and trying to walk purposefully.

It was clear now that the grand hall was at the center of the building, and the hallway I now walked marked one side of its perimeter, with smaller corridors and stairways branching off it. I quickly covered its length and found myself facing the outdoors again. I stepped outside, eager to breathe the fresh air, and was hit with an immediate reminder of exactly where I was. There were no dragons in sight, but the air was still heavy with their scent, as though it had sunk permanently into the fortress walls.

The carts that had crowded the courtyard when I'd arrived were gone, the crates they'd carried unpacked. A group of soldiers was gathered off to one side, executing military drills. Now that I had the time to look, I saw that there were a few ponies waiting in a paddock, for messengers, perhaps. Though it took an especially hardy breed to be able to tolerate the stench of dragons. In the old stories there were many mentions of the mountain ponies that had lived side by side with the dragons, but those were long gone from Ilvera.

I turned around. The fortress stretched above me, looking almost endless from where I stood. A few open shutters interrupted its smooth line, but for the most part it was a stark statement against the sky. I breathed in, and a new, unexpected scent struck me—something sharp and cold, like fresh snow in winter. A few floors above me, there was a small movement that caught my eye. I gasped—was that a wing? My pulse jumped in excitement.

A horn blew, and I shrank back against the wall as people streamed toward the main building. I hesitated. I wanted to investigate what I'd seen, but I was a stranger here. I couldn't be seen walking against the flow of the crowd, not yet. So instead I sighed in disappointment and let myself be swept into the grand hall along with the others.

The occupants of the fortress did not immediately sit at the long tables standing in rows along the length of the hall. Instead they stood at attention as one man ascended the platform at the far end. I shifted uncomfortably, drawing in my elbows as a boy swerved around me. The hall was emptier than I'd expected, given the size of the fortress. Even so, I had never been among so many Zefedi in such close quarters.

Many of them were in uniform, trousers and unadorned tunics differentiated by color. Brown for the guards and soldiers, I thought, looking around the hall. Black seemed reserved for some higher rank, as I saw several of them congregated near the front.

The doors that led to the kitchen opened, and a number of servants clad in undyed beige tunics ferried platters of food to the tables. The rich scent of red evelyn pepper permeated the hall.

This must be supper. I frowned. Gemed had said the kitchen was short staffed. Did he expect me to be working? Had I already misstepped? No—that couldn't be right. He'd told me to stay away from the kitchen, and he hadn't specified when I was to return.

Just as quickly as they had begun, the kitchen servants closed the doors and stood against the wall. The man on the platform raised one hand, and the crowd fell silent.

"By the grace of the Flame of the West we are gathered, and eat," he said. I could hear those around me repeat the words after him. "By the emperor's decree, the lords have accelerated their training. They will be here in a month's time," he said.

A buzz of angry murmurs carried through the hall.

"Quiet!" the man continued. He was clearly the lord of the fortress, and I looked at him long and hard. He was of average height and build, with long black hair tied in the Zefedi style. There had to be something special about him to be named the highest non-Aurati authority of the most important military center in Zefed. But from here, I couldn't tell what it was. "It is not for us to question the Flame Himself, but to follow."

He raised a closed fist in the air, and the crowd mirrored him, although they were certainly slow about it. I swallowed. I wished I'd memorized every word Father had ever spoken about his origins. I wished I'd delayed my coming until I'd wrung every last drop of knowledge from him. I'd thought myself canny enough to the workings of Zefed, but this was a situation I did not know how to parse.

The announcement about the lords appeared to be the only bit of news the fortress lord had to report. He descended from the platform without ceremony, and immediately the crowd advanced toward the food.

Soon enough I collected a bowl of soup, a piece of flatbread, and a spoon and picked a table where only a few others sat. They were about my age: two girls and three boys, all with the straight hair and lighter skin that marked them as descendants of the original Zefedi invaders. They barely glanced at me as I sat down at the end of the table. Once again I was glad of my own tawny coloring, which had never been Verran enough for some in my small village.

"Why shouldn't he? The dragons will be ready sooner!" one girl demanded.

"You can't seriously think that. The kits aren't ready to be bonded, and there aren't nearly enough people at the fortress to prepare them in time."

"But if Patak says they are—"

"Patak is a lazy bureaucrat who wouldn't know a dragon

from a dog if someone weren't standing right next to him, feeding him lines. The only reason he's here is that he can be trusted not to step above his station." This from a lanky boy with ragged black hair who sat nearest to me, dressed in a guard's uniform. I glanced at him carefully. Zefedi men did not usually cut their hair so short. What had happened to him? Nothing too terrible, I supposed, not if he was still allowed to work here.

"Face it," the boy continued. "This is because of the prophecies. *He* thinks he'll need the dragons to fend them off."

Immediately the tenor of the conversation changed. There was only one person who could inspire that tone of voice without even the mention of a name. The Flame of the West himself.

One of the other boys lowered his voice. "You can't say such things," he said.

"Why not? Everyone knows it's true." But the boy's actions contradicted his words—he stopped talking and went back to eating his soup.

I blinked down at mine. It bore some resemblance to the dish my father used to make on special occasions, spiced so strongly with red evelyn peppers that my nostrils opened in surprise as I inhaled. But where Father would have decorated the bowls with green sprout paste and a sprig of mint, this dish lacked decoration. Mass produced, to be eaten quickly and without complaint.

I took a mouthful—and had to stop myself from spitting it out. Too much salt. Too much . . . everything.

"Enjoying your food?"

I looked up. The boy with short hair was looking at me curiously. What could I say? Was Gemed under some delusion that he was a good cook?

After an uncomfortable pause, the boy smiled. "I was just teasing. Everyone knows the food is terrible here. Except for those at the top, I suppose." He nodded to the high table. I'd noticed that they were being served different plates than us, though I was too far away to see what was on them.

I smiled nervously back. "It's . . . interesting."

He laughed. "You're a diplomat!" He leaned closer, smiling. "So, what's such an illustrious personage doing in a place like this? I haven't seen you before."

He was flirting, I realized, and I didn't know what to say in return. I should have thought to prepare for this after my encounter with Vienne at the inn.

"Don't mind Sev," the girl sitting next to me said, giving me a friendly nudge in the side. She wore a light blue tunic. "He was practically raised by wolves. There's a reason he's on night patrol so much—it's because the other guards can't stand him."

"Oh," I said. Sev winked at me, unconcerned.

"But it's true that we don't see many new people at the fortress. I'm Lilin, by the way. I work in the nursery."

"I'm Maren. I'm the new food taster."

The others, who had been chattering and half listening, suddenly fell silent.

"That's . . . nice," the other girl said, frowning.

Lilin looked concerned. "They told you why there was an opening, didn't they? There have been two poisonings here in the last month alone."

"But they've caught whoever did it, right?"

The solemn faces around the table told me that they had not, and my stomach tightened. Suddenly I didn't feel hungry at all.

"Don't scare the girl off," said one of the other boys. "I, for one, want to know how they convinced Gemed to take on someone new. We thought it was impossible."

"It was a favor," I said. "He and my father were close, and I needed the work."

Sev's gaze turned thoughtful. "Not many people choose to work at the dragon fortress—and not under such circumstances."

"Then why are *you* here?" I shot back.

To my surprise, his cheeks turned red, and he stared down at his food. The rest of the table erupted into laughter, though I didn't think what I'd said was that funny at all. Clearly Sev was someone unused to being caught off guard. And it was doubly clear, to me at least, that he was like me in one respect: He was hiding something.

A hand clapped down heavily on my shoulder, and I froze. "Why aren't you at Lord Patak's table? Are you not a food taster?" Kellyn demanded, glaring down at me.

"I—" I didn't know what to say. Gemed had told me not to come back to the kitchen until later, but something told me that Kellyn would not accept that excuse. I bit my lip. I had to come up with something. *Think. Say something!*

"Gemed told her to start her duties tomorrow at breakfast," Sev said. "I heard him."

I flashed him a grateful look.

Kellyn snorted. "If you mean to keep your position, you'll remember that your meals are to be taken in the kitchens, *not* at the tables."

"I understand," I said quietly.

"Then go."

I rose and hastily gathered my food. Then I fled the great hall, certain that I felt her gaze burning into my back until I was well out of sight.

Once safely in the hallway, I leaned back against the wall and closed my eyes, my heart finally slowing. That had been close. And it could have been disastrous, but for Sev's intervention. Why had he lied for me? I was nothing to him.

But that wasn't something I could spare a thought for now. I had to get back to the kitchen, and I had to make sure I steered clear of Kellyn. Seer or no seer, she was still dangerous.

Gemed looked up as I entered. He and three other servants wearing beige tunics were busy clearing the kitchen for the next meal. "Where were you?" he said.

"You said you didn't have time to teach me," I said.

He scowled and snapped his fingers at me. "And I don't have time for this, either. Pots. Wash them!"

He indicated the gargantuan pile of dishes that was threatening to topple over by the door. I stopped my mouth from falling open with no small amount of effort. "Where?" I asked. I didn't see a water basin.

"Outside. Come back when you're through." He jerked his head in the direction of the hallway.

One of the servants tossed me a cloth as I passed her. I picked up the first pot and almost dropped it, unused to its weight. There had been stew in here once. Now there were bits crusted onto the sides and a rank smell. Gemed must have been telling the truth when he said the kitchens were short staffed.

A brief walk down the hallway led me through a heavy wooden door and outside, where I found a wash station with two empty buckets and a path. I set down the pot and picked up a bucket. The path was lined with bushes and appeared to lead into the patch of forest I'd seen from high on the mountain. There was a small measure of peace to be gleaned here from the slim trees that branched up toward the waning sunlight. But when I looked up, the twin waterfalls loomed ominously over me, bordered by the shards of black rock that made this part of the mountain impassable.

I followed the path until I reached a stone well, and lifted its cover. A mossy scent rose up from the darkness, and I could hear the faint rushing sound of moving water far below me. This wasn't a well, I realized. It was a shaft that had been made to connect with the Serpent.

Could it be used as a means for escape? It was wide enough for me to fit through the opening at the top easily enough, but what if the hole narrowed? A visceral image of getting stuck halfway down and slowly starving to death caused me to shudder, as unlikely as it was.

Still, it was a good thing to know. I hooked the bucket to the chain and lowered it down to the river, waited, and pulled it back up again. I lugged the full bucket back to the wash station and considered the pot. The cloth that had been tossed my way had been sewn around what felt like pebbles, creating a rough surface with which to scrub. I tipped the bucket so that water sloshed over its edge and into the pot, and set to work.

I scrubbed the pot until it was as clean as I could reasonably make it. Then I carried it back into the kitchen and exchanged it for another. Each time I returned, there was a different vegetable being chopped in preparation for tomorrow's meals, another look thrown my way that seemed half contempt, half pity. My fingers reddened and my arms became sore, and I couldn't tell how much time had passed except to note that the sun had finally set and darkness spread over the fortress grounds.

Three kitchen servants were in the dormitory when I finally came in to sleep. They looked up at me with interest.

"Suppose you're the owner of this?" The girl standing in the corner held up my pack.

I tensed. "Yes," I said slowly.

"What's your name?" she said.

"Maren."

"I'm Mol." She seemed to be the most senior of the kitchen servants. "Gemed may have told you the rules of the kitchen." I nodded. "Here are the ones you'll actually want to follow. If Gemed assigns you a duty, it's yours. But after that, you take your orders from me. After that, Torash, then Sim."

I didn't argue.

"You'll be doing the tasting for Lord Patak as well," she said, her words suddenly clipped. She was watching me closely for a reaction I was determined not to give. So I nodded in acquiescence, face as blank as I could make it. She looked a little disappointed and thrust a pile of clothing into my arms.

"That's all. They'll douse the lanterns soon."

There was a washroom I hadn't noticed earlier on the far side of the dormitory. I was the last to use it—a confirmation of the new order of things. I slipped out of my travel-worn clothes and into a long tunic for sleeping, cognizant of the sounds on the other side of the thin door. Mol had given me two uniforms that matched the one she wore—brown trousers, beige top—and I folded them neatly.

By the time I was finished, the other servants had turned down the lantern, leaving the room in darkness. I fumbled my way to the bed I'd chosen, grateful it was near enough that I only stumbled twice, and never over someone.

The blankets were thicker than I'd expected for servants, but as I huddled under the covers, I realized that it was because the room was so cold. Indeed, my blanket was almost not enough.

I closed my eyes and thought of summers in Ilvera, the shell bushes blooming, floating in the lake with Kaia for hours. *Kaia*.

When I found her again, we wouldn't be able to return to the mountain. She would be an escapee, and I would be a criminal in the eyes of Zefedi law. So we would run. We would go to find Tovin, and from there we would travel far away from the reach of the tyrant. We would find our freedom, even if it meant being forever lost to Ilvera. In the dark, I fixed my mind on the ember of resolution in my heart and willed it to burn bright again. *Kaia*. For Kaia, I could do anything. Even lie here and sleep among hundreds of Zefedi soldiers. Even taste the food of the man who oversaw the exploitation of the dragons. Even take one of them for my own. I would. I must.

CHAPTER EIGHT

Kaia dares me to jump the first time we climb the cliff above the lake together, but it takes until the third time for me to make the leap.

I'm fourteen this spring, and I jump just as the snow melts down the mountain. Hitting the water is like submerging myself in ice, and I come up gasping. I swim to land and run shivering toward her, all thoughts numb except one: that today I am brave enough to leap. Today I am brave enough to touch her cheek and lean in, press my lips to hers in the way I've thought of doing so many times.

I can feel her surprise as our lips meet, and when I pull back, she smiles like summer, and the touch of her hands on my skin chases the ice away.

The dream shifts, and I am in darkness—no, a forest. Dawn on the horizon.

Kaia, legs quivering and feet swollen from the long days running. She walks like a broken girl. The trees look familiar here, but the air feels different—damp and heavy. She sways on her feet, and the seers hold her up when her knees buckle. It is not a kindness. She is more exhausted now than she has ever been, but the seers who surround her do not stop, do not sleep. They crest a hill, and she sees

Lumina rise in the distance, white stone towers and impenetrable walls. There is fear etched on her face, and I reach out a hand, but I cannot touch her.

Something slapped hard against my face.

"What?" I snapped, sitting up, arms ready to strike back against—Mol, who was standing in the half-light of dawn, hand drawn back. There was a window in the room that I hadn't noticed before on account of its height. Too high to be of any use to me when it came time to make my escape.

"You're late. Get up." She grinned as I rolled out of bed. "And don't be cross with me. Gemed would do you worse in a blink."

I gritted my teeth but refrained from replying. *Head down, swim below the surface.* I fumbled my way over to the washroom, legs aching. I shouldn't have been so tired, but the combination of travel and nerves had taken their toll. I splashed my face with cold water, then wiped it dry with my sleeve. My vision was fuzzy, my limbs still shaking, somehow worse off for the few hours of sleep I'd snatched. The memory of the dream—the first time I'd kissed Kaia—sent warmth surging through my chest . . . but the warmth was quickly overwhelmed by fear. If Kaia and the seers had arrived at Lumina in truth . . . I shook my head. I had to keep moving. That was all I could do.

I opened the door to the dormitory to find it empty, Mol and the others having left me behind. I dressed hurriedly and followed. Gemed hadn't wanted me here in the first place. He wouldn't hesitate to push me out at the first opportunity.

The dormitory was cold, but the kitchen was already uncomfortably warm. The fire was stoked, and Mol and the other servants sat around the long table with heaping bowls of porridge. I moved to sit.

"Not you," Gemed said. "Hurry and put this on." He handed me a loose green robe made of far richer material than the uniform I was wearing. I pulled it over my head, and he picked up a serving tray arrayed with a spread of fruits, nuts, and freshly baked bread. "Let's go."

It was time. I swallowed, hard.

"Don't contradict the lord," Gemed said as we walked. "He'll make it clear what he wants you to sample. Follow his instructions to the letter. When you're done, you can come back to the kitchen and eat with the rest of us."

We had arrived at a door, and I had no recollection of how we'd gotten there—only that I was tired and would have traded most, if not all, of my Zefedi coin to lie down. Gemed placed the tray in my hands and stepped back. He knocked quickly on the door. An armed guard opened it from the inside and waved me in.

Willing my hands to remain steady, I entered.

Lord Patak's receiving chamber was a place of opulence, with furs on the floor and paintings hung and the air heavy with dark incense. It was designed to impress as much as the great hall, though in different ways.

The lord himself sat at a desk and did not look at me. He was occupied already with the woman standing across from him, arms folded. She was about my mother's age, her brown hair tucked into a businesslike knot. She wore cords that marked her as an Aurat, but they were silver—a color rank I'd never seen before.

"The dragons will not be ready when the lords arrive," she said fiercely. "You *must* tell the emperor to delay."

"Must I?" Lord Patak snapped back. "He wants the new crop of Talons now. How would you suggest I respond?"

"Tell him he's about to waste a year's worth of work on nothing. I don't care if the lords are ready. The dragons won't age faster just to please him. Besides, the instruments aren't finished."

"You've had months to prepare. If you need additional labor to be ready in time, perhaps you should accept one of the initiates Kellyn has brought here *for you*."

The Aurat rolled her eyes. "Sniveling weaklings who don't have the necessary talent. I will not accept an apprentice who has no chance of surviving."

The tray wobbled in my hands, and the lord registered my presence for the first time. "We'll continue this later, Neve," he said, waving off the woman.

She threw her hands up in frustration. "Go on pretending this is the right decision, if you like. When it comes down on your head, remember that I warned you."

She stormed past me and out of the room without another word. Lord Patak grimaced, then turned his attention to me. I placed the breakfast tray carefully at the edge of the desk and stepped back. Something about the man made my skin crawl.

"You're new," he said. His eyes were pale, a watery brown that made him look sickly. This impression wasn't helped by the heavy bags below them.

I nodded.

He pointed out a few slivers of melon, nudged a few nuts my way, and tore off a piece of bread. "There."

I reached slowly across the desk. His gaze was intense as I picked up a piece of fruit and bit down on it.

Cold. Tasteless—or perhaps that was because I could barely think over the panicked rush of blood through my ears. I swallowed. I felt dizzy—was I dying? No, I remained upright, on my feet. I reached for the nuts, and then the bread, still warm from the oven.

The lord eyed me intently. I looked down, avoiding his gaze. Time slowed to a crawl. I imagined poison uncurling in my belly, slithering through my veins.

"That's enough. You can go."

I made a short bow and fled, taking three wrong turns before I found my way back to the hall that led to the kitchen, the closest thing to a safe haven I had.

That morning I could barely taste the porridge Gemed served me. The flavor of fear was too overpowering in my mouth.

The next few days fell into much the same pattern. The kitchen servants and I tended to the food and the fires. Most meals consisted of simple Zefedi fare, pale imitations of my father's cooking, but I was grateful for it. It had only taken a day to lose my taste for rich flavors, and I was happy to retire to the plain servant food with the knowledge that if I was about to die by what I'd ingested, at least we would all expire together.

Breakfast and the noon meal followed Lord Patak wherever he went, but suppers were fortress-wide affairs served in the great hall. I tasted the lord's supper and stood a step back from the high table where he sat with his closest advisors until I was dismissed. These advisors wore colorfully dyed vests and gowns and adornments that seemed more appropriate for the tyrant's court than for a military fortress, though perhaps that was what they were accustomed to.

They rarely spoke about policy at supper. Nor about the tyrant, except to praise his name efficiently and move on to other topics, mostly centered around the amenities and lack thereof to be found in Deletev—the only place anyone spent time when they were not here, it seemed.

There was something strained about their evening chatter, as though they all knew there were other, more pressing matters to discuss. No poisoner had been caught, even with the guard shifts doubled. But at the high table no one would breathe a word about disturbances in the fortress and across Zefed, for fear of Kellyn and the other Aurati in initiate yellow, who sat quietly at the end of the table. Unfortunately, this circumspection rendered the fortress officials almost useless to me.

"How fares the fortress's favorite poison taster today?" Sev asked one evening as I circled the table, doling out yet another stew. The kitchen was still short staffed, which meant repetitive meals. Every evening after being dismissed from the high table, I joined the servers making their rounds of the great hall.

"Sev, don't say such things!" Lilin said, elbowing him.

"Why not? Is that not accurate?" He shrugged. "And I thought girls from Gedarin favored truth over pleasantry."

Lilin rolled her eyes. "Never mind him," she said.

"I won't," I said, smiling. After five days at the fortress, I'd picked up on the friendship between Lilin and Sev, built on a foundation of lively banter and jibes. It was an easy relationship that was almost endearing, until I reminded myself that we could not be friends. They were Zefedi, and not only that, Zefedi who had chosen to work *here*. They were my obstacles, my enemies. So I smiled at their jokes, but only so that I might make myself unremarkable among them.

"What's happening at the high table? You must hear some interesting things now that you're in the illustrious inner circle," Sev said.

I laughed at his description of my position. "They only gossip about Deletev, even though the fortress seems so busy! Is it really true, that the Talons are coming early to bond with the dragons?"

Lilin leaned in, lowering her voice. "I don't know that they can," she said. "The hatchlings can't be separated from the mothers until they're a month old. After that it's another six months before they're ready to start real training, and even then they need at least another few months to acclimate to humans before they're bonded. Bonding early could be dangerous."

I could hardly hold myself back from peppering her with questions. But I couldn't linger for much longer before someone took notice, so I settled on asking my most important one. "Can we watch the training?"

Both Sev and Lilin laughed. "Only a chosen few are allowed in the room—the Talons in training and Neve. She's the Aromatory," Sev explained. "And given everything that's going on, there's no way Patak will let that rule slip."

It made sense. The Talons were the emperor's dragon guard, a group of nobles—mostly second or third children—offered by their families to serve the emperor for life by mastering a dragon. But I'd never heard of the Aromatory before. Suddenly

I remembered the woman from Lord Patak's study, the one with silver cords. He'd called her Neve.

"What does the Aromatory do?" I asked.

"She's the only person who knows the tools and procedures for training the dragons," Sev said. "And it's a fact that if you don't train them properly, the dragons go right out of their minds."

My heart sank. This part of my plan, already threadbare, had just been ripped to shreds. I'd counted on being able to walk away from the fortress with a dragon, and I'd relied on my heritage as a Verran daughter to help me. But what use was my heritage, far removed from the days of the dragon riders as it was, if the dragons required proper training to stay sane?

I needed to know what the Aromatory used and how it worked, and I hadn't the faintest idea of where to begin. *Think.* Kaia wouldn't let this discourage her. I took a breath and held it before letting it out again.

"If it's so dangerous, why would the emperor want to speed up the process?" I said.

Lilin and Sev exchanged a glance. "Best not to talk about it here," Sev said finally.

If it was serious enough that Sev was the one quieting down instead of Lilin, I wouldn't press him on it now. Instead I finished serving the table and moved on to the next, pondering my new problem.

The following day was the senday, one day set aside each week for rest and reflection. The fortress was too busy for everyone to observe the full day, but there were a few precious hours in the morning that were mine alone. All week long I had been run ragged and collapsed into my bed the moment I was released from my duties. My hands were raw and my elbows bruised from scrubbing pots. The dragons—and the impossible problem posed by their training regime—were never far from my mind, but without the energy to move my legs at the end of the day, I couldn't even begin to form an intelligent plan. But after my conversation with Sev and Lilin, I was determined to use the morning wisely.

The animal feed—including the meat that went to the dragons—was kept in storehouses outside the main building. Deliveries were made daily to the nursery—all Lilin would say was that it was somewhere below the first level of the fortress, and that only those who worked there knew its exact location— and somewhere upstairs. And I'd also twice glimpsed carts of what looked like uncooked meat trundling toward the back of the fortress along the path that passed by the well.

Much as my heart drew me toward the hatchlings, it didn't seem worth the risk to go hunting for the nursery. Besides, I needed an older dragon. As best I could guess, the dragons upstairs were the ones being trained for the emperor's Talons, and would likely be as difficult to access as the hatchlings. That left the path.

Mol and the other servants had left the kitchen for the morning. The creak of a door echoed far down the hallway. Even Gemed was nowhere to be found. I steeled my shoulders and slipped outside.

The carts I'd seen pass this way had headed through the scrubby trees in the direction of the waterfall that knifed down the mountainside. I followed in their tracks, a twinge of fear mingling with the nervous excitement jumping under my skin. I had never been near a dragon before.

The sound of water crashing down grew more intense as I rounded a curve and came out on the other side of the trees. My heartbeat quickened. There, built into the rock of the mountain itself and curtained on either side by the mists of the waterfall, was a massive iron door.

I didn't see any guards. Was it because the lock was so heavy? Or because what was inside would frighten away anyone who came here unprepared?

There was a small window barred by iron rods built into the door. I hummed a call for courage under my breath. I was a Verran, a daughter of dragons. Those behind the door would not harm me. I had to believe that. Still, the rank stench of dragon assaulted my nose as I approached, and I put my face up to the window with caution, bracing my hands against the door. The iron was warm to the touch—*rage* suddenly jolted through me like a kiss of lightning, and I drew back, shaking pain out of my fingers. What was *that*?

I heard something shifting in the dark, and I leaned in once more, taking care not to touch the door again as I squinted, trying to make out shapes in the cave. These dragons were the emperor's prized possessions, the tools with which he quelled any who would stand against him. But this cave didn't give any indication of such reverence. All I could think of was a cage.

There was another shift, and I found myself speaking as I would to a skittish dog. "Shh shh shh, you're all right," I whispered. "Won't you come out so I can see you?" I hummed a nursery song that my mother had sung for me when I was small. I held my breath, waiting.

A moment later there came a roar that shook the very ground, and a burst of fire seared across the cave. I caught a glimpse of wings flapping before the flame turned in my direction, and I leaped aside. Something large crashed against the door, which shuddered but held. I scrambled back, terrified—and simultaneously elated. A dragon! What I'd seen on my first day at the fortress might have been a trick of the light, but this was real. My legs were trembling, but a grin spread across my face. Dragons were real, and I—Maren, a dragon girl from the dragon mountain—had just seen one. This was the creature I needed, a dragon strong enough to spark terror with an errant flame.

The dragon roared again, and I retreated. Even on the day of rest, it was impossible for a disruption that loud to go unnoticed.

I stripped off my clothing as soon as I got back to the dormitory. The scent of dragon and fire lingered too heavily for my comfort. When I returned to the kitchen in a fresh tunic and trousers, Gemed was waiting—and with him, a new set of tasks. More pots to be scrubbed, and after that, vegetables to chop for supper. There were always more vegetables to chop. I surrendered to the work in a haze of racing thoughts. I'd found a dragon. Now I needed to be able to train one. But how? Even if I had the tools, I didn't have the opportunity, not unless I got out from under my kitchen duties and the ever-present specter of poison in Lord Patak's food.

I decided it was time I paid a visit to Neve.

CHAPTER NINE

I watched Neve at supper that night. She sat among the Aurati at the end of Lord Patak's table, but I soon noticed that just as she never spoke to anyone, no one addressed her directly either if they could help it. No one would even look at her straight on. The set of their shoulders betrayed them as uncomfortable in her presence, for reasons that escaped me. Kellyn in particular seemed to resent her, as did the Aurati initiates who tailed Kellyn like chicks running after their mother.

Neve didn't eat the same food that was served to her table companions either. Instead she partook of the dishes served to the rest of the fortress, and even then, she only picked at the blandest of them—unseasoned rice, flatbreads meant to accompany heartier dishes, the plainest cuts of meat.

I didn't understand it. The dragon fortress existed to keep and raise dragons for the emperor's use, and Neve was an integral part of that machine. So why didn't anyone treat her with the same fawning attention they accorded Lord Patak?

For the moment that wasn't my concern. All that mattered was getting close to her.

It was Kellyn, finally, who gave me the idea for how to approach Neve. She was in the midst of pointedly boasting about one of her initiates as I rounded the table with a pitcher of wine, reminding me of the conversation I'd overheard between Lord Patak and Neve the first morning I'd tasted his food.

Neve needed an apprentice and would not accept any of the Aurati initiates at the fortress—initiates that Kellyn seemed to have summoned for this express purpose. I didn't know what qualified someone to be an apprentice to the Aromatory. I only knew the barest outline of what the Aromatory *did*. But if Neve was overworked—which it seemed she was—and she had accepted no one else . . .

It was an imperfect plan to match all my others, and it was bold—too bold for me. But Kaia would have leaped into it headfirst, and I knew she couldn't afford my hesitance now.

When supper was over, I followed Neve out of the great hall. I didn't dare approach her until she had already climbed the stairs to the second floor, so as not to risk being overheard.

"Neve?" I said, just as she started up the next flight of stairs.

She looked disoriented as she turned, and it took a moment for her gaze to settle on me. Her eyes narrowed. "You're the taster," she said.

"Yes."

"What do you want?"

"I want to help," I said.

She frowned. "You want to help *me*?"

I hoped I knew how to play this. "I've heard Lord Patak talking about how much work you have before the lords arrive. If you don't want an Aurat as an apprentice, I could help you."

Understanding spread across her face. "I know why you're really here."

My heart froze. She couldn't know, could she? I'd covered my tracks well—there was no reason for her to suspect me of being Verran.

"You don't want anything to do with me. You're just frightened of dying by poison and looking to get out of it."

I started to protest, then realized that it might be better to let her accusation stand.

She shrugged. "Nothing keeps you here. If you don't want the job anymore, you can leave."

"It's true I don't want to taste the lord's food anymore," I said. "But it's not just because I'm frightened. I do want to help you."

"And what if I told you that the apprentices I've dismissed in the past have been taken, disappeared? Service to the Aromatory will not make you safer."

"But you need the help, don't you? Or you won't finish in time. I've seen the toll it's taken. I've watched you."

She sighed and pinched the bridge of her nose between her fingers. "I don't have time for this," she muttered. "What do you know about the Aromatory's work?"

Hope leaped in my chest. "I know it has something to do with the dragons. Nothing else."

"Hmm. Come with me."

Neve led the way up to the third floor. She unlocked a door at the end of the hall, and we entered a room nearly as ornate as Lord Patak's. She went to the far wall and unlocked a small cabinet, then pulled out a selection of five mismatched bottles with glass stoppers. She set them down on the table and looked at me. "Sit."

I sat in the chair she indicated. She slid one bottle toward me. "Open it."

I didn't understand what I was doing, but I lifted the stopper anyway.

"Tell me what you smell. Be as specific as possible, no matter how strange it seems."

Warmth. Sun. A sharp, sweet tang in the back of my mouth. It was on the tip of my tongue—Father had brought fruit that smelled like this to the mountain once, after a long trip to Kyseal. "Orange," I said.

Neve did not react, other than to stopper the first bottle and pass me another one.

"Mint."

"Anise seed."

"Sand . . . desert sand."

"Risen dough."

And the last . . . Neve pulled a small vial out from under her shirt, where it hung on a chain. My nostrils flared as she opened it, placing the bottle exactly at the center of the table instead of offering it to me. The hair on my arms raised at the scent, fresh as bitter pine, sharp as ice. But there was something else, too, a spice that brought the blood rushing through my veins. A heat like the desert thistle my father sometimes brought home. It burned my nose and made my eyes water, and I came up blinking.

"Describe what you smelled," Neve said.

"Fire," I blurted without thought. "And ice. Like the mountains."

She tilted her head to one side. "Why do you say that?"

I bit my lip. I couldn't say anything that would betray that I was from Ilvera. So I shrugged. "Reminds me of them, that's all."

Neve nodded, as though this made some sort of sense to

her. She reclaimed the bottle and put the chain back around her neck, then leaned back in her chair, studying me.

"Your sense of smell is developed, but far from perfect. A true candidate would have been able to identify the desert where I gathered the sand."

"I can learn," I insisted.

"Stubborn, aren't you?" She paused, considering. "Very well. If you truly think you're able, I'll test you."

Had this not been a test?

"One of Lord Patak's meals will be poisoned. Identify the dish *before* you ingest it, and I'll take you on."

My jaw dropped. She—what? She was proposing to poison the fortress lord as a test of my abilities? What would happen if I failed?

I knew the answer. If I failed I would be dead, frothing on the floor beside Lord Patak's chair.

And yet I was already risking my life. Once I stole a dragon, I'd be given a death sentence, hunted by the emperor himself. My path was along the edge of a precipice, and every step was a chance to fall.

Whatever it takes.

I took a deep breath. "I agree," I said.

My legs shook as I made my way back down to the kitchens. I was one step closer to the dragons. One step closer to Kaia.

Kaia. She would shake me silly for what I was doing if she were here. But she would have done exactly the same for me, if I had been taken. She wouldn't have hesitated. She had promised. And here I was, quiet and set to trembling at every threat—but I was here. A poor substitute, perhaps, but I would not give up.

Once I had retired for the night and lay in my bunk, breathing calm into my limbs, my thoughts wandered back to the last oil that Neve had presented to me. My identification had been far from complete. I'd described it as fire and ice—but that was wholly inadequate to encapsulate what I'd smelled, and what I'd felt. The scent, whatever that had been, had woken something in me that felt like a monster writhing, struggling to break through my skin from the inside out.

"Again." Pain blooms across my palm, gone in a flash. An Aurat stands over me, a thin wooden wand in her hand.

I can't do what she's asking. I've stood for hours this way, my legs shaking, my feet throbbing. They tell me to open my mind, to pour myself down through the stone of Lumina. I've flung my thoughts away from this place, to the mountain, to the lake, to anything that is not the inside of this cell, these four walls, the ceiling above me, the icy stone below my feet. I close my eyes again. They wait impassively for me to hit a mark I will not aim at.

I list to one side—the wand kisses my arm with fire. I fail.

"Again."

I woke with a queasy stomach and reflexes that jumped at everything that moved. With each new dream of Kaia I was more convinced that somehow I was seeing things that were actually happening. If I believed what I was seeing as I slept, Kaia had reached Lumina. And they were *hurting* her. At least it seemed they wanted her for a reason. But what? And how long would it take for them to tire of her refusal to cooperate?

I tried not to panic as Gemed prepared breakfast for Lord

Patak. It seemed unlikely that Neve would poison the first meal, not when we had just spoken the night before. But perhaps that was a reason she *would* poison it, knowing that I would expect it to come later, when I had let down my guard.

I spent the day questioning every smell, every bite of Lord Patak's food until I'd convinced myself not only that I'd been poisoned, but that this poison was attacking my brain and slowly driving me mad.

Neve, on the other hand, seemed perfectly serene. I didn't dare look at her across the high table at supper.

I couldn't sleep that night. In the morning I got up before dawn and searched the fortress garden for something—anything—that could be used as an antidote. I dug up fresh ginger and was lucky to find callow bark growing in a forgotten corner. Kaia had once used it to play a trick on Tovin. In large quantities, it would induce vomiting. But there was nothing else I recognized that would directly counter any of the few poisons with which I was familiar.

"What are you doing?" Mol mumbled as I came into the dormitory.

"Ginger. For cramps," I whispered.

She rolled over and went back to sleep. I pocketed the herbs and carried them with me everywhere.

Aside from the perilous challenge I'd brought upon myself, tensions were rising at the fortress. Sev fell asleep at the table during the noon meal, and Lilin looked little better. "There's just too much to be done," she confessed. "I haven't slept enough in . . ." She trailed off. "Too long," she finished finally.

"And all this is because of the Talons?" I asked.

Lilin twirled her spoon between her fingers. "By the decree of the Flame of the West. We are but his hands, doing his will."

She had to be exhausted to say that much—Lilin had never let a word pass her lips in my presence that could be construed as criticism of the emperor. I left her to her meal.

Another day passed. Two more. I knew Neve expected me to be able to smell the poison, but I didn't trust in just my nose's ability. I inspected Lord Patak's food carefully before I ate it, judging each piece of bread against the last, comparing for differences. I stayed alive.

Two riders arrived at the fortress, their high-bred Zefedi horses skittish and balking at the scent of dragon. They were sent by the Flame himself, to inspect the fortress ahead of the arrival of the lords.

Supper was late as a result. Gemed changed his mind three times about the menu before settling on a cold soup, a roast, and light butter cakes to finish. I walked beside the servant who was carrying the dishes for Lord Patak and the two visitors.

The soup was a vibrant green that I barely tasted, and the roast was well-spiced. But when I leaned over the cake that the lord had passed to me to taste, I hesitated.

I had been in the kitchens as Gemed had flipped them out of the cooking irons. I had smelled them as he dusted them with cinnamon and painstakingly dripped three drops of aromatic oils over their tops. But they smelled different now.

It was an odor so slight. I closed my eyes, hoping that by blocking out my other senses, I would be able to put my finger on what it was. Something . . . bitter.

I couldn't identify it. I opened my eyes and looked around the table. Neve wasn't there.

Where had she gone? She hadn't said what I was supposed to do when confronted with the poison. I couldn't tell them she had done it—they would never believe me, especially when she wasn't here to speak on the matter herself. And I couldn't wait any longer for her to reappear.

"Wait," I said.

The word came out so quietly that I had to clear my throat and repeat myself, louder, before the table took any notice. Then everyone turned their heads to stare at me, as surprised as if an owl had started to speak.

"Well?" said the lord impatiently.

I looked down at the cake again. "There's something wrong with the cake."

The lord laughed. "How could you possibly know without eating it?"

I shook my head. "I can smell it. There's something wrong."

The lord gestured. The man sitting on my other side bent over and sniffed exaggeratedly before shaking his head.

"I know what that cake is supposed to smell like," I said. "I was in the kitchen while it was being prepared. It smells different now. Bitter, almost like almonds. I'm not eating it, and neither should you."

The lord's lips twisted. "Well. If you won't deign to do as you're told, then how are we to determine whether your claim is true?"

"I'd swear it on anything," I said. "Neve could tell you."

Lord Patak looked around the table. Neve still wasn't here . . . but I could almost hear the wheels turning in his head as he noticed who was: the two riders, advisors to the emperor, who were watching our exchange with interest. He grabbed my arm and pulled me down to him. "If you're doing this to make a fool of me, you'll be very sorry."

He pushed his chair back and stood up. "Pardon the interruption. Please, carry on," he said, bowing to the table. Then he turned to me. "You. Bring the cake."

He snapped his fingers at the guards standing at attention near the doors. They followed us to the kitchens, where Gemed and the other servants were cleaning up after dinner.

"Was the cake not to your liking, my lord?" Gemed said, straightening.

Patak snapped his fingers at me. Hands trembling, I placed the cake on the long kitchen table.

"Your taster insists that it is poisoned," the lord said. "Can anyone explain why she might think that?"

Gemed paled as the eyes in the room fell on him. To deny involvement would sound cowardly, but what else could he do, if he was innocent?

"It's a butter cake," he said. "All the ingredients came from the usual places. Cinnamon and orange oil to top. Nothing was tampered with in this kitchen."

"That you saw," the lord said pointedly.

"The cake was clean when it left the kitchen," Gemed said.

"Would you swear to that before the seers?" Kellyn had entered the kitchen behind us.

It was foolish to speak. But I couldn't see Gemed blamed for something I knew he hadn't done. "He didn't do it," I said.

"And how do you know that?" asked Kellyn.

"I assisted in preparing the cakes," I said. "They didn't smell that way when they left the kitchen. It must have happened when they were being carried to the hall."

"Or at the table itself," Kellyn pointed out.

A sick feeling spread through my stomach. "I didn't do this," I said. "I saved him!"

"I saw her," Mol said, stepping forward.

What? I turned toward her.

"She came in from the gardens a few days ago. She'd been digging around. She could have planted something there."

"So you poisoned the cake yourself in order to take credit for saving Lord Patak's life?" Kellyn said. "I've heard enough." She gestured to the guards standing behind her. "Take the girl."

"But—I didn't do anything! I dug up some ginger for cramps!" I pulled the ginger out of my pocket.

"Or to cover your tracks." Kellyn gave me a small, dangerous smile.

"Wait." Neve stood in the doorway. I almost melted into the floor in relief.

The smile dropped from Kellyn's face. "This doesn't concern you," she said.

"Am I not the expert in matters of scent?" Neve said. She spoke with the confidence of someone who knew her authority. She walked to the table and picked up the plate, examining it from this angle and that, then closed her eyes and inhaled.

Finally she set the plate down and looked directly at the lord. "Arryn oil."

The lord's face went white. "We have to lock down the fortress at once."

"There's no need," Neve said. "I poisoned the cake."

In another context, the shocked scene might have been a comical tableau. But all I felt was an inability to breathe properly.

"*You?*" said Lord Patak. "I don't understand."

Neve looked at Kellyn, then at me. "This conversation is best suited for more private quarters," she said.

"Fine." Lord Patak snapped his fingers again at the guards, who ushered us from the kitchens. I caught a glimpse of Gemed on the way out. His face was crestfallen.

Curious faces greeted us in the hall as we proceeded upstairs to the lord's chambers, but no one in our party spoke. Once we were all inside and the door was locked, Lord Patak threw the cake against the wall. The plate shattered, and I flinched away from the shards.

"*Why?*" he asked. "Was it you, last time?"

"I would not endanger you," Neve said. "I did this today—*only* today—as a test for the girl."

"A test?" he echoed. "What if she had failed?"

"I would have spoken up."

Kellyn's face was almost purple. "You weren't even at the *table*."

Neve shrugged. "Or the girl would have died. Does it really matter to you?"

Lord Patak paused, then shook his head minutely. "Not particularly, but it's just not *done*."

"*And* your little display has disrupted the fortress during this crucial period. The emperor will hear about your unacceptable negligence," Kellyn said.

Neve didn't react to Kellyn's threat—in fact, she sounded

almost bored. "Did you not say that I needed an apprentice? Did you not hound me about it all spring? I tested the girl days ago. This was the final trial, and she passed."

Kellyn looked, if possible, even more apoplectic. "She's a kitchen girl, not an Aurat!"

"And half the girls you've presented to me have been unable to tell the difference between onions and garlic!" Neve shot back.

They both turned and looked to Lord Patak expectantly, who threw up his hands. "What do I care for the whims of the Aurati? Neve, you think so highly of this girl?"

"She's not completely hopeless. Unlike Kellyn's initiates."

The lord ran a hand through his hair. "Poisoned by the Aromatory," he muttered.

"You were never in any real danger," Neve said firmly.

No one missed the glare Kellyn shot her.

"She's yours, then. Now get out of my chambers."

Kellyn made a sound of protest, but the lord waved her off. "Out, out!"

Half disbelieving, I trotted after Neve as she led the way back to the kitchen. "Collect your things," she said, standing by the door. "You won't be returning here."

Mol rushed to me as soon as I entered. "What happened?"

"Does it matter? Thanks for all your help, by the way," I said.

She crossed her arms. "What was I supposed to do, *not* mention it? You were digging up something suspicious in the garden! Besides, it seems like you got out of it all right. You could have gotten a lot worse than just dismissed."

"I haven't been dismissed," I said.

"You're not?"

"I'm going to be Neve's apprentice," I said. It was only now beginning to sink in. *I was going to be Neve's apprentice.*

Mol's jaw dropped. "How?"

"I—I don't really understand it myself," I said. "I have to get my things."

She followed me into the dormitory. "You know you can't trust an Aurat to keep to their word."

I paused in my packing, surprised. "That's a bit rich coming from you, don't you think?"

"Just listen, won't you? I know you think there's an opportunity here. Maybe you failed the Aurati tests when they came through your town and you think this is your way in. But you don't know what they do. What they're capable of."

I know better than you, I wanted to say. But Mol sounded so sincere it made me reconsider. In her own way, perhaps she *was* trying to help.

"Thank you," I said, finding that I meant it. "I'm going now."

I met Neve outside the kitchen, and she led the way back to the third floor.

"Here," she said, pointing to a door to the left of the chambers we had used for her test. "This will be your room from now on. Tomorrow after breakfast, report to me here."

She started down the hall. With nothing else to do, I opened the door.

There was a sleeping mat in one corner of the room, a bureau, and a table and washbasin in another corner. There was a small window, providing a partial view of the courtyard below. But as I stepped inside, something else tugged at my attention. A scent like ice in winter.

Perhaps all of Neve's apprentices had stayed here. I wondered what had happened to the last one. *Disappeared*, Neve had said.

I placed my pack on the floor and sat down on the sleeping mat. My stomach growled, and I realized I hadn't eaten any supper of my own, but I didn't dare return to the kitchen now. Instead I closed my eyes, letting the panicked energy from the test fade from my body, and waited for sleep to claim me.

CHAPTER TEN

I woke in the morning certain I had overslept. I hadn't dreamed, and though I was unsure what to make of the absence of a vision, I was grateful to have passed one night without worry. After a quick wash and a brush run hastily through my hair, I stepped back into the trousers I'd hung up last night and pulled my tunic over my head. I got halfway to the kitchen before remembering that I wasn't one of the servants anymore. The feeling that came over me was giddy, almost triumphant. I was still alive. I had succeeded.

From the look of the great hall it was clear I'd just missed breakfast. I snagged a bruised, barely ripe starfruit and darted back upstairs to Neve's door. The starfruit proved to be a mistake, as it was impossible to keep the sticky juice off my skin and clothes as I ate. Inwardly cursing, I threw the pit out the window and knocked on Neve's door.

There was no answer.

I waited. Were there instructions I had missed or misunderstood? I raised my hand and knocked again, then leaned forward and pressed my ear against the door.

The door gave way, and I stumbled forward, almost tumbling face-first into Neve's robes.

"Where have you been?" she said, shutting the door behind me. "Get lost? Have more important things to do?"

"I overslept," I said, blushing.

"Really," she said drily. "Well, go to sleep earlier next time." Her nostrils twitched slightly, and her gaze dropped down to my hands. "Eating, were you?"

Anything I said would likely get me into bigger trouble. I just nodded.

"Starfruit isn't ideal for eating on the run. It gets messy, and this work is about cleanliness and precision. You're late, so there's little time to waste. Come."

There were two doors leading off the chamber. She unlocked one of them and ushered me through, directing me to a small area partitioned off from the rest of the room by heavy curtains. "The most important thing is not to contaminate any of the scents in this room. Every time you enter, you must change out of your clothes and into these." She held up a set of finely woven white robes and a pair of slippers clearly meant for nothing but this floor. "Cover your hair and put on gloves as well."

I hurried to don the robes, leaving my own clothing on a shelf against the wall. Then I tied a scarf over my hair and drew on the thin gloves before opening the curtain and reentering the room.

My nose twitched. Glass beakers and stoppers, flasks, and brushes covered every counter and table. And it was all so . . . clean. No, that wasn't quite the right word. It wasn't just clean. It was sterile. The entire room smelled like *nothing*. Which wasn't at all what I had been expecting.

"It doesn't . . ."

"Smell?"

"Yes," I said.

"You'll get used to it. The scents are so concentrated that if they weren't under control, your nose would be overpowered. You'd lose your sense of smell completely."

"Oh," I said, my voice small. It was difficult to imagine.

"Indeed," Neve said. "Now, come over here." She led the way to a high table standing in the corner. A mortar, pestle, and a handful of rough stones sat on its surface. "Crush these."

"What are they?"

"Never you mind," she said. "For now, crush. They should be powder by the time you're through."

I placed one of the rocks in the mortar and gave the pestle an experimental twist. Nothing.

"Not like that, your wrist will crack." Neve grabbed my hand and adjusted my grip on the pestle. "This way."

Slowly, slowly the rocks cracked open. I looked up, expecting Neve to be watching me. Instead she had moved to a table on the far side of the room, her attention completely absorbed by an open vial. I watched her stare at it until she noticed me staring.

"What now?"

"I don't know what I'm doing. I don't know why I'm making powder. I don't even know what an Aromatory is. You're an Aurat—but I've never seen silver cords before."

"And there's a reason for that," Neve said, returning her attention to the vial. "Having buyer's remorse already?"

"No," I said carefully. "It's just that I'm trying to understand what it is we're doing here."

Neve finally set down her tools and looked directly at me. "I'm the Aromatory, the only one in the world. What I do is a secret of the empire."

"Why did you agree to take me on, if what you do is so secret? Kellyn would have preferred you choose one of her initiates."

"The reason Kellyn wants an Aurat at my side is so that she can replace me—but Aromatories don't retire. They die."

"Are you saying she wants you dead?"

"Quite." She raised an eyebrow at my shocked face. "Power and secrecy, that's the Aurati way. Kellyn doesn't care about me personally. She's interested in the knowledge I have. Now that I've chosen you, don't be surprised when she asks you to take your vows."

"To become an Aurat?"

Neve nodded.

"Is that a requirement, if I'm to be your apprentice?"

"No. Not while I'm the Aromatory. The fact that you're not one of Kellyn's sniveling brats is one mark in your favor at the moment. Besides, you might not survive the trials even if you did agree to take your vows, and that would be detrimental to both of us."

"What do you mean?"

Neve smirked. "You don't think that just anyone can decide to be an Aurat, do you? You would skip the initial testing, under the circumstances, but there would be the training. And then the midsummer trials. And then you'd be one of *them*, or you'd be dead. Either way, no use to me."

Dead? "I—what?"

"Enough about that," she continued. "As far as I'm concerned, all you need is a keen sense of smell and an excellent understanding of discretion. You've the former. We're now in the process of determining if you have the latter as well.

"No more questions. If you last longer than my previous apprentice, perhaps I'll tell you something else. For now, do what I say and nothing else."

After that we worked in silence. The powders I ground were grainy and uneven, and Neve's words rang in my ears. So anyone who walked through the doors of Lumina was betting they were good enough to pass the trials. And if they didn't . . . I counted out the days in my head. Despair stabbed at the center of my chest. Midsummer was only five weeks away. *Kaia*. She would never cooperate with the Aurati—my dreams told me they were already finding her wanting.

What was I going to do? Five weeks was far too soon. I didn't even know how to train a dragon yet, let alone steal one. I tried to calm myself. Running through the list of everything I still needed—everything I was still so far from attaining—would only lead to panic. And panic would only make things worse. There was nothing *to* do but stay the course, though that didn't make me feel better. Somehow I made it through the rest of my work without breaking and was relieved when Neve gave me a curt nod at the end of the day and sent me on my way.

"What happened last night?" Lilin asked at supper.

"What?" I shook my head, forcing myself to focus. I was still jumpy and distracted, and had almost gone down to the kitchen for serving duty before remembering my change in status. Last night felt so long ago it could have been years. I looked to the high table. Some of the lord's advisors were sitting there, but Lord Patak himself was absent.

"What was all the commotion at the high table? No one would tell us anything," Lilin said, clearly impatient for my answer.

"Someone poisoned the lord's cake," I said. I didn't know if Neve's involvement would become common knowledge, but I could imagine so many worlds in which it might go very badly indeed if others knew what she had done. I decided to leave that part out.

"How did you know? You couldn't have tasted it," Sev said.

"I could smell it. They didn't believe me at first."

Lilin leaned forward. "So what happened?" she said eagerly.

"Neve intervened. She confirmed I was telling the truth."

"But you're not tasting the lord's food today," Sev said. "So have you been reassigned?"

"Neve asked for me. Afterward."

The surprise was immediate. "*Neve?*" Lilin practically shrieked.

Sev didn't do anything nearly so theatrical, but he leaned forward. "Really? You're working with the Aromatory?"

I nodded.

"Doing what?" he said.

"I don't think I can say," I said. No one at the fortress knew the specifics of what Neve did. If I talked, she would know it was me.

"I heard she hasn't taken an apprentice in *years*. And you're not even an Aurat! Are you?"

I shook my head.

Lilin sat back in her seat. "Kellyn must be beside herself. She's been on Neve about a new apprentice as long as I've been here."

"Of course she has," Sev said. "Neve is the most important person here."

"Don't say that," Lilin said. "What if they hear you?" She nodded toward the high table.

"I said what I meant." Sev lowered his voice. "The lord could be replaced in a heartbeat. Same with most of the advisors. But Neve is the only living Aromatory." When I glanced up, he was staring at me inscrutably.

"What?" I asked.

"It's strange, that's all. Gemed, Neve. Two people known for their hostility, both taking you on." A blade of ice slid down my spine. "You must be some kind of charming."

I shrugged. "Coincidence, I suppose."

"Of course," he said, frowning, but he let the topic drop for the rest of the meal.

Water laps at my feet. I am standing at the edge of the lake atop the mountain, and when I look across to the far shore I see them—spiraling towers of white stone gleaming in the sun, more glorious than I had ever imagined. Wind rustles through my hair, and massive shapes cross the sky above me, their wings casting great shadows over the lake. A song fills my ears, golden and resolved and luminous. When the music ends, one word echoes from across the water. Follow.

I woke with a sob caught in my throat. I had dreamed of Ilvera, the way it had been before the tyrant, and I was unprepared for the emotions that swept through me: Joy, for the vision I had been granted. Sorrow, for the knowledge of what had happened since. As I lay in the half darkness of early morning, I became aware of something else: a high-pitched note in my room, almost a cry, that at first I wasn't sure was even real. But it persisted, even through the pillow I pressed over my ears, and after a while I gave up trying to go back to sleep.

I was tired and still distracted by the sound as I set to the tasks Neve assigned in the morning—sorting almost identical herbs by scent, washing vials and other instruments in particular ways, and, of course, more grinding. There didn't seem to be any rhyme or reason to how Neve apportioned the materials. All she did was hand me a stone or dried plants or flowers, and tell me to crush them.

So I did, setting my wrists and arms to work until they ached and the ache spread up to my shoulders and all the way down my spine. To pass the time, I found myself humming, a lilting patternless tune that followed the minute curves of the sound in my head.

"What are you doing?"

I jumped. In my inattention, Neve had managed to appear right beside me without warning. I looked down at the rock I'd been crushing. It was a creamy color, almost pearly under the light. The powder it created shimmered.

"No," Neve said. "I'm talking about you. What are you humming?"

"I don't know," I said. "It's just been in my head today."

"Well, stop it. You're distracting me."

I thought I'd ceased humming after that, but not ten minutes later, Neve set down her work with an exasperated huff. "Get out, and don't come back until you can keep quiet."

"But—you said the lords will be here next week."

"And I'll work faster without incessant humming in my ears. Get out."

I obeyed, stripping off my work attire and putting on my everyday clothes in a daze. It was early in the afternoon, and there were few people about on this floor.

I didn't know where I was going, only that the sound was growing in my ears, leading me forward. The word from my dream echoed. *Follow.* I bypassed the twin set of staircases that stood opposite the great hall and went up the servants' passage instead, which was tucked neatly out of sight in a corner. Up one floor, then another.

At the fourth floor I slid open the painted screen that disguised the passage and stepped out onto the landing. This was just a nondescript hallway. But there was a muffled thump above me, as though something had fallen. Another thump and then a scraping sound, like something sharp being dragged across the floor. However thick the stone ceiling was, it wasn't enough to fully deaden the sound. I returned to the passage and climbed on, my heartbeat tripping as it quickened.

I cracked open the screen to the fifth floor and peeked out to see two guards standing watch in front of a pair of gargantuan doors almost twice my height. I waited, but the guards showed no sign of moving. After a few minutes I had to concede that I was unlikely to get to those doors anytime soon.

I turned and started back down the stairs, but something caught my eye. There was a section of the floor behind the stairs that looked different from the stones around it. I knelt down, studying it more closely. Dust. The absence of dust, rather. The rest of the floor was coated in it, but something had shifted over these stones, and there was a draft . . . I looked up. The air seemed to be coming from the wall itself.

I put my hands against the wall and pressed against the stones. *There.* The wall gave way before me, opening up a dark crawl space. After a quick glance behind me to make sure I was alone, I ducked inside.

The hidden passage was so narrow I could touch the walls on both sides without stretching, which was a small relief. As long as the passage didn't branch, I wouldn't get lost. I closed the hidden door behind me, cutting off the light.

I walked the space with caution. I had no guesses as to who could have installed it—whether it had been built with the original fortress or carved out later. After a few minutes I saw a pinprick of light ahead. As I approached, I saw it was a peephole, and I bent down to peer through it.

There wasn't much to see. It was a room, an office, though I couldn't tell whose. I left it and continued on. Three more holes, three more rooms. The temperature in the passage was rising— or was it just my nerves? No, it was actually getting warmer, and I began to sweat. Another peephole up ahead, this one slightly larger than the rest.

This room was no mere office. It was a chamber larger than any other I'd seen in the fortress, besides the great hall, but that wasn't what made it notable. Three walls were solid stone, but on the far side of the chamber it was as though the fourth wall had been cut out, leaving behind an enormous opening. Through the gap I could see the tops of trees—the beginning of Anator Forest. I imagined that if I stood right at the edge of the open chamber, I might be able to see all the way to Deletev. Of course, that view came hand in hand with what I assumed to be quite a drop for anyone who stepped too carelessly. Something flicked across my vision, and I gasped.

There, just on the other side of the peephole, were the dragons.

They were about the size of the wild pigs that roamed the mountains, their bodies sitting close to the ground, supported by strong legs. Their tails were easily as long as their bodies or longer, and their faces were surprisingly expressive with curved snouts, big eyes, and small ears. Tiny fangs glinted at the corners of their mouths. Their movements reminded me of river otters swimming, sleek and sinuous, even in what I assumed was their youthful clumsiness—Lilin had told me the kits weren't yet a year old. Their scales looked smoother than I'd pictured, and each dragon had distinct coloring: deep black, vibrant blue green, and a third the color of sand. Their scales shimmered as they moved, like the undersides of seashells in sunlight.

They were beautiful. They were mesmerizing. And they were singing. That was the sound that had haunted me since waking, a cacophony of notes that were at once unfocused and bell-like, and the instant I thought of it as song, I couldn't think of it any other way. A familiar song, I realized. The same song that had played through my dream last night. A shiver ran down my spine. *Dragon dreams*, my mother had said. I'd been told to follow the song, and this was what had come of it. But what dragon was sending me these dreams?

Most of the dragons had their wings folded against their

bodies, and though I craned my neck trying to get a better vantage point, I could not find one with wings unfurled. They seemed to be playing, bounding after balls or nipping at each other's tails. *Playing*. I had never dreamed I'd see a dragon at play.

They weren't terrifying the same way the dragon I'd found chained in the mountain had been, and their size made them poor prospects for my purposes. But in this instant I wanted nothing more than to call out to them. I leaned closer, trying to see as much as I could through the hole in the wall.

There was a rich scent coming from the chamber—something dark, wintry, and unexpectedly familiar. It tickled my nose, and I turned my face into my sleeve. Close by—very close by—I heard a sneeze.

I froze. The sound was too close to have come from the chamber. I began moving as silently as I could back in the direction I'd come from. Whoever was here had broken the same rules as me, but without knowing who, I couldn't be sure they wouldn't turn me in if they caught me.

I burst out of the hidden passage and closed the disguised door behind me. Then I ran down a full flight of stairs and across the hall into an empty corridor before pausing to catch my breath. I was safe, for the moment. But who had been in the darkness with me?

Looking down, I cursed myself for my foolishness. I looked like I'd rolled in a pile of dust. I brushed off hastily, hoping that I would be able to get back to my room to change without drawing attention.

I got down to the third floor without incident, but as I rounded the corner to my room, I ran straight into two of

Kellyn's initiates coming from the opposite direction.

"Sorry!" I said, fighting the urge to brush off my clothes once again. I greeted them properly, fingers touched to my forehead followed by a bow. Despite seeing each other daily at the high table, we had never been introduced, and I had to confess that I often struggled to tell them apart, especially as they wore identical yellow robes.

They bowed back. "Shouldn't you be with Neve?" one asked.

I couldn't think of a reason not to tell the truth. "Neve found me annoying today. She sent me away."

The taller of the two laughed. It was rare to see the initiates without Kellyn, and I found myself looking at them with fresh eyes. They weren't so much older than me, and they were much less intimidating without their mistress. If Kaia were here, she would find some way to turn the situation to her advantage. Perhaps I could do the same.

"Has she always been so difficult?" I asked, adding a hint of gripe to my voice.

The shorter Aurat smiled. "Kellyn can't stand Neve," she said conspiratorially, lowering her voice. "But she's the Aromatory, so she ranks higher. Though Kellyn will be after you soon about becoming an Aurat yourself."

Neve had said the same thing. "Do you think I would be a good candidate? I've never been tested."

The two looked me up and down critically. "It's hard to say. One can never tell who is strong enough to survive until the trials."

That wasn't helpful. "What was it like when you joined?" I said.

The taller girl practically glowed with excitement. "It was shocking. I never thought they would pick me. I almost didn't go to the testing. When they called my name, I didn't think it was real. Of course, I wanted to be a seer."

"Just like everybody else," the other initiate said. "I'm quite happy *not* to be. Girls who become seers, they change. It gives me the shivers."

I could tell I was losing their attention, but I had one more question. "Is it true, what they say about the midsummer trials? That the initiates who don't pass are . . . killed?"

All warmth seemed to drain from their faces.

"Please," I said, trying to look vulnerable. It wasn't difficult. "I need to know."

The two exchanged a knowing look. "It's true," the taller girl said finally. "If you don't pass your trials."

The other initiate smiled thinly at me. "You won't be able to hide behind Neve forever. Best do what you can to prepare now." Her tone made it clear that she didn't think there was much I could do—and that she knew what the outcome of my trial would be. She nodded abruptly and pulled her companion along, leaving me alone in the hall.

I was more confused than ever, and more sobered. I would have asked more questions if it hadn't been so obvious that to the Zefedi, becoming an Aurat was something to aspire to. Something for which they were willing to risk death. The empire must be teeming with any number of girls jumping for a chance to join the Aurati, despite the dangers—and the seers most of all. So what need had they for a Verran girl like Kaia who didn't want to be taken? What real business had they ever had with Ilvera?

◆ ◆ ◆

"So. Assistant Aromatory."

I glanced up from my supper to see Sev looking at me intently. It was clear by his expression that he'd already tried to get my attention. "Sorry," I said. "I was just—"

"Contemplating the immense power you hold in your new exalted position?"

"No," I shot back. I hadn't been able to get what the Aurati initiates had confirmed out of my mind—the fear of what it might mean for Kaia. "I'm a glorified servant. If that."

"If you say so," he said. "Lilin and I have been talking."

Across the table, Lilin nodded.

"Day after tomorrow they're sending some of the dragons down to Deletev for the festival. Lilin and I have been excused for the celebrations. Come with us."

"Really?"

"Of course!" Lilin said. "The dragon festival is the best part of the year. I heard even the emperor was there a few years ago."

"I'm not sure I can go," I said. "Neve will need my help." Not to mention that an emptier fortress was an opportunity for exploring that I shouldn't pass up.

Lilin scoffed. "The Aromatory got along fine before you became her apprentice. I'm sure she'll let you go if you ask. The festival only comes once a year."

I found myself teetering on the edge of declining the invitation when Sev leaned back in his chair and stretched, his sleeves falling down to expose his forearms. My gaze snagged on a smudge of dirt above his wrist.

Sev quickly adjusted his sleeve, and I frowned. That could have come from anywhere. But something in my gut told me otherwise. Perhaps if I went with them, I might find out why a fortress guard was hiding behind walls, watching what he wasn't meant to see.

"All right," I said. "I'll ask."

CHAPTER ELEVEN

I was surprised when Neve gave me permission to go without discussion. She scarcely even looked up from her work as she told me it would be educational and waved me out of the workshop. It seemed an odd thing for her to say, but I didn't question it. I was going to Deletev.

On the morning of the trip, I left my uniform in my room and dressed instead in one of the Zefedi outfits I'd borrowed from Kaia. I waited for Sev and Lilin in the courtyard near the gate with no small amount of trepidation. Was I making a mistake? Would this excursion help my quest or only waste my time? I hadn't heard the dragon song since finding the little ones upstairs, but I didn't know whether to interpret that as a good sign.

My thoughts were interrupted by the low carts that came around the corner of the fortress, each pulled by two mountain ponies. One large box made of thick iron sat on each cart, tied down with heavy rope. The dragons must be inside them, though they made no noise. The carts pulled into a line in the courtyard—I counted ten in all—and guards surrounded them, checking that everything was secure. Someone tapped on my shoulder, and I turned to see Sev and Lilin.

"Ready?" Lilin said. She had discarded her beige tunic for a green dress with long sleeves that gathered at the elbows before belling out around her wrists. The skirt was wider than the Verran style, and I wondered if that made it more cumbersome as well. She flashed her papers at one of the guards and hopped aboard a cart when he nodded at her. Sev and I followed, and I sat warily on the floor of the cart.

"Are you sure it's all right to sit like this?"

"So close to the dragons? Of course," Lilin said. "Otherwise we'd never get down to the city at a reasonable hour."

I settled myself as best I could. The iron box was warm in the sunlight, and when I pressed my palm against the surface, I thought I could feel the anxious thrum of the dragon inside. These older dragons hadn't been singing when I'd found them in the mountain—they had been so angry. I bit my lip. Would they respond if I sang to them now?

The drawbridge was lowered, and the carts trundled forward, and my impulse to connect with the dragon dissipated against Lilin's laughter. This was the first time I'd been outside the fortress walls since my arrival. Now the light seemed brighter, the forest greener, the air clearer as we bounced against each other in the cart. Even under the circumstances, it was impossible not to feel a rush of excitement as the fortress receded behind us and we began the journey to Deletev, accompanied by armed guards on horseback.

The ponies made brisk progress, and we covered the distance quickly, passing the wayfarer's inn by midmorning. Soon enough we crested the final hill, and I craned my neck to see the road unfolding before us and, there in the distance, Deletev.

For most of my life I'd found it easy to forget the rest of the world existed. Deletev was an uneasy reminder that as much as we Verrans proclaimed our independence, Ilvera still fell under the flag of the empire. The fortress existed because of our mountains, and Deletev existed because of the fortress. Now I looked on the city under the impartial light of day, and I saw the influence of dragons everywhere. It was in the arabesques on the high city walls and gate. The height of the towers, as though dragons might land at any moment. Even the way the road leading to the city wove and turned, like a dragon's flight.

The other travelers on the road stepped aside to let us pass, and Lilin stood up as we entered through the city gate. Sev grabbed my hand, and we jumped down together into the busy street. Because of the festival there was a clear intended route, and we swept along it with the crowd.

"Where are they taking the dragons?" I asked.

"The stadium," Sev said soberly.

"Never mind that—we're in Deletev!" Lilin said. "What do you think? Food first?"

My stomach rumbled appreciatively, and Sev laughed. "Come on, then."

We followed the ever-winding street to the market, and I was immediately overcome by the crush of people around us. Father had told me that as the capital city of the kingdom of Eronne, Deletev was one of the largest cities in Zefed. It seemed to be populated by a multifaceted mass of people from all walks within the empire, and even some from farther afield. Most of the people spoke Zefedi, but I heard the occasional snippet of Celet and Lirusan—even the odd Verran greeting. Here I felt myself relaxing—in such a crowd I could count on anonymity.

I was thankful for the coin I'd stuffed in my purse almost as an afterthought. In the Deletev market I purchased tender blue plums that rarely made the journey up the mountain, and beef skewers roasted over a small cook flame as Sev and Lilin hunted down their own lunches. Then we wandered, my mood brightening as my hunger receded.

I was cheered by the colors and dazzled by the scents. I longed to take the time to inhale, parsing out each flavor that passed before my nose. As it was, there was no time to stop and savor, as Lilin had set her sights on a carpenter's stall ahead of us, and I didn't want to be separated from her.

The carpenter's table was set both with functional objects and curios. A beautifully carved box lay alongside a featherlike item that seemed to have no purpose other than to delight the eyes. Then there were the dragon figurines, at least a dozen of them varying in size. The largest was as long as my forearm and looked heavy enough to be a paperweight, while the smallest was no bigger than my thumb. I bent down to study it more closely. It could have been the more detailed sibling to Kaia's dragon carving.

"Souvenir?" the carpenter said. "There's a battle tonight."

"Mm," Lilin murmured. She wasn't looking at the dragons. Her eyes were on another carving, a sailing ship.

"A dragon battle?" I asked.

"Cruelty is what it is, really." Sev's voice curdled with anger. "It's where the weaklings and sick ones are sent, to see who can earn back a chance to avoid the emperor's oubliette."

"Think you're above it?" the carpenter snapped back. "Don't come to the city during dragon season, then. Get on with you."

Sev grabbed Lilin's hand and pulled her away from the table, and I quickly followed.

"Why'd you have to pick that fight?" Lilin said. "I was looking at something."

"It's just wrong," Sev said. "You know it as well as I do."

Lilin glared at him and left us behind in search of another amusement. I eyed him with renewed curiosity as we followed. So he was a guard in sympathy with the dragons ... who spied on training sessions that were strictly off limits. I didn't know what to make of him.

Late in the day, Sev and I reunited with Lilin. A few hours apart seemed to have allowed them to forget their argument, and we sat on the edge of an empty fountain, eating our supper. A part of me knew we should start looking for an inn, since the carts wouldn't return to the fortress until the morning. But I wasn't certain I wanted to turn in at all. I was still swimming in the energy of *different*, and I didn't mind the hours of sleep I was sure to lose. At least, I thought I felt different. Though maybe it was only the walking and the food and the fresh air. Somehow I'd become accustomed to the fortress—a frightening thought indeed.

Most of the people passing us by were of Celet or Lirusan ancestry—I could tell by their warm brown complexions, sun kissed by the summer. Fewer were those with Old Zefed blood. And then there were the people of the Seda Serat, the islands to the east across the ocean—the emperor's latest chosen conquest. I understood that the Flame of the West had one natural state: war. I wasn't certain why he should settle on the Seda Serat, especially considering how long they'd traded with Zefed.

The tyrant's ire had clearly spread throughout the empire. I observed three groups of Seratese people passing through the square as we sat, recognizable by their darker brown—nearly black—skin and thick hair done up in dozens of small braids. Each huddle was followed by glares and undisguised whispers, and none of them walked alone. Considering the atmosphere of the crowd, I didn't blame them.

"Well?" Lilin said. She was playing with a bauble she'd bought cheap, as its head was dented on one side.

I thought she was talking to Sev, but when I looked up she was staring expectantly at me. "Sorry?"

"What do you think of the festival?"

"It's . . . overwhelming," I said.

"Not as many people as last year," Lilin said.

There could be more people in one place than the crowd I'd faced today? That seemed impossible.

A makeshift stage had been erected across the street, and two actors had brought out a scroll so long it had to be intended for comedy. Now one was reciting items to the other, who checked them off the list.

"Poison?"

"Check!"

"Comet?"

"Check!"

"Tidal wave?"

"Check!"

"Drowned in his own tea?"

"Now that's simply ridiculous!"

"Ah, but is anything too ridiculous for the shadow prince of Ruzi? As you know, he's stalking the emperor as we speak, readying to attack him with—what did the latest prophecy say again?"

"A feather pen!"

They were joking. I just hadn't realized that anyone in the Zefedi empire would dare to make such jokes about the Flame of the West. And a prince of Ruzi? Something stirred in my memory. The people I'd met at the wayfarers' inn had mentioned Ruzi as well—that the kingdom was falling apart, that there was a lost prince. I looked over at Lilin and Sev, wondering whether this was something I could ask about without compromising my own story. I decided to try bluffing.

"I thought there was only one prophecy—what do they mean by the *latest?*" I asked, nodding over at the actors.

Lilin lowered her voice. "Have you not heard? My uncle told me that the first prophecy the Aurati presented to the emperor this season was that he would be killed by the shadow prince of Ruzi. But that was only the first. Now the conspiracy includes him and several dozen others, depending on the day."

What others could Lilin be speaking of? I thought back to my own prophecy: fire. It was terribly vague. And what *would* happen if the emperor died? The crown prince was young, I remembered. Too young to rule.

"Or maybe they aren't as reliable as they used to be. I heard the Aurati presented four conflicting prophecies to the emperor in a single day. Their powers are slipping," Sev scoffed, crumpling up the leftover paper from his meal and tossing it aside. "Let's move."

"I'm not done. Neither is Maren," said Lilin.

"Fine," he grumbled, slumping back down in his seat. "Take all the time in the world."

"Is there something wrong?" Lilin said archly. "You've been in poor spirits all day."

A muscle twitched in his cheek. "Maybe I'm just tired of doing this, is all. Watching dragons be bonded to those lords who don't know anything about how to treat them. Bringing them down to the slaughter."

"No one's forcing you to do it," Lilin said. "You think you're so much better than us, then what are you doing working at the fortress at all?"

Sev didn't seem to have an answer—at least not one he was willing to share. He looked away.

"I thought so."

"At least I don't pretend not to see," Sev retorted. He turned to me. "What do you think?"

"About the dragons?"

The expressions on their faces told me it should have been obvious. "I—"

"You don't think." Sev's voice was flat. It wasn't a question.

"I didn't say that," I said. "I just . . . I'm not trying to stir up trouble." A blatant lie if ever there was one.

"I don't believe this," Sev said. "Do you know what happens to the dragons who lose in the pit fights? Do you? And I'm not talking about the dead ones either." He stood up and paced before us. "The emperor keeps them. Broken wings, some of them. Blind. Doesn't matter what state they're in—as long as they're alive, he throws him into his own pit. His *oubliette*," Sev spat. "No light. No space to move, no fresh air to breathe. They start to go out of their minds down there. And what does he do? He threatens people with them. Dragons will eat anything if they're starved and mad enough, you see. A bit like humans that way."

My stomach turned. Dragons chained, without air, without song? How could anyone, even the tyrant himself, do such a thing?

"You're being dramatic," Lilin said.

"I'm telling the truth. You're being willfully ignorant." Sev glared at me. "I thought you were different, Maren. But if you really don't have an opinion, then you won't mind coming to see the battle tonight."

Maybe it was the way he threw down the challenge, or the way he looked as he said it. But for some reason I felt defiant— determined to prove him wrong about me. I stood up.

Lilin shook her head. "I'm going to find a room for the night. You do what you want."

Sev shrugged and started walking. I looked one more time at Lilin, who turned away. Then I followed him.

The stadium was huge, with walls and spires intentionally sheared to evoke thoughts of the dragons within. As we approached, I realized that the shimmering material lining some of the arches were scales. I could already hear cheering and jeering coming from inside.

Sev flipped two feathers to an attendant standing at the door and ushered me forward, his hand resting briefly on my back.

Inside, the stadium opened into stone bleachers. We had to

climb halfway to the top to find two empty seats next to each other. It was a popular thing, a pit fight. I looked around. Everyone I saw was jovial and energetic. The floor and walls of the pit below were scored with the scars of previous battles—countless claw marks and black scorches, and dark stains that were likely dried spills of blood.

And the smell. This place smelled like dragon and smoke. Beside me, Sev shifted. His face was pinched, eyes unhappy. He didn't want to be here, but he was—to show me. The crowd roared suddenly, and I turned back to the pit to see the great black gates on either side crank open.

The summer night was warm already, but the air seemed to ripple with heat as the dragons entered the pit. They were about the size of two mountain ponies, large enough to dwarf a man standing at his full height, though still not as big as I'd heard the full-grown dragons in service to the Talons grew to be. I leaned over to Sev, though I almost had to yell to get his attention. "How old are they?"

"Yearlings," Sev said. "These are the ones that didn't leave the fortress last year. Now they fight for another opportunity to be bonded."

"Who are they?" I asked, motioning to the people flanking each of the dragons. From this far away I couldn't see the expressions on their faces, but they were all armed with long spears and light shields. They slouched, as though trying to make themselves as small a target as possible. The dragons were similarly reticent, approaching the center of the pit reluctantly.

"Stadium attendants," Sev said sourly. "No real training, no understanding of how to work with them."

The distance between the two dragons was rapidly closing. I didn't know what I expected—an announcement of some kind. Instead the attendants suddenly withdrew what looked like glass bottles from the packs slung across their shoulders and threw them hard at the ground, where they shattered. Then they sprinted for cover.

I leaned closer. As soon as I did, the scent hit me—fire and brimstone, so acrid it made my eyes water, and I sneezed and sneezed. By the time I wiped the tears away, the dragons had gone rabid. They stood on their hind legs, arched their backs, and roared. Their wings—what wings!—unfurled to their full length, and streams of fire escaped their mouths, burning out within a few feet. And then they sprang.

This wasn't a duel; it was a brawl. Unguarded, wild aggression. The dragons tore into each other with claw and fang, ripping and biting. Their wings flapped uselessly, tails lashing, and roars of anger mingled with howls of pain. These dragons weren't fully grown, and this was what humans made them do? For entertainment?

Tears, real tears, pricked the corners of my eyes. It felt like my skin was too tight for my body, which was yearning to leap up and run away. I looked over at Sev. His face was stony as he watched, but when he turned to me, his composure wobbled. There were no words that either of us could say.

There was no way out of this crowd before the battle was over. So when Sev reached over and grabbed my hand, I held it like a lifeline. Like it was the only thing that could keep me upright in this horrible, horrible place.

The blue-green dragon was gaining an advantage over the

brown one. It had managed to rip part of the brown's wing open and score it down the left flank. The brown dragon was limping, still roaring but backing down, backing away. I could tell that whatever had caused its berserker rage was fading, beaten down by pain. But the favored dragon was still advancing, still breathing fire. It lunged, caught the brown dragon by the other wing, and bit down.

The brown dragon screamed, and the world went white with pain.

I swayed in my seat. Someone—Sev—held me upright as I forced myself to remain conscious. The buzzing in my ears faded as the crowd's cheering came back into focus, and slowly the pain I felt began to recede. The brown dragon was going to die. I was sure of it, it was all I could see, until—

The attendants were on the field again, this time waving long lit torches that wafted strong fumes that made me feel suddenly calm, heavy like a stone in deep water. The blue-green dragon swayed and sat back. The brown one simply fainted, and the battle was over.

Relief flooded through me, though around us there were many people grumbling. How dare they complain, when this cruelty was finally over? Sev ushered me through the crowd, which was slow to move, slow to accept that their entertainment had come to an end.

The air outside the stadium was a rush of cool clarity, and all of a sudden I was aware of the sweat dripping down my back and the damp hair plastered to the sides of my face. I dropped Sev's hand—I'd forgotten I was holding it—and darted into an alley, where I vomited up my supper.

When I was through, I turned away and rested my cheek against the stone wall of a nearby building, determined never to move. Footsteps approached, and I cracked open my eyes to see Sev. I closed them again. I couldn't muster the energy to be embarrassed about my weakness, or bring myself to speak to him.

"Come on," he said. "We can stop by the fountain on the way back."

The farther we got from the stadium, the more it seemed like that world didn't even exist. No one sat at the fountain. Most people hurried past, likely on the way to their accommodations. I splashed water on my face and washed the bile from my mouth, though I could still taste it.

An inn across the way caught my eye. "I need to sit for a moment," I said. "There?"

Sev looked up at the sky. "All right," he said.

The place was mostly empty, and the Lirusan woman standing at the bar waved casually, inviting us to sit wherever we wanted. We took a table in the back, and I sank into a chair.

"It's awful," I said at last. And it was. Stories of the atrocities committed by the tyrant had been drummed into my head from an early age. But it was different to see them for myself. And as much as we Verrans hated the emperor's Talons, I'd always thought of the dragons as being noble warriors. A romantic, childlike view, perhaps. But that was what I had thought. What I had just seen wasn't like that at all.

Sev nodded.

"Will they be all right? I was afraid they wouldn't stop the fight."

"Sometimes they don't. But that's rare. They can't afford to lose the dragons."

My hands were shaking. I placed them flat against the table, palms down. "I don't understand. If you hate this so much, then why *do* you work at the fortress?"

For a while he didn't say anything. Then he spoke. "I suspect it's for a similar reason to why *you're* here."

My heart stopped. "What do you mean?"

"I've seen the way you act," he said. "You're not like the others. You don't worship the Flame the way they do. You're here because for whatever reason, being at the fortress is better for you than being elsewhere. I took a chance, showing you this. Lilin . . ." He sighed, frustrated. "Lilin's like so many of the others. She doesn't care to think too hard about the ways in which her work contributes to what the dragons undergo. She doesn't hurt the dragons herself. *She* only serves the people who *do*, so what does it matter? But you're different. I knew you would be."

My first reaction was one of relief. He hadn't seen me in the hidden passage. He didn't know about my plan. And yet . . . he'd still been watching me closely enough to notice more than I wanted him to. I would have to be more careful in the future. "But if you're not like them, why do you do it?" I asked.

"Like I said. Everyone has reasons they think make the trade-off acceptable." Sev leaned toward me, taking my hand between his. Warmth spread through my chest at his touch. "How are you feeling now?" he asked.

I took my hand back, putting it under the table. "Better," I said. And I *had* been feeling better—until he'd held my hand. "Should we go find Lilin?"

"I'm sure she's fine," Sev said. "If this place has rooms available, we can stay here. I'll go see."

I dug a few feathers from my purse and put them on the table. "Here. For my room."

For a moment it looked like he was going to argue. Then he pocketed the coins and went to speak with the woman at the bar.

"We're in luck," he said when he returned. "There are rooms available—unusual for the festival."

He passed me a key, and we rose from the table. At the staircase I paused, grabbing Sev's arm to stop him. "Why did you show me this?" I asked.

"Because you're like me, I think," he said. "And there are precious few of us in that fortress to begin with."

I blushed. I couldn't help it, even as I suspected him of other things. Because I understood what he meant—it was good to know that there was someone else who knew how it felt to be an outsider. To know that you weren't so alone.

CHAPTER TWELVE

I stood in a hallway so long I couldn't see its end. The walls were white, the floor so black it was as though I stood upon a starless sky. My feet made no sound as I walked.

"Maren." I turned. Sev was beside me, holding my hand.

I opened my mouth.

"Don't," he said, placing a finger to my lips. "Promise me, Maren."

I didn't know what I could promise him—instead I leaned in and kissed him on the lips, my arms winding around him as the hallway dissolved and we tumbled into an ocean, the water closing over our heads as we clung to each other. The world tilted again, and we were in a landscape of snow, and all the while his hand was in mine, his mouth against my skin, his voice in my ears.

I woke up, breathless. I—that had been—I had no right to feel this way. Kaia needed me. We were *heartmates*. If I dreamed of anyone, it should be her. I needed to know how *she* was. Sev was Zefedi, my enemy, and I was losing all pretense of resolve if I thought he might understand anything about me. I'd betrayed myself and Kaia with this traitorous urge to—to *connect*. It was a moment of weakness; that was all. Every bone in my body was dedicated to getting Kaia back. I accepted no compromise, and I certainly accepted no confused dreams.

Nevertheless, I was angry when I caught sight of Sev as I climbed aboard the cart leaving Deletev that morning. This was his fault. If he hadn't taken hold of my hand, I wouldn't have—I refused to think further on it. At least he had been assigned guard duties on the way back, so I wouldn't have to speak with him. The winner of last night's battle was inside the cart, and it was imperative to transport the dragon back to the fortress as quickly as possible. The defeated dragon remained in Deletev, to be shipped on to the emperor's palace in Gedarin with the other unfortunates after the festival was over.

The trip back was uneventful, leaving me ample time to stoke my anger. I was here for Kaia, and Kaia only. Anything else was a distraction, and I would not have it.

When we arrived, I jumped down from the cart as it was still moving and stormed up the steps, where I collided with Lilin coming from the opposite direction. "Oh!"

She stepped back, her expression carefully neutral. By her neat appearance it was clear she had arrived before us, and I felt a momentary flash of guilt that I had been too preoccupied with my stewing over Sev to notice she hadn't been on the cart.

"How did you get back?" I asked.

"Caught a ride with a trading caravan," she said. "I didn't feel like waiting around for you two."

I looked down at my boots. "I'm sorry. We shouldn't have left you last night."

She tossed her hair back over one shoulder and shrugged. "Well, you're not the first girl to have her head turned in Sev's presence. Took you longer than I expected, if I'm being honest."

"What?" I blinked, confused. "That wasn't why I went with him."

"If you say so." She made to push past me.

Was she jealous over him? "Wait, Lilin!" She stopped. "We're not—there's nothing between us. I just wanted to see what he was talking about. That's all."

"Look," she said, lowering her voice. "I like Sev. But you could have a *place* here, with Neve's support. Don't let him distract you. He may be charming, but he's not as loyal to the Flame as the rest of us, and he's not exactly careful about what he says, is he? I'm not the only one who's taken notice, so you'd do well to watch yourself with him if you want to stay out of trouble."

My heart sank. She was right. Of course she was right. Whatever Sev was doing skulking around secret passageways, it was irrelevant to me. I needed to get to Kaia before midsummer. This trip to Deletev had burned two precious days, and what had I learned? Nothing.

In Neve's chambers I worked hard, moving items more forcefully than necessary.

"What has gotten into you?" Neve said.

I looked up. Neve had never invited personal conversation before, which meant either that she was in a contemplative mood or that my own mood was far more transparent than I'd realized. "It's nothing," I said.

"*Nothing* doesn't threaten to break my instruments," Neve said. She crossed her arms. "Out with it now."

I couldn't tell her the truth. It was too mortifying. I went scrounging for another excuse. "I saw a pit fight yesterday, in Deletev."

Neve inhaled sharply. "Ah."

"Is this what we do here?" I asked. "Drive dragons out of their wits? And please don't tell me that it's none of my business. Please."

Neve looked up at the ceiling. "Bring me the powder you were working on before you went to Deletev."

The change of subject was so abrupt I blinked.

"Come on, there's no time for dillydallying."

I went to the shelf and took down the powder. It had been a bright yellow herb. Crushing it for hours on end had mellowed it into a kind of rusty yellow with a sharp, spicy scent that made my hair stand on end after just a whiff.

Neve held out a wide, shallow bowl. "Put some in here. Just a pinch."

I did as she said, glad that I was wearing gloves. While most of the items we used were inert, some of them stung.

Neve donned an additional protective robe and handed me one to put on over my uniform. Then she took a pot of freshly boiled water off the squat stove in the corner. Standing back from the table, she put out her arm and poured the water over the powder. It hissed and spat, and a scent roared up in the room, heavy and hot and unbearable. I gagged and stepped back from the table, putting a hand over my mouth. It was exactly the same as what I'd smelled last night, except a thousand times stronger up close. My eyes were watering, my stomach clenching and oh gods, I felt *rage* exploding within me, calling for blood, demanding release—

The water cooled and stopped bubbling. The smell dissipated slowly while I paced the far side of the room, arms crossed. When it was gone, Neve spoke again. "What you have just encountered is fire root," she said. "It's one of the most dangerous scents we make."

"I smelled that in the stadium last night," I said. "The dragons went berserk."

"Fire root stokes aggression. In combination with other things, it's used to make dragons attack."

I could barely contain my excitement. *This* was what the Aromatory did. These scents controlled the dragons.

"That's all?" I said. "Throw it out and watch the carnage?"

"No, that's *not* all. The pits are a crude, lawless place. They have the undiluted powder for no reason other than to make the dragons go mad. There's no finesse. No training involved. It's brute instinct, and anyone involved in those brawls is lucky they don't end up dead." She shook her head. "Here, come closer. What you're looking for is a smooth texture, a color like rust. It should sting to the touch but not be overly painful. Mixing with water is the test. If you see this reaction, it confirms the powder is potent enough."

"All right." I leaned over the bowl. Its contents matched the description Neve had given, more or less. "What next? Do you bottle it up?"

"No. Grinding the raw material is only the first step." She set the bowl aside and brought out a clean glass jar, into which she spooned the remaining fire root powder. Then she took off her necklace and opened the vial she had tested me with. My nostrils flared as the familiar scent spread through the room—

pine and ice . . . and flame. It raised the hairs on my arms and commanded my attention.

"What is that oil?" I asked. "I've never smelled anything like it."

"And you won't anywhere else," Neve said. "It's a rare oil, distribution restricted by the emperor's decree."

Of course it was restricted. The tyrant would never chance losing control of the dragons.

Neve emptied the vial into the jar in one swift movement and put a lid over it just as quickly. "Now it sits." She covered the jar with a dark cloth and went to the cabinet along the short wall. She opened the door and set the jar on one of the shelves, then shut the door again, blocking out the light. "There."

"How long does it sit for?"

"Weeks, normally. But we don't have that time now." A lone horn sounded, and Neve paled. "The Talons. Early, just as Patak said." She wiped her hands hastily. "Clean up. And I don't just mean wiping your hands. Wash thoroughly. Make sure you're spotless, and come back here after lunch."

"But—"

"Just do it."

I dutifully set my things aside and went about peeling off the scent-drenched uniform. Back in my room I washed, scrubbing my hands with harsh soap until I couldn't smell the fire root on my fingers. I donned fresh clothing, though it was harder to shake the hot, heavy haze of the fire root from my head. Then I went down to the great hall for the midday meal.

Lilin sat in our usual place, but Sev was not at the table. I scanned the hall and found him seated against the wall, about midway between the main doors and Lord Patak's raised platform. I hesitated, torn. The lords were here to bond with the dragons, which meant I was running out of time. The thought of approaching Sev still made my chest tighten and my stomach flip. But I needed information, and he would tell me the truth after what had happened between us last night.

I steeled myself and sat down across from him. "Neve said the lords are here."

"And a good afternoon to you, too." Sev's voice was hoarse and tired, but I wasn't here to inquire after his well-being.

I leaned in and lowered my voice. "She said they're early. Why?"

He shrugged eloquently. "Who can say when it comes to the Flame of the West and his whims?"

"*Tell me.*"

Sev's expression stilled, and he glanced about the room before replying. "Wants to snap up the dragons before someone else does, doesn't he? He hears whispers, just like everyone else. Can't keep a muzzle on the rumors flying about, or the prophecies."

Prophecy. I'd been so distracted I'd let the prophecies slip from my mind. If the Aurati seers could be trusted—and Sev seemed to think they could not—that meant that somehow the missing prince of Ruzi would kill the emperor. It seemed the tyrant had a valid reason for paranoia. And Lilin had mentioned other prophecies, other conspirators.

I realized I'd been silent for longer than I should have. "So the lords will bond to the dragons?"

Sev nodded. "One each. The Talons are selected by the

Flame himself, and the dragon bond, once formed, can't be broken. A dragon carefully trained is a companion for life. Loyal to the end."

I sat back. "If the bond is unique, how can the trainers do their work?"

Sev smiled grimly. "Bonding is different from training, I'm given to understand."

Another stake driven into the ground, separating me from my goal. If the dragon's bond was unbreakable, I would need one that was not yet bonded—a yearling. Perhaps one of those that had faced down a screaming crowd in the arena, fought for its life, and come out standing. I should have paid more attention in Deletev. I might have stolen one then, if I'd gone about it right—

Nonsense. I would have had a dragon without the means to train it. It would have ripped me apart. There was no use in worrying over something that had already happened. I could only look to the future. I knew something of the oils, but I needed to know more. And I needed a dragon—and a way to steal it, and then get us both out of the fortress. It wasn't even worth thinking beyond that, considering the magnitude of what I must do first.

As if to punctuate that dismal point, the doors of the great hall slammed open. Sev jumped to his feet along with the rest of the fortress, and I followed suit. The lords of Zefed, Talons in training, had arrived.

There were seven of them, three men and four women, each dressed identically in jet-black uniforms with hair bound severely back. Unsurprisingly, they all looked to be Old Zefedi—descendants of those who had first come from the land over the mountains, the birthplace of the first Flame of the West—with straight dark hair, angular faces, and lighter brown skin than the Lirusan or Celet people. Theirs were the old families, the people who had been raised up into the nobility and royalty of the empire.

I'd expected them to be accompanied by entourages befitting their station, but that wasn't the case. They seemed more like soldiers, attended by only a few servants carrying a modest amount of luggage.

They advanced down the center of the hall to Lord Patak and halted. Patak stood. "Early come and yet welcome, kin of flame."

One of the lords, a young woman whose face seemed carved of stone, stepped forward. "Well met, my lord. We have come in search of wisdom."

Patak waved aside the words with a hand. "No need to stand on ceremony now. There will be a feast tonight with ample opportunity for that sort of thing. For now, sit and eat. I'll have the servants shown to your rooms."

At first the lords looked uncertain. But Lord Patak gestured to a table that had been cleared for them at the front of the hall, where Mol and the other kitchen servants stood at the ready with platters of food. After a moment the Talons approached the table and sat. Only then did the rest of the hall relax, while the Talons' servants exited the hall with a few fortress guards. And it was only after I'd sat down again that I realized that somewhere in the flurry of motion, Sev had disappeared from the room.

When I returned to Neve's chambers, there was a traveling case on the table that I'd never seen before. I watched as Neve undid the buckles on the case and flipped it open. Inside was a grid of cushioned glass vials, and she ran her fingers over each one, inventorying its contents.

"What is that?" I asked.

She didn't look up. "Nothing that concerns you."

"It has to do with the dragons, doesn't it? Am I not your apprentice?"

Neve shut the case with a loud click. "Provisionally," she said. "You are not ready to learn this." She sighed, locking the case. "But neither are they, and that's the hand we've been dealt. Very well. You'll come with me to the first training session this afternoon. But mind that you're to observe, not to speak. You'll do exactly what I ask of you and nothing else. I don't think I need to remind you of what dragons are capable of doing when they are startled."

I nodded, trying to keep the grin off my face. I was about to come face to face with a dragon—*and* learn how to bond with one.

Neve and I climbed to the fifth floor. She carried the case, and I walked behind her, mindful of her warning to stay out of the way. No hidden passage for me today. The guards at the door bowed to Neve and let us through.

Neve waved at me to wait as she walked to a man in the center of the chamber and shook his hand. I contented myself with looking about, unable to contain my awe. The space was even grander when I was standing in it, and the dragons! They were at least three times as large as they'd been the last time I'd seen them, though they were still a far cry from the size of the yearlings that had battled in Deletev. They still took my breath away as I watched them bat lazily at each other. Their song was a hum in my head, lazy and contented.

The door opened behind me, and I turned to see the Talons in training enter the room, forming a line in front of me without speaking.

They had arrived without their servants, each in uniform, with their hair unbound. It was a symbol of trust, my father had once told me. They were about my age—younger than I had expected them to be, given the enormity of their responsibilities.

"Welcome. I am the head trainer," the man next to Neve said. Behind him, his apprentices held open vials of oil, herding the dragons together. The air was scented with a misty lavender fragrance that soothed my mind. "You have arrived here sent on the most sacred of missions by our leader, the Flame of the West. You have been called to serve by bonding with a dragon. Do you accept this duty?"

"We do," the lords said in unison.

"Very well," said the trainer. He turned to Neve. "The floor is yours."

Neve nodded back. "Thank you. You are dismissed."

Reluctantly the trainer and his apprentices left the room. The door closed behind them, leaving seven young dragons unattended in a room with only one person who knew how to control them. And I wasn't the only person aware of it. The group of lords shrank inward, no one person willing to put themselves closer to the dragons that were resting at the other end of the room.

Neve reached into her satchel and brought out the case. My hands shook slightly, and I pressed my palms together to still them. This was it. The secret I had come here to learn.

"This is a dragon master's case. It is the most important instrument in a Talon's arsenal. Without these oils you cannot hope to create a bond with your dragon. And while that bond will ease and strengthen as time goes on and you work with your beasts, you will not be able to maintain it by yourself, in the absence of the oils. You have been given leave to approach a dragon and prove your worth, a signal that the Flame has put his trust in you. Should you mishandle the instruments you have been given, it will cost you your life."

She beckoned me forward and handed me the case. I kept my gaze fixed firmly on the middle distance—I wanted to draw as little attention as possible. "There are twelve oils in this case. In sufficient quantity, any of them is enough to provoke a response from a dragon, even when used by people completely untrained in the art. Your responsibility is much more particular. You must be able to use the oils to create a lasting bond with your dragon. You must make the dragon trust you like one of its own before anything else can be accomplished."

Here Neve reached inside the case and selected the largest vial. The liquid inside was almost clear. "This is mirth wood oil. It is the root of all your interactions with dragons. Without it, you would be incapable of creating a bond with them."

She opened the vial and held it up. I inhaled deeply, waiting. If this oil was the key to forging the bond, then it had to have some spectacular, overwhelming scent.

Pine, ice, and flame. This was the same oil that Neve had combined with the fire root powder earlier today, the one I hadn't been able to identify during her test.

Neve approached the dragons, holding the vial aloft. The dragons tensed and rose to their feet, necks outstretched. They were curious now, and a few of them chimed their interest. Their noses followed the vial as Neve walked back and forth before them. She then stoppered the vial abruptly and walked back to the Talons, seemingly unaware that the dragons, now attentive, were following her. I was surprised to notice that they weren't tethered to anything either—they were free to roam around the room.

"Each of you carries a unique scent pattern, a signature so faint that only the canniest of noses can sense it. Most humans cannot, but every dragon can. Now, each of you hold out your wrists. Roll your sleeves up."

The lords rolled up their sleeves with military precision, though it didn't seem as though they were eager to do so. Neve unstoppered the vial once more and walked down the line, dabbing the oil against each of their exposed wrists. "The mirth wood oil mingles with your scent and makes it uniquely palatable to the dragons. They may choose to bond to you and your scent once you wear this oil."

"What do you mean, *they* choose?" asked one of the lords.

"Exactly what I said," Neve said without looking at him. "Scent and oil are only the tangibles. But the intangible counts as well. Your heart must be open to the dragon. A closed heart will drive the dragon away. And yes, they may choose not to bond with you. Approach carefully, for if you cannot bond with a dragon today, you will not get a second chance. Noble brats are replaceable. Dragons are not."

Her words shocked the room into silence. I was used to Neve's blunt way of speech, but I was confused by what she'd said. If a person's unique scent did not match a dragon in this room, why did it preclude their bonding with a different dragon, on a different day? I filed the information away, though something about it didn't sit right with me.

"Now," Neve said, having finished distributing mirth wood oil among the lords, "find your dragon."

By this point only a few of them looked at her incredulously. "How?" asked one, tossing her hair over her shoulder.

"With truth in your heart," Neve said simply. "That is all the advice I can give you for this."

A few snorted in disbelief, but they all, one after the other, started across the room. Neve crossed her arms, looking after them.

They looked afraid, as I would have been in their position. They had no armor and only bare wrists to offer the dragons, whose nostrils flared and smoked as they approached. As much as I was enthralled by being in the same room as the dragons, I was glad that my role was limited to holding the dragon master's case as Neve supervised.

Two, then three of the lords stopped at a safe distance, arms hanging at their sides. The one in the lead—the young woman who had led the group from the beginning—stumbled to a halt when faced with the small sparks of flame the kits were producing—playfully, I thought. Then, as the sparks died down, she walked forward again, wrists held high in a stance of supplication.

The dragons wavered as I watched, rearing back from this unfamiliar attention. The woman ducked under a wing—I held my breath—and stood straight in front of the tallest of the dragons.

The kit flinched back, snorting out startled blue-green smoke. Then, slowly, it stood straighter, spine lengthening and relaxing, wings flaring out to the sides before folding back against its torso. It bent down until its head was beside the woman's, inhaled deeply, then exhaled as if it was sighing.

Something broke inside of me. By all accounts it was a triumph. But the taming of the dragon—even this small first step—was a sight that rang inside me like a discordant note.

Emboldened by their leader's success, the other lords moved forward. My shoulders tightened, though I wasn't sure why I felt such disgust. These dragons and Talons would be partners for life. They would never be forced to brave the pit battles or the emperor's oubliette. These creatures would be nobility.

But not free. Never free.

A yell rent the air, and I whipped my head around. One of the men had not been able to coax a dragon into gentleness. Instead it had attacked, raking a score of deep scratches across the lord's arm. Now the dragon was spitting fire as the lord stumbled back.

Neve sprang into action. She grabbed two of the oils from the case without even looking at them. "Ring the bell!" she shouted, and pointed toward the door. Two of the remaining lords raced past me, and I heard it ring—a harsh toll that brought running footsteps. A moment later the trainers burst into the room with large vials in their hand. I stumbled back against the wall, out of their paths.

At the other side of the room Neve leaped over the fallen lord and hurled the two vials to the floor, shattering the glass. Oil splattered, spreading the overwhelming scents of lavender and damp stone. The riled dragon staggered back and fell on its hind legs, its fire dimming until only smoke poured from its nostrils, and then nothing. The other kits were similarly affected, though it took me a moment to understand what they had done. While the first dragon had attacked, the others had moved to shield the humans who had already offered a bond.

I shivered. The trainers approached the dragons, moving efficiently to restrain them against the wall, but it was clear they were almost unnecessary. Neve had already taken control of the situation.

It was silent in the room aside from the one lord mewling in pain. Neve bent down to examine him. "This one needs to go to the infirmary. Tell them that once he's healed, he's to be sent home."

I stared as one trainer helped the lord to his feet. He was crying openly now, begging to be given another chance. He knew that failure in this realm meant his own fall from fortune. From what I'd heard, perhaps even death. What had he done wrong? What had the dragon found wanting?

My hand went to my wrist. I was a dragon daughter. But would that even matter when it came time for me to bond with one?

CHAPTER THIRTEEN

The remaining lords, who had entered the room so confidently, now left cowed even after their success. One of their own had failed. Even for those who had passed, this was only the first test. The trainers began to wipe the floor clean of oil as Neve approached me and took the case back. My arms, relieved of their burden, fell limply to my sides.

"Is that normal?" I asked.

Neve's gaze flicked across the room. "We'll discuss it in private," she said. "Let's go."

We left the training hall together and began the descent to Neve's chambers.

"How could you have let this happen?" I jumped. Kellyn stood behind us on the stairs, clearly furious.

Neve scowled. "No one *let* anything happen. As I've warned you all before, these dragons should not be bonding. They are too young."

"And what would you have us do? Make our excuses to the emperor and stop the process entirely?"

"It's too late for that now. The process cannot be interrupted, unless you'd like to report to the Flame that this entire brood is unusable."

Kellyn pinched the bridge of her nose, inhaling sharply. "Then things are proceeding as they should?" she said, her voice measured.

"If you call the unnecessary loss of a Talon and very possibly a dragon as well an acceptable scenario." Neve shook her head. "Go snoop somewhere else. I have work to do."

"I need a word with your new apprentice," Kellyn said.

"So speak."

Kellyn crossed her arms.

"Fine, fine. Maren, report to me after your little chat."

I didn't want to be trapped in a stairwell with Kellyn, but there was no way out of it. Neve's footsteps receded from earshot. We were alone.

"Let's cut to the chase, shall we? I was lenient on you when you just wanted a job in the kitchens, but things are different now that you're the Aromatory's apprentice. If you intend to continue on this path, you must become an Aurat."

I swallowed. "I thought the Aromatory was separate from the Aurati."

Kellyn laughed. "Neve may have given you that impression. But Neve is not the head of operations here. I am. The Aromatory has always been an Aurat. The Aromatory will always be an Aurat. Neve has insisted that she cannot do without you, given the accelerated training schedule. But after the Talons depart, you will leave the fortress and travel to Lumina for your initiation. Is that understood?"

Lumina. I was torn between laughter and fear. I could have a personal escort to the very place I needed to reach—but I couldn't very well hide a dragon beneath my cloak on the way there.

"Thank you," I said, remembering that any girl in Zefed would kill for the opportunity to join the Aurati. Some likely had. I had to play the part.

She frowned. "Do not think that just because you are excused from the testing, it will be an easy process. An apprentice can be replaced. Even the Aromatory's."

"I understand," I said. And I did. I could not afford to be complacent. Joining the Aurati was an honor—but I understood that offer to come hand in hand with a threat.

I caught up with Neve as she was unlocking the door to her chambers. "Don't tell me—you are to become an Aurat," she said.

I nodded. "She said that it was required."

She opened the door and went into the studio, placing the case on the countertop. "You know that if you join them, one of us will be dead soon enough." Her tone was resigned.

Death watched me from every corner. I was tiring of it. And the trouble was, I had begun to like Neve. She was unlike any Aurat I had ever heard of or met.

"If you don't want to be . . . replaced, then why take an apprentice at all?" I said.

"Because one was going to be foisted upon me regardless." Neve paused. "I could hold the knowledge hostage, I suppose. But if I died without passing it on . . . Without the oils, the dragons would be uncontrollable. I don't want to be responsible for what might happen to them next."

"Why did *you* become an Aurat?" I asked. The more time I spent with her, the less interested she seemed in anything to do with the emperor's plans.

Neve gave me a sad smile. "Don't you know? Every girl child in the empire must aspire to go to Lumina. It is the highest of honors."

She wasn't going to give me a straight answer. I decided to change the subject. "Will the lord be all right?"

"Yes," Neve said. "Physically, at least. But this is exactly what I was afraid of. Of all the shortsighted schemes, trying to rush along the training of new Talons is one of the worst."

She opened the case, fingers trailing over the two empty spaces.

"So now what happens?"

"The poor unfortunate gets sent home in disgrace. And I must continue helping the dragons acclimate to the lords. In fact, the events of the day probably quickened the process, at least by a few ticks. Shared trauma does that. Once they've fully bonded, the difficult work begins."

"And what happens to the dragon he tried to bond with? Surely it's not . . . disposed of?"

"Of course not. It will be raised here for another year. Yearlings are harder to bond with than the young ones, but they are more resilient. Those who win their pit fights will have one more opportunity to bond. Sometimes a Talon loses their dragon, whether through illness or battle. In such cases, the Talon may attempt to bond with one of the yearlings. Not all Talons make this choice, though."

"But I thought dragons could only bond once?"

"And the yearlings aren't bonded," Neve said. "Besides, bonding is an art as well as a science. Did you know, the people of Ilvera used to bond with dragons without mirth wood oil?"

She chuckled at my dumbfounded expression, likely mistaking it for surprise at this revelation. I was just shocked that she knew about Ilvera's history with dragons at all.

"It's true. No one knows exactly how, but the phenomenon is well documented. And don't look so surprised. A solid grounding in dragon lore benefits my work as the Aromatory. Past women in my position have theorized about whether bonding by oil is stronger than the so-called natural bond between the Verrans and dragons, but that's speculation. Without further evidence, we'll never know.

"Now, that's enough about that." She opened a cabinet and pulled out several more bunches of dried lavender. "Here. We're going to need more of this."

I was distracted as I pulled out my tools. Neve's words about the Verran history with dragons were impressive, but *this* was what I had come here to discover. The herbs I crushed were made into these oils, the powers of which I'd just seen demonstrated. These oils were what I had been missing. I needed to get my hands on a set . . . or what if I could make my own?

If I made my own set of vials, I would be able to abscond with the Aromatory's knowledge without anyone knowing what I had taken. Then all I would have to concern myself with was stealing a dragon, just as I'd originally planned. But that was tomorrow's problem. For now, I had something I could plan for.

That night I ate supper with Lilin and Sev. The two seemed to have gotten past their fight in Deletev, but Sev was oddly subdued.

"Tell me about the dragon attack," Lilin said, leaning eagerly toward me.

I winced. While the exact details of the encounter remained unknown, everyone in the fortress had heard that one of the lords had been unsuccessful at bonding with a dragon. "It was difficult to watch," I said. "The dragon seemed all right, but the lord—"

Sev stabbed at a piece of meat with his fork. "The dragon will be sent down to Deletev when it's old enough to fight," he said sourly. "That's hardly all right."

"I know. I'm sorry," I said. Much as I'd tried not to think about what had passed between us in Deletev, Sev was never far from my mind. I could imagine how unhappy he must be at this turn of events.

"Another waste," he said. "I'm sure it was the lord's fault, anyway."

"It will have another chance to bond," I said.

"Only if it wins."

"There will be new dragon kits soon," Lilin reassured him. "There's a restless mother downstairs."

Sev shrugged her off. "Why are you still talking about that? Dragons are not so easily replaceable. And if the Flame himself wants more dragons, he'd do well to reconsider his policies. They're worth more than a threat to give grown men nightmares."

Lilin's face grew pinched, and she quieted.

"What happens after the new kits hatch?" I asked, hoping to draw her out.

She flashed a smile at me. "There are usually three or four

in each hatch. They stay with the mother for a few days after hatching, but once their eyes are open and the wings unfurl, they go to a nursery. After that, we start spending time with them." There was a warmth about her as she spoke. It was clear that she enjoyed this part of her duty.

Laughter erupted from the Talons' table, and I looked up. It was strange, that in a place of such urgency, there were people who could find levity.

Abruptly Sev shoved the bench back from the table and stood up. He picked up his plate and left the hall without a word.

The next few weeks fell into a new pattern. In the mornings Neve set me to minor tasks while she prepared the next lesson, and I watched as closely as I dared out of the corner of my eye. Sometimes she brought me to the training floor to assist her—on other days I followed and crouched in the hidden passageway, taking careful notes as she introduced each oil. Every lesson started with the administration of the mirth wood oil and a renewal of the bond between the lords and their dragons. I saw an incremental change in the way they interacted, the comfort they began to feel and take in one another's presence, a change in the quality of their songs. However the dragons might have been with my ancestors, these creatures were different—inextricably altered by captivity and the ties that bound them to their Zefedi masters. I watched with a sinking heart, but could not look away.

And every night, I crept into the Aromatory's studio and, after catching up on what I was supposed to have done during the day, began to prepare my own case of oils. Neve had given me a key to the studio reluctantly after she'd admitted there wasn't enough time for her to watch over all my activities, train the lords and their dragons, and finish the oils necessary to complete the cases. While she was training the Talons, I was meant to be in the studio—and if I did most of my work after the sun had set, she was too harried to notice.

My task was slow going. During the day we strained the oils in progress using tightly woven cloths that separated the oil from the discarded matter. Then we repeated the entire process, forcing more and more aromatics into the oil until Neve was satisfied with its strength and purity. Since Neve checked the jars daily, I could pilfer only a small amount of oil at a time, and I worried every night about whether mixing the oils at various strengths would cut their potency too much to be of proper use. And I had no pure mirth wood oil.

I'd searched the studio from top to bottom for it, and for the cases Neve and I were filling with completed oils, but had so far been stopped by the locks on several cabinets and one large chest in the corner. The only way in was to break the locks, and if I did so, I'd only be giving myself away. For the time being I carried on as best I could, trying to soak up all of Neve's lectures. There were twelve oils in total. Lavender was the first oil she introduced—to calm. Spiny pine, to energize. Moss rock caused contentment. Fire root was the last oil to be taught. For that lesson Neve insisted each lord wear protective gear, and she reviewed the procedures in place in case of uncontrollable rage or fire on the part of any of the dragons.

They all managed to escape unscathed but for a few singed brows. The lords took it as a victory, though they had also learned caution during their time with the dragons. That night I stumbled into bed earlier than usual. The late hours I'd been keeping, combined with the adrenaline from my days with Neve and the dragons, were finally taking their toll on my body. I was exhausted.

Kaia, thinner and paler, hair unkempt. I stare at her across a dark cavern lit only by a coal brazier at the center of the room, above which hangs a small bowl suspended by thin gold chains. She is flanked by two Aurati seers in ceremonial green robes who march her to the brazier and bow low to me.

Not to me, I realize. I am no longer myself—I stare out of eyes that are not my own, that meander around the room and refuse to focus on anything for longer than a moment, no matter how I long to drink in the sight of Kaia after so much time apart.

"Great one," they intone, "we bring this girl before you as an offering."

Disgust ripples through the body I inhabit. The rest of my thoughts slip between crevices, impossible to grasp long enough to make sense of them . . . except for the hint of something new. Something I haven't felt in centuries. An opening in the stone, a presence, an eye peering. Someone is here. Someone sees.

Before me, the Aurati push Kaia up to the fire and hold her arm over the bowl. I will her to struggle, but she stands still, a grim, determined expression on her face. A knife is wielded—it cuts into her arm, and then she sags to one side as blood spills into the bowl.

"No!" I shouted, startling myself awake. I sat up, my heart pounding. Kaia was in danger.

It had been some days since I'd dreamed of her, and I'd taken the absence of vision as a sign that I was moving in the right direction. But now I wished I could will myself back to sleep, to search out the being who was sending these visions. I had to know more—but I knew enough already. *Whatever it takes, I will make it so.* Kaia had fought. It was clear in the blood beneath her fingernails, the gauntness of her cheeks. Whatever they had wanted her to do she had fought. She had done everything she could to get free, and now—of course the Aurati would have found her wanting. Of course she would be *finished*.

In the dark I counted the days, heart racing. I'd lost track of time in the frenzy of training—if anything happened to her, it would be my fault.

There were two weeks left until midsummer. Two weeks to get from Eronne to Oskiath, and into the Aurati stronghold. I had to go *now*, before Kaia's time ran out. I hoped my imperfect oils and half-spun plan would be enough to save us both.

I got up and moved in a strange, panicked haze. Up. Clothing. Pack. I collected my clothes and everything I had brought with me, as well as a few things I'd picked up here. I stuffed them all into my bag.

A heavy knock at the door snapped me out of my blurred state.

"You're late, so I expect to hear that you're so ill you can't get out of bed," Neve's sharp voice called from the hallway.

I threw the pack under my bed and kicked off my boots before opening the door. "I'm sorry," I said. "I overslept."

Luckily, Neve didn't look at me too closely. She seemed distracted. "I don't have time to deal with you right now. Go to the studio and work on the pearls. I need powder so fine it could blow away."

I nodded and closed the door. Neve had inadvertently interrupted my panic, allowing me to think clearly. I couldn't possibly walk out of the fortress now, in the broad light of day. Tonight. I would leave tonight.

I didn't follow Neve to spy on the training session. Instead I went to the studio and took down the milky lake pearls to grind—for clarity, used to enhance communication between Talon and dragon—as she'd asked. Then I went to one of the cabinets and reached carefully past the empty bottles to the back of the shelf where I'd hidden the vials I'd been working on. They were wrapped in nondescript brown paper, the same sort that held sleeping stones and moss rock. Now I took down the parcel and wrapped it in my shawl. These oils were amateurish and perhaps useless, but they were what I had.

Pure mirth wood oil. I still didn't have any. Now that I was planning to leave, the time had come to try getting past Neve's locks. I wasn't sure I'd be able to hide the damage I was about to cause, but I had no choice.

The lock on the chest would not give, so I used a knife to pry the latch from the wood itself. Splinters flew as it gave way, sending me stumbling back. That wouldn't be covered up so easily, but I couldn't think of that now. I knelt down and raised the lid.

It took me a moment to recognize what I was seeing. Talon cases, almost identical to the one that Neve took to the training room every morning, except these were sleek and new. I counted—there were enough cases for all the Talons in training.

I reached into the chest and touched one with trembling hands, then drew it out and set it onto the floor. It was surprisingly light. When I undid the clasp and opened the top, I saw why. The case held only four vials, leaving eight slots still unfilled.

I withdrew the vials from the case and opened each in turn, sniffing carefully. Fire root and lavender, spiny pine, and . . . mirth wood oil. How long would it take for these to be missed, if I took them?

Far longer than it would take to realize the fortress was missing a dragon. I swapped out the vials with my own crude oils, then hid the case below its fellows, closing the lid on the chest and replacing the lock as best I could. I slipped the vials into my shawl with the others I had already collected, and knotted everything into a sturdy package. As long as Neve didn't notice that the box had been tampered with before I left, I might get away with this.

I had to hide my shawl somewhere. My room was safest, I decided. I'd seen no evidence that it had been searched in prior weeks. I removed my apprentice uniform and washed my hands thoroughly before leaving the studio.

As I rounded the corner, I saw Sev standing in front of my door. I couldn't make a hasty retreat. He'd already seen me. I fought the urge to hide the shawl behind my back as I walked over to him.

"You're not with Neve today?"

I shook my head. "Too much to do."

"Oh." Sev leaned back against the door, then seemed to change his mind and stood up straight again. "Why have you been avoiding me?"

I could feel a blush rising up my neck. "I haven't," I protested.

"You *have*. I've barely seen you at meals—when I do, you wolf down your food and practically run from the hall."

Say something. Anything. "I've just been occupied with the training." I couldn't put the scarf down without drawing his attention to it, but the longer I stood there, the more it felt like a hot coal in my hands.

He moved toward me, and I stepped back against the wall. "Maren. I'm worried about you."

I couldn't help myself. "What are you talking about?"

"Look, being the Aromatory's assistant is a big step up from food taster. But I've seen you—you're getting too close to Neve. You have to remember who you're dealing with. You're working for an Aurat."

"I'm aware of that," I said. "And I'm very busy today, so if you'll excuse me—" I made to brush past him, but he caught my arm with his hand.

"I care about you," he said, frustrated. "I'm trying to help you."

On any other day I might have indulged the conversation longer. But I could not risk him discovering what I was holding. I wrenched out of his grasp. "I know what I'm doing, and I don't need advice from you." I pushed into my room and slammed the door behind me.

"Maren, please. You can trust me," he said through the door.

I leaned back against the door, shaking. Everything that was about to happen, I had already set in motion. There was nothing he could do for me.

I heard Sev's footsteps receding down the hall, and I sighed.

I didn't know how to interpret his sudden concern, but I couldn't afford to let my guard down now, at the last. Whatever Sev had said about caring for me didn't matter, because tonight I would have a dragon. Tonight I would finally be on my way to Kaia.

CHAPTER FOURTEEN

My heart stuttered for hours as I lay awake in the dark with one hand on my pack, the other over my stomach, which was so tightly knotted I was in danger of vomiting.

I could do this. This was what I had been working toward for so long.

As I heard the sounds of the first watch going off duty, I knew it was time. There was a window of opportunity during the changing of the guard, but it was fleeting. I took one more deep breath and stood up. Then I put the vial of mirth wood oil in my pocket and the pack over my shoulders, and slipped out of my room.

The hall and stairway were empty, but I still hugged the wall as I crept past the kitchen and cracked open the door that led to the back of the fortress. The only light outside came from the torches near the guard stations, which made it easier to avoid them, but more difficult to navigate the rest of the grounds. I moved slowly, favoring caution as I made my way to the cave where the yearling dragons were kept. As I got closer, however, I was surprised to see that things had changed since I'd been here last. The door was open, and five sleeping yearling dragons were chained to each other in a new paddock that had been constructed up against the face of the mountain. It was lit by four torches staked in the ground.

I swore under my breath. I hadn't counted on an active guard in front of the dragons. I would need a distraction at the very least.

I crouched behind a large bush and thought. I could go back inside and wait for another night. No—every day was crucial for Kaia's survival. My entire body thrummed with the need to act *now*, to not let another moment go to waste. I slid to the very edge of the paddock and sidled along toward the dragons, using the bushes and scrub as cover. Thankfully there seemed to be only two armed guards, and they were both facing away from me. I grabbed a rock from the ground and threw it in the opposite direction. Their heads whipped around as it landed, and in that moment I sprinted to the paddock and threw myself through a gap between the bars.

I landed hard, the packed earth jarring my ankles, and froze, holding my breath. No alarm raised. No fire engulfed me. I rose up from my crouch.

I had seen the dragon kits in the training room and two yearlings in Deletev. But now, these yearlings were even more overwhelming up close. It was hard to tell when they were asleep like this, but they had clearly grown since the battles in Deletev. Almost twice my height and solid across—more than large enough to carry the weight of an adult human.

There was a dull ringing in my ears. I pressed my hands to my sides and concentrated on slowing my breathing. Calm. Resolve. *Whatever it takes.*

I moved toward the dragons, keeping to the darkest part of the shadows. As I moved closer the ringing in my ears became clearer. It wasn't just in my head. The dragons were dreaming.

A brief smile curved my lips. If the dragons were dreaming, maybe I could use their song to keep them asleep. I looked back at the guards. They'd returned from investigating the rock I'd thrown, but there was no sign that they were suspicious.

Very softly, I began to hum. I took one step, then another. Now I could see that while their chains were too finely wrought to be accessed by claw, the shackles had been designed to be easy for humans to open and close. The only catch was the necessity of being close enough to release them.

The ripples of heat emanating from the dragons' bodies distracted me, and I tripped over some loose stones. My breath caught in my throat as I fell to my knees. I clutched at the strap of my pack—still intact. I grounded myself with one slow exhalation. Then I reached out. My hand touched metal, and I fought the urge to scramble back. If the dragon even rolled over in its sleep, I could be crushed. I needed to be quick.

I pulled the pin from the shackle and lowered it silently to the earth. Then I moved on, managing to free most of the dragons' limbs. I couldn't bear the thought of leaving any of them chained up. The last dragon I freed was the blue-green yearling that had won the fight I'd watched in Deletev. This was the dragon I would take.

I dug in my pocket for the vial of mirth wood oil that I'd carefully measured and poured from its original portion. What had Neve said, the first time the Talons had bonded? Open heart. I closed my eyes, willing fear to roll off my skin like water. I could do this. This was what I was meant for.

I opened the vial and tipped it over my wrist, feeling oil drip onto my skin.

The blue-green dragon snorted and a back leg twitched. Other than that, there was no response. I stoppered the vial and crept closer, holding out my arm like an offering.

The dragon slept on.

This was no time for sleeping. I pursed my lips and whistled the opening notes of the Verran call to arms. *Wake up!*

The dragon's eyes shot open. I stumbled back, fighting my instincts to run.

There was no time. "Please," I whispered, holding the dragon's yellow gaze. "I need your help." I reached out my hand, wrist up. When the dragon did not react, I placed my palm against the scales on its shoulder, right below a long scar. Anger jolted through my body, and the dragon reared, spitting fire. I dropped to the ground, one arm over my face, barely avoiding the jet of flames. In the distance I could hear the fortress bells sounding the alarm. The dragon roared as it unfurled its wings and launched itself into the air—and flew.

It was a magnificent sight, and one that made my stomach drop like a stone. That was it. My one chance, gone.

"Hey! You there! Stop!"

Ice flooded my veins. I turned to see the guards running toward the paddock, swords and torches in hand. The rest of the dragons were awake and shaking free of their shackles. There was no time to bond with any of them now, but maybe they could still help me. I whistled the call to arms again and ran, ducking under the paddock bars.

The fortress guards were well trained, but they were not equipped to handle four angry yearling dragons bearing down upon them. I swept past them amid snarls and shouts.

I had to get out of the fortress, but there was nowhere to go. They had seen my face. I glanced over my shoulder to see a second group of guards on my heels. I sprinted, boots pounding against the ground. Up ahead a structure rose out of the darkness. It took me a moment to realize what it was.

The well.

I took a breath so deep it threatened to burst my lungs. Then I hooked one hand over the edge and jumped in.

Down, down I fell until my arms scraped against the mossy sides of the well and my progress slowed. I sucked in my stomach and hunched my shoulders, praying to whatever god would listen that I not be trapped here, suspended between earth and river until I withered away. Shouts above me, the rush of the current below. I wriggled and my shoulder wrenched, leaving me gasping with pain. Another movement and I was plunging down into the water.

For the first few moments there was only shock at the cold. Then came the panic. Water crashed over my head, buffeting me about like a doll until I couldn't tell whether I faced the sky or the riverbed. All I knew was that I was moving, the current carrying me somewhere in the black—and then a sharp, crisp bite of air as I popped to the surface, gasping.

Alive. I was alive—but the weight of my pack was threatening to drag me back down. I couldn't lose the oils, not when I had lost so much already. So I sputtered and kicked, fighting to keep my head above the surface. I could now see I'd been swept free of the fortress and into the cover of the forest, but my muscles were stiffening and starting to fatigue. I had to get out, or else—I thrashed and beat at the water, slowly making my way toward the riverbank. At last I pulled myself up onto land, where I collapsed in the mud.

There was water in my ears, eyes, and nose. The adrenaline was leaving my body, and I was shivering and exhausted. But I could not stay here. I had to get up.

Why?

I had failed. Miserably. What did it matter what happened now? *Kaia wouldn't have failed*, I thought bitterly. But the image of her was just enough to lift my hands from the mud. To drag myself to my feet. No one else was coming for her. There was only me.

Whatever it takes.

The guards had seen me go down the well, so they would look for me off the river, but I had no time to cover my tracks. I ran into the forest. I had no other choice but to keep moving, one foot in front of the other, away from the fortress.

A strange sound drew my attention. I looked up, my vision doubling—but the sound did not come from the trees. It was in my head. A song, furious and pained. An enraged cry of confusion. One of the yearling dragons I'd freed must have escaped the fortress, and it was somewhere close by.

My heart leaped. This was it—one last chance. My teeth chattered, but I whistled, mimicking the dragon's song as best I could, and waited. There, off to my right. I whistled again and was rewarded by a glimmer of fire.

The yellow dragon paced among the trees, unsure of its

unfamiliar surroundings. Hope, in front of my eyes. My hands shook as I fumbled for my pack. It was soaked through, but the vials would be secure. They had to be. The dragon beat its wings, and I stilled until it settled again. The wet knots in my shawl were impossible to manage, and finally I ripped the fabric, spilling the vials to the ground. I stooped and scrambled for them in the dark, keeping one eye on the dragon. I hummed a calming melody as the vials went back into my pack one by one until I had gathered them all. The one remaining vial of mirth wood oil, I kept in my hand.

I took a deep breath. The dragon was still at a safe distance, but I remembered the way the Talons in training had approached their charges. For this to work, I would have to go to the dragon, close enough to touch again. I stepped forward until I could see the glint of its eyes in the dark. Then I unstoppered the vial and poured a few drops onto my wrist.

It took a moment for the scent to hit my sniffling nose, but when it did, I knew I had made a fatal error. This wasn't mirth wood oil—this was fire root. I stoppered the vial, but it was too late. The dragon might be confused, but fire root oil was a command it knew.

Sniffing the air and rearing, the dragon roared. A plume of fire burst from its mouth, singeing my hair with heat and setting several trees alight.

I staggered backward and fled through the trees that were now illuminated by the dragon's flames. Branches whipped against my body, and my boots jarred against the uneven ground. The dragon wasn't moving as fast as I knew it could, but still it gained. Heat touched the back of my neck and I smelled singed hair and fear pushed me to run faster—faster—until—

Something barreled into my side, and I fell heavily. My assailant and I rolled down an incline, and my head struck a rock. Stars lit up my vision, but I punched out anyway. I heard a grunt, and then my arm was twisted behind my back. A hand clamped over my mouth, muffling my cry of pain. As another burst of flame lit the night, I caught sight of the colors of the fortress guard uniform and a familiar face: Sev.

I shook my head, trying to clear the sudden ringing in my ears. He said something that I could not hear. I didn't understand the desperation I saw on his face, but I quieted. He released his hold on me and put a finger to his lips. Then he drew me to my feet, leading me to a small hollow. The ringing in my ears had dulled, and I could hear the dragon bellow somewhere close by as we huddled there. Sev dug his fingers into the ground and reached for my hands. I didn't understand what he was doing until he started smearing dirt over my skin—he was trying to mask the scent of the fire root.

There was movement in the dark. I tensed, and Sev grabbed my arm.

"Don't move," he whispered, lips brushing my ear.

I waited, holding my breath. There was rustling in the trees, and soon a group of what could only be men on the hunt passed by our hiding place.

I exhaled only when we could no longer hear their footsteps or the sound of their grumbling to one another. But a moment later, there came a fierce cry of anguish that rattled through me. Sev pulled me upright. "They found the dragon. It will give us cover."

I hesitated.

"We have to move," he said. "When the dragon is contained, they will come for you."

"Why are you doing this?" I asked, the words sounding strange and slow to form as my temple began to throb.

"I'll tell you," he said. "Once we are out of danger."

For now, I could see no better option.

He did not take my hand as we ran, but stayed a few feet ahead of me without looking back, trusting that I would follow. He had his own bag across his back, which only deepened my confusion.

We ran until the forest quieted around us, and my feet slowed to a trot, then a walk. But it was only when Sev fell back to match my pace that I broke, overwhelmed by all that had happened, and wept as I walked. Sev didn't speak. He only led us away from the fortress. By now I imagined it would be almost out of sight behind the trees, the tallest spires the only visible parts. But I didn't turn to look.

I guessed we were near the northern edge of the forest when Sev angled toward a group of tall trees standing together and pulled aside what looked like an innocuous pile of branches to reveal a hideaway burrow. "Come on," he said.

The space was barely big enough for two bodies—it clearly had been made for one. The packs we wore forced us to stand face to face, the tips of our boots touching. I could smell him—the lemony soap he had used to wash, his sweat. Even though my body was shaking with cold, I could still feel my cheeks warm at how close we were.

"We're safe here for now," he said. "But we need to put more distance between us and the fortress."

"Why are you doing this? What do you want from me?" I asked, my teeth chattering.

"The answers to your questions would take more time than we can spare."

"Give me a reason," I said. "One reason to trust you through the night."

His face was cloaked in darkness, but our bodies were close enough that I felt his pause of consideration, his stillness.

Then I heard him fumbling with his pack. "Give me your hand."

I reached out, and he took my wrist, guiding it into the bag. I could feel something wrapped with a thick cloth. Sev brushed aside the cloth, and my fingers touched something that felt like a smooth stone—but it had a pulse, like a steady beating heart against my fingertips. Recognition shot through me, and the ghost of a song echoed in my mind.

I drew my hand back. "You—you stole—"

"Yes," Sev said, cutting me off. "So maybe we can make a deal, if we survive the night. Good enough for you?"

Everything I thought I knew about Sev fragmented. My mind raced. Could this be a trap? Had he been sent to capture me through trickery? No, that didn't make sense. If the other fortress guards had sent Sev, they would have had to know that *I* would try something. Whatever Sev's game was, it was his own.

And besides, he had a *dragon egg*. Now that I'd touched it, I could feel a presence reaching out tentatively to my thoughts, curious to know what I was.

"All right," I said at last. "I'll trust you for the night. How do you propose we get out of the valley?"

"They'll search the roads first, so we'll cut through the forest and make for Deletev. It's better that we're traveling together—they'll be looking for just you at first."

"There aren't many paths through the forest. How will we make good time?"

"I made a plan."

Of course. He'd come to the fortress prepared, with an escape route. I felt even more ashamed of my slipshod effort. No wonder I had failed. I'd jumped first, assuming my patchwork knowledge of Zefed would catch me. But it turned out I knew nothing.

I nodded. "Let's go."

We listened. There were crashing sounds in the distance—guards rushing through the underbrush, perhaps—but nothing nearby. We crept out of the hole, and Sev replaced the branches before we left. I wanted so much to question him further, but we both knew who else might be stalking these trees. So we were silent, and the tension between us grew taut as a trip wire.

As the sky began to lighten, I could see that Sev's face was haggard, but determined. He glanced at me every so often, pretending to be turning against the branches that hung low across the path we were on.

Finally I broke the silence. "There's no need to check up on me."

He looked at me straight on this time. "Are you all right?"

What a question. "We're away from the fortress now," I said. "If you want me to be all right, you could start by telling me what you think you're doing."

"I could ask you the same question," he said. "What apprentice of the Aromatory attempts to steal a dragon, knowing it would mean certain death?"

I lifted my chin. "I don't need to answer to you. And I don't need your help."

A shadow of a smile crossed Sev's face. "Don't you? You clearly need a dragon for something. I have one."

Equivocating any longer seemed pointless. "You have an *egg*. That's useless to me." True words, though the presence in my mind seemed to rumble with displeasure.

"Better an egg than empty hands."

I rolled my eyes. "So you have an egg. What do you need me for?" The answer dawned on me even before Sev opened his mouth. "You don't know how to train it."

He nodded. "No one outside the Talons knows how dragons are trained. I assumed it would be straightforward enough—I didn't know of the Aromatory until I arrived, and Neve keeps her secrets well. I almost gave up. But then you came along, and I thought . . . it seemed like you were like me. Like you actually cared about the dragons. I had a hunch about you. Turns out I was right."

"And what do you need a trained dragon for?"

He looked around the forest uneasily. "Let's make it to Deletev first. Better cover there."

"No." I stopped walking, crossing my arms. "If you want my help, you'll tell me what this is about *right now*."

A twig cracked, and we jumped at the sound. Sev's hand went to the knife on his belt. He raised a finger to his lips and shook his head, then slipped away from my side. Suddenly every errant rustle in the trees was an enemy, every sleepy birdcall a warning. I drew my knife too, holding it at the ready.

There was a crash, and I whirled in the direction of the sound, readying myself to fight—or to run.

A tall man in a guard's uniform came into view, his sword raised. I froze as he saw me, my legs refusing to move. He opened his mouth—and then Sev was out of the brush and upon him. The two fell to the ground, their bodies tangling, and I backed up reflexively.

Visceral grunts and sounds of struggle broke through the air. The guard was pinned to the ground now, but managed to free one hand. Sev took a hit to the throat and reeled back. The guard reached for his sword, which had fallen out of reach. *Now. I must move now.* I darted forward and kicked the sword to the side, then stamped down hard on the guard's hand, eliciting a howl of pain. Taking advantage of the distraction, Sev hooked his arm around the guard's throat and drove his knife up, under the guard's ribs.

The blade made a wet sound as Sev pulled it free, and my stomach lurched. The coppery scent of blood filled the air as the guard's body collapsed.

I couldn't look away from his face. He was one of the older fortress guards, not someone I'd ever spoken to. But I'd seen him standing, breathing. Now he was just *gone.* I knew the harsh reality of mortality, but I'd never seen it like this.

"Trust me now?" Sev said. He wiped his knife on the grass before sheathing it. "There will be others out there. We have to run."

I didn't argue with him this time. We ran. The forest path was fully visible now in the daylight, and anyway, the trees were thinning. Our cover was disappearing. From our trip to Deletev,

I knew that there were only flatlands before us—farms and fields—spreading all the way to the city walls.

We left the forest and entered a field, moving quickly. Most of the land was useless for hiding—the grass only reached waist high in most places.

"Where to?" I shouted to Sev.

"Farm," he spat back. "Look for the flag."

It wasn't the first farmhouse, or the second or third. There was a stitch in my side, and my breath came in labored huffs by the time the fourth farmhouse came into view. A red flag flew from the roof.

"Plague?" I recoiled.

"Decoy," Sev said, grabbing my hand.

We darted around the back of the house. One window was shuttered over with wood. Sev tore it aside and ushered me through before replacing the shutter.

We entered a large central room that contained a squat black stove and a long farmhouse table. I imagined a farmer and his entire boisterous clan of children and hired hands hunched over their breakfasts, readying themselves for the day. From the looks of things, though, I doubted anyone had lived here in years.

I turned and peeked through the cracks in the boarded-up window. The fields were still—fallow—except for the breeze that rustled through the wild grasses. I couldn't see anything of the forest beyond but the treetops.

"See anyone?" Sev said.

I shook my head.

"The guard was probably just a scout. It will be some time before he's missed. You're safe, for now."

I raised my eyebrows. "Me? What about you?"

He smiled, the sort of grim smile that made me remember the way his knife had flashed in the forest. I resisted the urge to take a step back. "I was ordered to look for you before I stole the egg. When they find the guard, they'll assume my body's somewhere in the forest as well. I've got a good two days at least before they realize I'm not dead. You, on the other hand . . ."

Sev was right—he was in the clear. Then I thought of something else. They would assume I had taken the dragon egg as well. Anger curdled in me as I realized how easily he had framed me for the theft. It was devious and underhanded, but I had to admit, neatly executed.

Sev felt under the table and brought out a tightly packed bag. He opened it and withdrew a loaf of traveler's bread. It was flat and round and very stale, but he managed to break off a few pieces and offered one to me. I waited until he started to eat before biting into mine, and I held it in my mouth until it softened. In the newness of this temporary safety, my head was spinning.

I had failed. No second chances for bonding with a dragon. And even if the egg Sev had stolen hatched and survived without a mother, it would be too young to be of any real use for at least a year. Kaia didn't have that much time.

I had to get to her. But I was no longer certain of how to do that.

Sev was looking in my direction, and I wondered what he saw. I was still clad in the fortress uniform, but now it was ripped and soiled and a liability. My face and hair were probably little better. I flushed before I realized he wasn't really looking at me. He was looking at the pack I had dropped at my side.

"Why do *you* want a dragon?" he said. "Who are you working for?"

Myself and my own heart, I wanted to reply. "I have my reasons," I said instead.

"Surely you must be no friend to the emperor," Sev said. "So we must be friends ourselves."

"The enemy of my enemy? I don't think so."

He shrugged. "Why not? Tell me what you desire, and we will get it for you."

We? I bit my lip. Whoever Sev was, and whoever he worked for—they had to be plotting a move against the emperor. I didn't know how to judge him anymore. I could not trust anything he said, and certainly not any murky promises made on behalf of his unknown associates.

I looked at Sev and thought of the way he had dispatched the guard. Neat, methodical. Then I thought of the way he had looked by dragon fire, his face drawn and pleading. Whatever this quest was, it was personal.

"Who are *you* working for?" I asked. "How can you make such promises?"

"I know people with long reaches. They helped me get into the fortress. They'll hide us until the time is right to strike."

"A dragon takes years to train properly."

He leaned back against the table. "I can wait."

I couldn't. "You want me to throw my lot in with yours?"

"That depends."

"On what?"

"How much you need to be persuaded to share your knowledge."

His voice was cold, the underlying threat clear enough. I thought of the blade of his knife, wiped clean on the grass. I swallowed.

"Knowledge is nothing without the proper materials," I said. "What makes you think I have any of those? The Aromatory controls everything."

Sev rolled his eyes. "You're smart, Maren. If you tried to steal a dragon, that means you have the materials." His voice changed, softened. "I trusted you with the knowledge of the egg. Tell me how we can help you."

What did he have that I wanted? I had less than two weeks before midsummer. My plans were shattered, but the countdown continued. If I had no dragon, I needed another way into Lumina. Another way to rescue Kaia.

"Let me see the egg first."

After a considering pause, he nodded. I worked to keep the surprise from showing on my face. I hadn't expected him to agree without objections. Perhaps he really was desperate for my help.

Sev opened his pack and withdrew a tightly wound cloth package, which he placed carefully in my open hands.

It was about the size of a loaf of bread, and heavier than I'd expected. He had wrapped it thoroughly, and I sat down on the dusty floor before attempting to unravel the fabric. The layers of cloth gave way slowly to reveal a hard pebbled shell the color of a muddy river. My breath caught in my throat. Carefully I laid my palm over the top of the egg. It was warm to the touch, and a quiet, curious buzz spread through my fingertips at the points of contact. The egg was well, despite the upheaval to which it had been subjected.

I blinked back the exhausted tears that had been brimming in the corners of my eyes. The egg was a strangely calming presence, a heartbeat of certainty beneath my fingers, and I knew immediately that I did not want to leave it. But that meant committing myself to Sev's cause. Should I?

It was a question that I didn't expect to have answered, but the egg seemed to quiver in response, its buzz turning brighter. I couldn't help but snort in disbelief. The unborn dragon thought I should trust Sev? It was about to be hatched into a life of service to the boy.

I looked up. Sev watched me with an intense expression I could only describe as hunger. What would Kaia do? It was easy to imagine her subduing Sev and stealing the egg, but that wasn't a path forward for me.

"How much do you know of the Aurati?" I said finally.

Surprise crossed his face. "As much as anyone. Why?"

I chose my words carefully. "They stole something from me. Something precious. You say you can help me. Can your friends find me another way into Lumina?"

Sev looked up at the ceiling, considering. "It would help if I knew what was taken from you."

Kaia was too close to my heart to trust him with . . . at least, not yet. "First, convince me that you can be of use to me."

A bark of incredulous laughter escaped him. "I saved you from a rogue dragon. I killed a guard before he could alert the others. Have I not proven myself *useful* to you?"

I leaned back, fingers tightening around the egg. His mask had dropped entirely, leaving me unsure of my footing and slightly dizzy. Sev the fortress guard had been quick to smile and quicker to speak. This Sev was guarded and dangerous—a formidable enemy, if I chose to make him one.

I would not be afraid. "You did those things as much for your own benefit as mine," I said finally. "Besides, breaking into the Aurati stronghold is a more delicate task."

A muscle ticked in his jaw, betraying his frustration. "If your aim is to infiltrate Lumina, you won't do better than what I can offer you."

"All right," I said, deciding to play along. For a while, anyway. "We have a bargain. I'll share my knowledge in exchange for your help with infiltrating Lumina."

I could see the tension leave his shoulders. "Then we need to get moving. The fortress will be on the hunt for a girl by herself. We can fool them better together, but you need a wash.

"We both do," he amended as I raised my eyebrows at him. "If we enter Deletev by the west gate, that will be safer than coming from the south. We can resupply and head north from there."

"Fine." I handed the egg back to him reluctantly, and he wrapped it up again.

"Let's go."

CHAPTER FIFTEEN

I watched the people around us as we entered the west gate of Deletev, keeping an eye out for anyone who might pose a threat. Sev placed a hand on mine and tugged me close to him, as if he meant to embrace me. "Stop looking around," he whispered against my cheek. "You look paranoid."

I flushed and pulled away. The first part of our plan was simple: make ourselves presentable. Sev led the way without hesitation through the business districts, and I watched him, hoping to spot something that would help me unravel his character. He flipped a coin to a child playing with a doll on the side of the street, whistling as he did so, but I could see the tension in his shoulders. He was ill at ease, and I was sure I looked no better. I tried to let my arms move freely as I walked and only succeeded in a near collision with someone walking behind me. I sped up to fall into step at Sev's side. I *was* being paranoid. These were townsfolk on legitimate business. If the fortress guards had found us, we would already be under attack.

Sev and I parted ways at the fountain in front of the public baths. I paid to enter and was given a towel, sandals, and a rough chip of soap. Inside I hung my boots in a shaft of sunlight, and took a change of clothes out of my pack. Everything was damp from the river, but at least it was clean, and perhaps it would dry a little while I washed. I hung up the clothing, stored my bag on a shelf where it would be easily accessible, stripped quickly, and stepped down into the bath.

The water was warmer than I had expected, given the season. But it was a welcome warmth that soothed my muscles and made me aware of how rigid with stress my body had become. I tried to focus on relaxing. The water flowed through my hair, and I worked it loose of its braids before submerging my head. Then I resurfaced and grabbed the soap. The grime washed away, revealing yellow and purpling bruises on my arms and thighs—injuries I didn't even remember the specifics of.

It was a quiet day at the baths, or perhaps I'd come at an unusual time. There were only a few other bathers present, all spread out across the water. I kicked idly, and the water rippled around me. Sev would be waiting. If I wanted to slip away, now was the time. But in truth, I had difficulty coming up with any plan better than what I'd already agreed to. And I was tired, so bone-deep tired—and there was so much more to do.

I lingered until my fingers began to prune before surrendering to the inevitable. My boots were still damp when I stepped out of the pool and toweled off, but in all other respects my condition was greatly improved. I was finally clean, save for some dirt that had refused to come loose from under my fingernails. And I was dry and warm. I donned the new outfit and put on my boots. For now I let my hair hang loose so that it would dry. I took a moment to rearrange my pack, knotting the Aromatory's vials back into the ripped shawl as best I could. Then I stepped back outside to meet Sev.

I looked around the square twice before my gaze snagged on Sev standing against the fountain, watching the entrance to the baths. His new clothing was fashionable enough to match any of the well-to-do people in the city, and his dark hair was bound back out of his face. He was even standing differently—taller, I thought. He looked . . . handsome.

There was a new sack at his feet, which he slung over his shoulder as I approached. "I asked around about caravans heading to the coast," he said. "Just in case someone asks."

"And we'll be heading . . . ?"

"North. This should be enough supplies to last us for a while."

It was not that large a sack. "Where's our destination?"

"Let's talk after we make it clear of the city. Too many ears." Sev nodded his head meaningfully and started off around the fountain.

Too many Aurati, he meant. It felt like we were tripping over an Aurat or an initiate every few minutes, each walking purposefully to one place or another with their cords circling their shoulders. Maybe there was an Aurat assigned to each of the major businesses in Deletev.

We were walking through a quiet residential district when a crowd began to form. It happened subtly at first, but soon the street was busy enough for traffic to slow, and there were puzzled mutterings around us. I looked over at Sev, who frowned. The calm I'd begun to feel evaporated.

"Is the gate closed?" I asked.

"The gate doesn't close except in times of emergency," Sev said.

No, it was worse than that. As we drew closer, we saw a trio of Aurati before the gate, stopping everyone intending to pass through. And off to the side was a Talon sitting on the back of a dragon.

I stared. I couldn't help it. I had never seen a full-grown dragon before. This was no Talon in training, no traumatized yearling. This was an emperor's war machine, a dragon with scales so blue they were almost black. It stood easily twice my height and wore a complicated-looking harness and saddle, on top of which perched its master. The dragon's face was narrow, and the points of its fangs gleamed silvery in the sun, even when its mouth was closed. If it had the inclination, it could certainly have bitten my head clean off my shoulders.

Sev looked over at me. "It's going to be fine," he said, though he didn't sound convinced of his own words.

"We can't turn around?"

"Not without attracting attention we don't want."

I leaned into Sev so that only he could hear me. "So what's the plan?"

He bit his lip.

"You don't have one." It wasn't a question. I grimaced, then looked him up and down. We didn't look enough alike to be siblings, and we didn't have any specialized gear that we might use to pretend to be traders.

I wove two small braids into my hair and tied the rest back, then grabbed Sev's hand. "We'll have to be paired," I murmured. He looked down, and I was once again reminded of my lack of troth ring. Sev wore only one, I realized—a thin, unadorned band over his family finger that could have been the match of my own. Which made sense, considering his aims.

"Recently acquainted," I amended. "We're traveling north to meet your family. For a birthday celebration."

"A birthday celebration?" He looked faintly amused.

"Or something," I snapped. "It's your family—you come up with it. Just make it quick. And convincing."

Sev put his arm around my shoulders as we moved forward. The Talon was a grizzled man of about fifty years. I wondered what battles these two had seen. How easy we would be to overpower, if they realized what we carried. The Aromatory's vials were airtight—they had to be. But what of the egg? Would the dragon smell it?

There was nothing to be done about it now. The dragon's tail flicked restlessly as it surveyed the crowd. Those in line gave it a wide berth, which meant my view was close to unobstructed. Unbidden, the dragon dreams surfaced in my mind. Was such a creature truly the cause of my visions?

The dragon turned its head, and I found myself caught in its gaze. When the Aurati seers had studied me in Ilvera, I had felt scrutinized, but that was nothing compared to the way the world receded from me now. *I am your friend*, I thought. *Whether you know it or not.*

I was jostled from behind and stumbled. The dragon snorted, and the Talon leaned down toward its head, as though the two were sharing a whispered commiseration. I tensed, ready to run—and the moment passed. It was our turn to face the Aurati. If there was such a thing as luck, we had caught a thread of it: None of the three Aurati were seers. Still, my heart beat faster as we stepped forward. Sev took my hand, interlacing our fingers.

"Name?" one asked.

"Peregrin Malta," Sev said smoothly, transforming before my eyes into a Zefedi nobleman. He let go of my hand to perform perhaps the most embellished bow I had ever seen, but reclaimed it the moment he was fully upright. I tried not to let my surprise show on my face and realized that the Aurat was looking at me intently.

"I'm—Sybelle." And then, when it became clear she was waiting for my parentage: "Sybelle ben Gao." I wanted to bite my tongue, but it was the only thing that had come to my panicked, blank mind. Sev squeezed my hand. The Aurati didn't blink.

"What's your business traveling today?"

Sev yawned. "We're on our way to Oskiath," he said, raising my hand slightly. "My family wants to meet her."

He was playing the role of insouciant lord effortlessly. I only wondered whether he could pull it off dressed as we were, traveling by foot. And whether the reason he did it so well was because he'd been born to it.

"So soon?" the Aurat said, her gaze falling on our hands.

"Father wishes all troth rings to be made on his land," Sev said. He rolled his eyes. "Tradition, you know how it is. And I couldn't let this one out of my sight for that long." He put his arm around my shoulder and squeezed me close. "Ever since I found her diving for pearls out on the beach in Gedarin, I knew. And it's been a month already!"

I wasn't familiar with this aspect of Zefedi culture on the subject of troth rings, but it seemed to mean something to the Aurati. I caught the smirk that passed between the two who hadn't yet spoken.

"So what's all this about?" Sev said, waving his free hand expansively at the crowd. "Someone lose an heir? Rob a treasury?"

"Not for you to know," the oldest Aurat said. "Now, you were saying—"

A loud shout interrupted her. I turned, craning my neck to see. Two men faced off in a small pocket of space that had formed in the crowd.

"What did you say to me?" one man said.

"Nothing," said the taller of the two. They were both dressed in nondescript Zefedi clothes, but this one was Seratese, with tightly braided hair and ebony skin.

"You're right, nothing." The Zefedi man spat on the ground. "Just like you have nothing to say about how your people started this war."

The Seratese man shook his head, speaking in unaccented Zefedi. "If you must point fingers, look to our emperor. I don't want trouble. I was born here, like my father. I'm of Zefed."

It might have ended there, except that the crowd surged, and the man stumbled forward into his antagonist. It was like putting a match to a bowl of oil—instant chaos erupted as punches and shouts flew. The two older Aurati raced into the crowd without hesitation, slim batons raised. The Talon and dragon remained by the gate. Perhaps they were present only for the possibility of capturing a fugitive. Or perhaps a dragon was too powerful a weapon to bring to bear on a mere street brawl.

Sev and I backed away from the action, toward the gate. He caught the eye of the remaining Aurat guarding the gate, who waved us through distractedly. My heart leaped as we passed under the gate and exited the city.

"I had no idea it was that bad with the Seda Serat," I said as soon as we were out of sight. "That poor man. He did nothing wrong."

He nodded, face grim. "The emperor has done well at shifting the blame for his war. Most of those people back there have forgotten how it started. They believe him when he says their misfortunes are caused by something other than his own greed."

The war. In Ilvera, we didn't speak much about the emperor's wars—whether one had concluded or was forthcoming. Sometimes the mountain made us feel almost outside time, untouchable.

"Is this something your friends will change?" I said. "Stop the war?"

Sev looked away. "All you need to know is that they keep their word."

"And what word is that, exactly?"

His face tightened. If I hadn't been watching closely, I might not have noticed. "Vengeance."

"Yours?" He didn't deny it. "What happened to you?"

Sev's eyes slid away from mine, and I knew whatever he was about to say would be a half-truth, at best. "My family died for speaking out against the emperor. I'm the only one left."

"You can't be the only one whose family—" I blurted before reining myself in. "I'm sorry. That's not what I meant."

He shrugged. "You're right. Imagine what would happen, though, if everyone who's ever been wronged by the emperor joined us? Do you think any number of Aurati could put us in our place? When our dragon is grown, we'll destroy them." The venom in his voice left little doubt that it was personal for him, and rightly so. But I wondered now what kind of people would support such a quest. What motive they might have for sending an untried boy to topple the Flame of the West.

Maybe I was reading too much into this. Most Verrans would gladly have seen the emperor dead, myself among them. And Sev was hardly an untried boy, unable to gauge the depth of the waters he was swimming in. He'd survived at the fortress, after all.

And yet. "They must not like the emperor."

"No."

We walked for a while in silence. "These friends of yours—"

Sev interrupted me. "There are no friends in this game. Only players."

That was uninspiring, to say the least. But also no less than I expected, given the circumstances. I amended my sentence. "It sounds like they are letting you take all of the risk. What do they hope will happen if you succeed?"

Sev cut a glance my way. "Why do you care, so long as you get what you want?"

Because I care about you. I shoved the thought away, only to suddenly realize I was still holding Sev's hand. I let go, dropping my gaze so he wouldn't see my embarrassment. "Can't a person wonder?"

"Wonder all you like. All you need to know is that they will get you into Lumina if you uphold your end of the bargain. Now, let's move."

North of Deletev the road splintered. We stayed on the main throughway for most of the afternoon, then took a road that forked left. According to a sign, we were heading toward Ruzi and Oskiath. These were the great valleys of Zefed, lush farmland that sprawled across the belly of the empire. And yet something about it was not right. We were in the heat of summer, but several fields were already sparse and picked over.

"Has there been a drought?" I said. "Or cord beetles?"

Sev looked at me strangely and shook his head. "Supplies, for the war. He's been demanding more than there is in storage, so there's been an early harvest."

Early meant undergrown crops. And if everything was being sent to the east, what was there for the people in Zefed to eat? For the first time I wondered whether there was a reason other than pure malice for the recent demands that had been made of Ilvera.

I saw Sev watching me and schooled my face into a neutral expression. Had I given myself away with that question? Perhaps not. There had to be places in the empire untouched by the food shortage.

Late in the day we reached the beginnings of another forest. "We'll camp here for the night," Sev said. "It's a two-day journey to the other side."

"And then what?" I said.

"Oskiath," he said, nodding to me. "And the people who will help you with your quest."

So he'd been telling the truth to the Aurati. Oskiath. My father's homeland.

I had never been there before, but I'd heard of it enough. Fields of heather and plums so sweet they melted on your tongue. My father had told me stories about the way his village fountain danced with water, and how he had run through its spray every summer as a child. He had grown up in a privileged household, though he had always been vague on the specifics.

I sighed. I was Verran first and always, but my father's stories ran through my veins—as much as I hated the empire, I could not forswear his history. It was a part of me.

I thought of the letter of introduction he had given me and wished I had memorized its contents before disposing of it. I could not be Maren of Ilvera in Oskiath, but I might have had a stronger foundation of knowledge.

I adjusted the pack on my back. I could have done better—but for now I had to tell myself I was doing *enough*. I had the oils and the promise of an escort into Lumina. There were still almost two weeks before Kaia would be judged.

"Shouldn't we press on? Talons might already be after us, if Deletev was any indication."

"Probably," Sev said. "But there's no reason to suspect they're close. And when it comes time to run, it's best to have well-rested legs."

We picked a spot out of sight of the main road, but not too far that we lost track of where we were. The night was warm enough that there was no need for shelter beyond a blanket laid out on the ground. Sev sat down and opened the bag he had procured in Deletev. He set aside a small frying pan and unpacked fresh rice and pork buns and a jar of pickled vegetables, and smiled at my surprise. "We'll have enough travel rationing to do in the coming days."

He handed me a bun, and I wolfed it down ravenously. Another was waiting before I had finished the first. We ate in companionable silence, and when we were through, we settled onto the ground.

I wasn't tired, I found. By all rights I should have been. Instead I felt . . . restless.

"Did you ever think you would end up here?" he asked.

I rolled onto my side, facing him. "What kind of a question is that?"

"One I spend too much time on. I wasn't born for this. I was raised in peace. I wanted to be a sailor. Of all the lives I could have lived—*this?*" He looked at me, clearly inviting a response.

I bit my lip. "We don't have to make small talk," I said. "We've agreed to see this through. What else is there to ruminate on?"

"Nothing. But it'll make for a boring few days if the only things we say to each other are about the food." He looked back up at the sky above. This far away from the city the stars shone almost as bright as the ones in Ilvera. "Let's pretend we met somewhere else. Somewhere where all of this was just a bad dream. How would it go?"

Somewhere where all of *what* was a bad dream? Sev's nightmare had only started when the emperor had cut down his family. If not for that, Sev would have been perfectly happy living out his life in the empire—and in a notably high position, if I'd read him correctly. As for me, Ilvera's back had been broken to form the very foundation upon which his family stood. The wrongs against us were so much older.

"Where your family was never killed?" I said quietly.

"And the Aurati never stole from you."

I smiled. I could play along. "That's easy. You and I would never have met. I wouldn't be important enough to exist in your world."

"You're selling yourself short."

"You're noble by birth, I can tell. You might have been a Talon, or close to. I'm no one."

Sev made no move to deny my claim about his parentage. "You're not no one," he said instead. "I would have noticed you anywhere."

"There are hundreds of girls out there who are just like me. You think I'm special because you need me for your quest, but you'd think the same of anyone else in my position."

"Not true. I'd never think that highly of Lilin."

I couldn't help myself. I laughed. "Lilin and I are hardly in the same situation."

"You mean to say that stealing secrets from the Flame of the West isn't on everyone's agenda these days?"

I laughed again. I liked this easy banter, I realized. Strange to admit, but it was true. Sev was thoughtful and perceptive, and even though our entire conversation was hypothetical, his words made me glow. I suddenly recalled what my father had told me—how my own light burned just as bright as Kaia's. I had dismissed the notion then, but here, talking to Sev, I could almost start to believe it.

"No," I said after a while. "I never thought my life would be like this."

Sev sighed. "Get some rest. I'll wake you up for the second watch."

CHAPTER SIXTEEN

A woman kneels, her hands poised over a small fire. She looks familiar to me in a way I cannot articulate. The fire flickers, and she speaks. I lean closer, listening. "The flame will be extinguished." Her words are slow and indistinct. "The dragon will rise." Her face twists in anger, and she sweeps her arms down dismissively. The fire goes out.

The morning was gray and cool and misty between the trees. I watched the fog creep out of the night on tiptoe, as though it was trying not to wake anyone up. I sat with my knife held over my crossed legs and waited, and watched. Sev slept soundly, and I was envious. My dream had woken me before my watch, and it had troubled me ever since.

Most of my dragon dreams had been easy to understand, but not this one. The woman had been dressed in the cords of an Aurati seer. She had been making a prophecy—one that promised the rise of the dragons. I shook my head. How could that be? The dragons and Talons already occupied one of the highest positions in Zefed—unless the seer's words meant that the emperor's dragons would be freed?

A twig cracking nearby had me scrambling to my feet before

the animal entered my line of sight. It was a young spotted deer, its nose twitching with curiosity. My shoulders relaxed, and I almost laughed. The deer had nothing to fear from me. Hunting would be messier and more time consuming than we could afford. Instead I stayed very still and watched as it moved through our campsite. Once it was gone, I walked over to Sev and nudged him with my foot. He woke instantly, hand flying to his knife.

"Morning," I said.

He grunted something that might have been a greeting before stumbling behind some bushes to relieve himself. I cleared my throat loudly and looked the other way.

"How much farther?" I asked.

"Another day through the forest. Then we go into the mountains, through Wolf's Gap."

I passed my knife from one hand to the other. "So there will be wolves?"

"No. That's one of the words the Celet people once used to describe a place that was to be avoided, when they didn't want to speak the real reason. Wolf's Gap means 'beware.'"

That wasn't reassuring. I frowned at him as he came back around the bushes. "What's the real reason?"

"It's better not to talk about it here."

"Really? You're pulling that again?"

"There's a tunnel. Vir's Passage," Sev said, sighing. He looked nervously up at the sky. "The last journey. Trust me—it's better to leave it be. The only reason we're cutting this close is to save time. And there will be fewer people on the road."

"And that won't make us seem desperate?" I said doubtfully.

"Best hope we don't come across anyone on the road, then," he said. He packed his things and handed me a dense traveler's loaf. "Come on."

The egg was silent.

For most of the morning we walked without interruption. This forested part of Zefed reminded me of Ilvera, and the thought made my heart ache. I needed a distraction.

"How will you kill the emperor?" I asked. Sev stumbled. "You do intend to kill him, don't you?"

"Yes. I do." He didn't ask me why I'd brought it up. "The same way my mother died. By blade."

"Blades are common. Why wait?"

"You don't understand. I need the dragon."

I didn't understand. Unless this had less to do with him and more to do with the people he associated with. But what was so essential about a dragon, when an arrow or a sword or even a large rock would do the trick?

"You're right," I said. "I don't."

Sev abruptly stopped walking. "The Flame of the West was only able to build his empire by the might of dragons. It's not so far a leap to think that a dragon will bring him down."

He was lying. No one would go so far for a symbolic gesture. The only reason someone would steal a dragon was to use it, and use it well.

"You're just like the rest of them, aren't you?" I said.

"What are you talking about?" he said.

"In the fortress you spoke like you were different. Like you cared about the dragons. I see now that only lasts until they can be useful to *you*."

Sev recoiled. "I do care. And don't pretend to have the high ground here, when you were going to do exactly the same thing."

"But I *don't* have a dragon," I said. "And besides, whatever happened would have come down on only one person: me. You talked about the dragons' welfare like you wanted to change the world. But changing the person in charge is not the same as changing the system. The dragons will still be in captivity, just as they are now."

"And what of it?" he snapped. "Wherever you came from, it clearly wasn't a place that taught anything about governance. What do you think is going to happen when the emperor falls? Everyone's just going to get along? No. Someone is going to have to rule. And the easiest way to secure that power is to have a dragon."

I was almost crying, I was so angry. "Who's going to rule? *You?* Who are you to decide that?"

His jaw clenched. "Someone has to!"

I was afraid he might be right, and I hated him for it. I wished I could run behind a tree and stamp my feet or weep. Instead, I gritted my teeth and gave Sev a wide berth.

After going some distance in uncomfortable silence, I heard a bird let out a shrill cry that pierced the air. Another bird cried out, and another, until it seemed the very forest was screaming. I met Sev's eyes. All animosity was set aside. He put a finger to his lips but kept walking, scanning the trees around us. Suddenly a cloud of birds shot into the sky. Sev swore. "They've found us."

The roar of a dragon punctuated his words, clawing its way down my spine. Through the trees I glimpsed two huge shapes pass overhead. Talons.

"Maybe they won't land," I said. The forest was dense. It was difficult to imagine something as large as a dragon being able to cut down through the branches . . . until one did, landing so hard it shook the earth. It was far enough behind us that I couldn't see it, but its presence was unmistakable.

"We're almost to Wolf's Gap," Sev whispered. "When we're clear of the trees, run for the river."

Menacing crashes shook the earth, and an acrid scent filled the air around us. I nodded once, and Sev and I ran. The trees quickly thinned, and I could see bright daylight beyond the forest. The ground shifted under my feet, earth giving way to stone. There was less than a minute before we would lose our cover.

Another dragon snarled above us. "Go!" Sev shouted.

We burst free of the trees and sprinted across a sudden landscape of flat, smooth rock.

"Get across the river," Sev said in between labored breaths. "It's two—two up."

I didn't know what he meant but couldn't spare the breath to ask him. I could hear the river now, but the sounds of our pursuers were growing louder too. My boots squelched onto the river bank, and Sev threw himself into the river without hesitation. I followed, wading through water that came almost to my chest. I couldn't hear anything over the rush of the current around me. My hands and feet were numb. I had no thoughts except to get to the other side, and then we were out, gasping on the other bank.

"Where now?"

"Into the valley!" Sev said, heading down a trail that cut between two tall hills.

Sev was muttering under his breath—counting, I thought—as we ran. Strange. I'd thought this way was little traversed, but there were candles planted along the sides of the trail and paintings on the rocks that I could not slow to study.

Small paths broke off and snaked away up the sides of the hills, some of them so steep I could imagine only goats climbing them.

"There!" Sev pointed to one of the trails, this one a little shallower than the others.

I took the lead, Sev following. As the hill grew steeper, I was forced to use both arms and legs in an ungainly crawl. My head was down. I couldn't see where the trail led. I could only have faith that it went somewhere safe and away. But as I heard wings beating and felt a draft of wind hit my face, I knew that our time had run out.

I looked up.

The dragon's wings cast shadows over us as it circled with its rider. I looked back at Sev. There was nowhere to go and nowhere to hide. A weighty, sickening silence fell, and the hair on the back of my arms stood up.

Fire suddenly bloomed across my vision, and then I was falling.

There was a flash of white-hot pain, and the world went black.

The mountains swam back into view when I opened my eyes again. I was lying on the ground. My back ached, and my hands were scraped, and my head was impossibly heavy. A dragon crouched on the hill above me. As I watched, it flapped its wings and bared its fangs. There was smoke in the air. I forced myself upright in a hazy panic. Where was Sev?

Now that I was sitting up, I realized I had tumbled down the hill to the base of the trail. Sev must have fallen too. I turned my head slowly. He was a few body lengths distant from me, struggling to get up. Not that standing would help. The second dragon landed heavily on the trail behind us, blocking our retreat. There was nowhere to go.

The dragon on the hill began to descend, its claws catching rocks and sending them skittering down toward us. This was it. We were going to die.

The Talon behind us threw back her hood, revealing black hair and a weathered face. "Lay down your weapons," she called.

Why, to make it easier for them to kill us? We had no weapons that would be of any use against a dragon. One good blast of fire and we'd both be incinerated. Surrendering was the easy path, but I couldn't bring myself to kneel. Not after everything I'd done.

My hand clenched tighter around the hilt of my knife. I squared my shoulders and took a deep breath before drawing my blade. Then I charged down the trail toward the second dragon, letting loose a loud, savage cry. I could hear Sev running behind me as my vision narrowed to one point: the Talon.

She raised a wrist and whispered a word. I ducked and rolled as the dragon swept its tail across the path, batting Sev against the rocks as easily as I might have swatted a fly.

I screamed, stumbling to a halt. Sev crumpled to the ground and lay there, unmoving.

The Talon and dragon turned as one toward me. The other Talon nudged his dragon the rest of the way down the hill, trapping me between them.

"Lay down your weapons," the first Talon called again. "Or I'll kill your friend."

Sev. I did as she said, letting my blade fall to the ground.

"Good. Now take off your pack and throw it to me."

I looked away from the dragon, and my eyes fell on a small opening in the mountain. Vir's Passage.

I swallowed hard. Then I slowly shrugged off my pack, careful as I crouched down. Having injured Sev, the Talons seemed content to wait me out.

My fingers brushed the shawl that held the Aromatory's oils.

Before I could second-guess myself, I unknotted the shawl, my hands shaking as I gathered the oils together. The vials clinked in my palms as I stood up. Then, in one swift motion, I smashed them against the rocky ground.

Glass shards bit into my hand as the dragons roared and reared back, thrashing from side to side. One Talon was thrown from her dragon, cursing as she fell.

I snatched my knife and pack, ran to Sev, and grabbed his arm, pulling him up. Thankfully, he was conscious again, though disoriented.

"Come on!" I pushed him to move, herding him toward the cave entrance. Fire lit the sky, and furious shouts tore through the air, but I didn't look back. I moved forward, hands out as the passage narrowed, then widened. I hoped there were no sinkholes ahead—I would not be able to see or avoid them. All I could do was keep moving, because whatever lay ahead of us, it could not be worse than the certain death we had just left behind.

On and on we went, until the sounds of the outside world faded to nothing, and all I could hear was our labored breathing, our stumbling feet. Now the passage opened into a cavern—I knew it was large from the way it echoed.

I stopped. I could feel Sev shaking beside me. "Are you all right?"

"Tera's bones, Maren. What have you done?"

The air was stale but breathable. Sev moved, fumbling in the dark. A moment later a smoky lantern flared to life, and the space was illuminated. It could have been a bear's winter den, but everywhere were remnants of offerings: coins and brightly colored streamers of cloth and tarnished plates and goblets that must once have held food and wine. I looked back at Sev. Even in this dank half-light I could see his face was dangerously pale.

"Maren. You've brought us to the caves of the dead."

"Would you rather I had let you die?" I said. "I could have left you there."

He shook his head ruefully.

"I saved your life, and you're more frightened of a Zefedi folktale than the Talons coming after us?"

"They won't set foot in Vir's Passage. The dragons are too large to fit, and besides, these caves belong to the unjustly slain. The Talons know they are not welcome. Neither are we. The dead will not let us pass."

"Too late now," I said tersely. "Are you hurt?"

"My shoulder," he admitted, grimacing. "And my side. Here—take this."

He couldn't hold back a yelp of pain as he maneuvered his pack over his head and passed it to me. My stomach fell. He was seriously hurt, if he was giving me care of the dragon egg. He was more afraid of dropping it than he was of my stealing it.

"Sit down. You need to rest."

"No," he said. "We have to get out of here." But he swayed as he spoke.

"*Sit*," I said, taking his hand and helping him down to the ground. "Let me see it."

Sev shook his head. "It's nothing. Just need a moment." But when he leaned back, he fell, collapsing to the ground in a boneless heap.

"Sev!" I set down his pack. Blood was blooming on his shirt, and I pushed up the fabric to inspect the wound. It was long, stretching from one hip bone up his torso, but at least it was shallow. I placed my hands against his neck. His pulse was steady, but he was so cold. I had to do something, but exhaustion was taking over, leaving my hands and legs shaking. I felt too slow to think, tongue too heavy to speak. I sat, letting my head fall forward between my legs. Perhaps this was it. The pair of us had escaped from Talons only to freeze in a cave with only the dead for company. Fitting, really.

A calming presence intruded into my thoughts. I straightened, surprised, and reached carefully into Sev's pack. The egg thrummed against my hands. Unbelievably, it was alive and whole. And, in spite of everything, so was I. We still had a chance.

I removed my sodden jacket and unlaced my soaking boots, then stripped down to my underclothes. There were tapestries hanging on the walls—I offered a silent apology to whoever had hung them before tugging one down and wrapping myself in it. It smelled musty, but it was heavy enough to provide some warmth.

I used some of our precious water reserve to rinse the grime, blood, and glass from my hand, wincing as I did so. At home Mother would have used long needles to tease the shards free of my skin, but this was the best I could do here. I rinsed Sev's wounds as well, and ripped one tapestry into long strips that I used to staunch the bleeding. Then I placed another tapestry over his body and finally upturned my bag and spread out the contents to dry.

When I finished, I gathered the egg in my arms and sank down to the cave floor. I blew out the lantern, and let myself drift off to sleep.

CHAPTER SEVENTEEN

I have seen the tyrant's army sweeping across the land, and now he has turned his sight on our mountain. Our ring of councilors— dragon and human side by side—is divided. We might descend to the lowlands and meet them in combat, but we are too few to stand against them on such a vast battleground.

We vote to remain atop the mountain, where we are still safe. I am uneasy, but for today I stretch in the sun, wings spread wide, and watch my kits frolicking with their human companions. War is coming, knocking at our door. But I will not let them have today.

I felt uneasy as soon as I woke up. My dream had been filled with the dread of what was to come. It was impossible not to feel that same foreboding spilling into my reality. I sat up and lit the lantern, then looked over to where Sev lay. He was sleeping, but poorly, tossing and muttering. I leaned over him and pressed a palm to his forehead. He was feverish, and there was little I could do to help his wound without anything to clean it properly. I sat back on my heels. The fever might work itself out. But I didn't know how long it would take, and in the meantime, the Talons might be setting traps outside.

I stood up and took the lantern with me around the cave. While it was a natural formation, it had clearly been shaped by human use. I frowned. If what Sev had said about Vir's Passage was true, how had people come here without inviting harm upon themselves? This seemed to be a main chamber of sorts, but there were three passages that led deeper into the mountains. I looked down each of them but didn't see any indication of their purpose, and I was leery of leaving Sev alone in his condition.

If only I could go outside to find something to help him. On the Verran mountain we knew which herbs would bring down a fever. There had to be something similar here. Or yarrow oil—if only I hadn't smashed it on the rocks yesterday.

The moment I allowed the thought to breach my mind, I could not hold back the nausea that followed. I'd lost *everything*. The oils were gone, and with them the only thing I could contribute to Sev's quest and his patrons. Without them, he had no need of me. Without mirth wood oil, I couldn't even attempt to make more of my own.

Maybe I could keep Sev from finding out. After all, there was no need to discuss it further until after the dragon hatched. But even that was the faintest whisper of a hope for a best-case scenario. And nothing about my life since leaving Ilvera could be called a best-case scenario. But try as I might, I could not think of a different choice I could have made. There had been no other option that would have allowed us both to escape. And even if I was that mercenary, Sev had carried the dragon. The egg would have been gone as well.

But it wasn't.

I could take the dragon egg—Sev was in no position to stop me—and I could be gone. And yet ...

And yet I wouldn't leave him.

It was a surprising realization. Before I'd come down the mountain, I had cared nothing for Zefed or its inhabitants. Whether they lived or died made little difference to me. But Zefed was different than I'd expected. Sev was different than I'd expected. *I* was different than I'd expected. When I had started this journey, I would have given everything I had to get Kaia back. But ... not this. I would not be responsible for Sev's death, alone and unknown.

Having decided that I would not leave Sev to fend for himself, there was little else to do but wait. So I did. I lay down, curling myself around the dragon egg, and closed my eyes once more.

The lantern had gone out by the time I woke, and the cavern was quiet. I lay with my eyes open, listening. There was nothing except for the sounds Sev made as he slept, but I could not shake the creeping sensation that raised the hair on the back of my neck.

I lit the lantern with shaking fingers. The cave was empty except for us.

I took out the traveler's bread, but it was soggy all the way through and could not be salvaged. I placed it against the wall and pulled out an apple instead. I took tiny bites, chewing until the fruit was mush in my mouth before swallowing. I didn't know how much longer we were going to be in here, or how we were going to get out. We couldn't afford to waste food. Sev didn't wake, but I forced some water down his throat and put the back of my hand against his forehead. Still too warm, but he was sleeping more soundly.

I waited and sang a Verran song of traveling. There weren't many of those—we didn't tend to go far from our mountains. And they were all sad, anyway. Mournful and melancholy, which matched perfectly the way I felt now. The notes echoed down the caves, making it feel like I sang with an accompaniment of many.

I stopped singing. The thought of others in the darkness only unsettled me more.

We could not stay here for long, and a way out wasn't about to present itself. I would have to find it. I slung the pack with the egg onto my back, afraid to leave it unattended. Reluctantly I picked up the lantern and walked down one of the passages. The cavern where we had stopped was clearly some place of gathering, or worship. These side passages were not adorned to nearly the same extent. Which meant that they led somewhere, and that maybe we could use them to get out.

A quiet shuffling echoed down the passage, and I nearly dropped the lantern. "Who's there?" I said, whirling around. Had the Talons decided to follow us after all?

There was no one—and yet there was *something* here, its attention heavy upon me.

"We're sorry to disturb your peace," I said. "We mean you no harm."

A cold wind whipped through the passage, and the lantern went out. I shrieked, dropping into a crouch. Images of ghostly fingers wrapping around my neck flashed through my mind. Someone was laughing—several someones.

Your words come too late, the voices chorused.

I clapped my hands against my ears as though that would block the words that were already inside my head. This was how they did it, I realized. The ghosts wouldn't kill me—they would turn my mind against me until I did it myself.

I could feel them, an icy pool of darkness deepening within me. *You have trespassed here. You'll never survive. You have nothing of worth.*

You were destined to fail from the beginning.

You were always second best.

I was. I always had been. Kaia had run ahead, and I had followed her without question. She had accepted my adoration, because I had nothing else of worth to give. She would never have followed me.

You were never good enough for her. You'll never be good enough to save her.

You're already too late.

You lost the dragon. You lost the oils.

Tears streamed down my face. Of course they were right. I'd already failed. Kaia's and Sev's fates were sealed, all because of me.

Ghostly figures shimmered into view around me, translucent at first but quickly growing more solid. What would happen when they were fully formed?

Lie down. Go to sleep. Let yourself go.

You have done nothing.

You are alone.

But—that wasn't true.

I had tried. I had given more of myself than I thought possible to give.

And I wasn't alone. I had the dragon egg.

The thought was like a spark. Suddenly the dragon's presence filled my mind, its anger chasing out the ghostly intruders.

The ghosts fell silent, but did not retreat. My mind was mine again, for now. The dragon's presence was alert, but I didn't know if the unborn hatchling was strong enough to fend the ghosts off a second time. I could still feel inky tendrils probing the corners of my thoughts. *Think.* I needed to counteract the ghosts' assault or else lose myself again—but how?

I had to push them out completely, using my own entire self. No fear. No darkness. No doubt.

"I *am*—" I croaked. I dug my fingers into the dirt. I had survived losing Kaia. I had left my mountain and walked among my enemy, and I had survived. I had befriended a Zefedi boy and broken bread at the same table as Aurati initiates. I had seen a pit battle and bathed in a public bath and touched a dragon egg. I had lost the yearling, but I hadn't given up—I had changed course. I would find a way past the loss of the oils. I had done so much, and I was still here.

I started again, closing my eyes. "I am Maren ben Gao Vilna of the Verran mountain. I have left my home, and I have fought and bled for my quest. I have met Aurati and faced down dragons and matched wits with Zefedi invaders. What I have done, I have done to survive. Like Ciara, mother of dragons, I will soar. I have not failed. I will not give up. I am second to no one. I am *worthy*, and I will not be overtaken by you."

Had it worked? My mind was quiet. I could sense the dragon in its egg, waiting.

I opened my eyes. The ghosts had faded. In the corners of my vision I could still see glimmers of their shapes wavering in and out. Sev had said these were the ghosts of the unjustly slain. They had tried to drive me to my death, but I couldn't bring myself to despise them.

"I am sorry for my trespass and thankful for what safety your domain has provided. I would not have done it if I had another choice. We will be gone as soon as we are able," I said. "I will make amends, if you will only tell me how."

A breeze lifted sweaty strands of hair from my face. The ghosts seemed to be considering.

You are dragon touched. There was only one voice in my mind this time, soft and sad.

"I am."

Another breeze like a sigh.

You and yours may stay safe in our domain for three nights only. If you wish to make amends . . . bring down the tyrant.

The ghosts melted completely away, leaving me in utter darkness.

I sagged in relief. "Thank you," I whispered. I reached out, found the lantern, and hurried back to the main cavern.

I paused at the threshold, holding my breath. There was no one there but Sev. As I watched, he rolled onto his side and let out a groan of pain.

"Sev!" I crossed the cavern and helped him slowly into a sitting position.

"You're still here," he said.

I nodded. "How do you feel?"

He grimaced. "Not well. It's my side."

"Here." I passed him my water skin. There wasn't much left.

"How long have we been here?" he said between shallow sips.

"Maybe two days," I said. "It's hard to tell in the dark."

He groaned. "And you haven't seen anything?"

"If you mean the ghosts, then yes. I saw them."

"*What?*" Sev's gaze darted around the cavern. "We have to go *now*. It may already be too late."

"No, we're all right," I said. "We have an accord. They're gone now."

He stared at me. "That's not funny. We're lucky to be alive right now—you cannot make jokes about this."

"I'm not joking," I said. I conveyed what had happened, leaving out the specific thoughts they had used to attack me.

His face grew even paler. "You're not joking," he muttered. "You just made friends with the guardians of Vir's Passage."

"I wouldn't say we're friends, exactly." They were probably watching us even now. "They said we have three days to get out."

"That's not long." Sev closed his eyes, face tightening in pain.

I wanted to distract him. Perhaps if I got him talking? "What did the emperor do to them?"

"The emperor has always been suspicious to the point of paranoia. When he was a young man, newly crowned, he came to suspect a rebellion. He believed the perpetrators were being harbored in a nearby city called Vir, and so he sent his armies to quell the uprising. The people were not prepared to fight. They fled, sending those too weak or young to hide in these hills. The emperor's troops pursued them." Sev swallowed. "The soldiers cut down every last child. These caves are where their bodies were entombed by the people of the surrounding cities—the last citizens of Vir."

I gasped in horror. "How could he? Most of those people must have been innocent."

"That is the emperor's way. He wanted to make an example of them. So he did."

I had thought by the way Sev had spoken that these deaths were generations old. But to hear that they had happened in my lifetime? Fury built in me, that the tyrant would treat his own people so.

"And they became ghosts?"

"They became known as the guardians of these lands to those who shun the empire, and people began to leave them offerings, for their protection and their peace. Those who seek to harm the land or those who dwell on it meet their ends here."

"Then is it so surprising that they would let us go? We mean the land no harm. And we're no friends of the empire."

"Intentions are not something you can count on. They're vengeful spirits. They were cut down mercilessly, and they do not forget, regardless of whether people pray to them for peace. Those they claim, die screaming. And besides, one can't trust ghosts to interpret your motivation the same way you want them to," Sev said. "Regardless of our motivations, regardless of what they told you, we should not linger here."

After what he'd told me, I agreed. "Eat first," I said, forcing some dried meat into his hands. "Do you know where the tunnels lead? I went down that one but didn't make it far."

He shook his head. "I've only ever heard about the one entrance."

"Well, that won't work."

"Do you have a better plan?" Sev said. "Those tunnels could lead anywhere. And our food won't last long."

"I'd be happy to take the same way back. Just as soon as you come up with a way to do it without getting us captured, or killed."

Sev leaned back, exhausted by the effort required to eat. "I see you'd rather we were killed by ghosts instead, or lost in the tunnels until we starve to death."

"We have three days to come up with something. That's not nothing." We glared at each other before Sev looked away.

A cracking sound echoed suddenly throughout the cavern.

I jumped to my feet, knife out, facing the tunnel we'd entered through. "What was that?"

"I—I think it's the egg," Sev said hoarsely, his face almost gray.

He couldn't be serious. I opened his pack and looked inside. Sure enough, there was a short jagged line down one side of the egg. I put my hand on the shell and felt the dragon's presence strongly. It was impatient. It was ready.

I couldn't hide the panic in my voice. "What are we going to do?" The nursery in the fortress had tools and procedures, all designed to keep hatchlings healthy. We were in a haunted cave and had nothing. To make matters worse, I was almost certain that the dragons outside would be able to sense the hatchling once it arrived. How would we be able to protect it?

And if we somehow did manage to get out of the caves and away from the Talons, how would we feed it? We would soon run out of food for ourselves. I had never asked Lilin about what hatchlings ate.

"You have to make it stop," I said.

"Don't be ridiculous. It's coming now, and there's nothing we can do about it." Sev's voice was calm, but his hands were shaking as he reached out and touched the egg.

He was right. There was nothing I could do about the circumstances of this hatchling. There was no getting out of it. This was happening.

"All right," I said. "All right. Let's think. What do we need?"

"Shelter," Sev said automatically.

"Blankets, then." I grabbed one of the blankets that had dried out and set up a makeshift nest. Then I took the egg and placed it gently on top of the blanket.

"Nothing to do now but wait," Sev said.

I sat cross-legged on the ground.

The egg remained silent.

A few minutes later, in as casual a manner as possible, "Have you ever observed a hatching before?"

A short pause. "No."

A pit grew in my stomach. We were going to kill this dragon. It was going to hatch, and we were going to make a mistake because we had no idea what we were doing—and it would be all Sev's fault. And mine.

I brought my knees up to my chest, hands clenching my sleeves. Sev's hand crept across the distance and gripped mine.

"It's going to be all right," he said.

He couldn't know that, but I didn't argue. I found myself leaning until our shoulders were touching, reassured by the contact.

We sat. We waited.

My stomach rumbled. Sev's eyes drifted closed. The cavern was quiet.

A sudden pressure built in my head. A keening started as low as the buzz of a bee, then grew louder and higher. And then there was a wobble, and the crack on the side of the egg lengthened.

Sev started upright. I reached out instinctively, but he batted my hand back down. "It has to find its own way out," he whispered.

The keening grew in my head. Another tap and another crack. A chip of egg fell away, and for a second I saw gray skin, and then there was an explosion of song in my head, a cacophony of confused melody that was nevertheless curious and excited.

The egg cracked again, and the dragon's head emerged into the air.

It was a spindly thing with stone-gray skin. The dragon sneezed and shook its head. Then it thrashed, struggling to break open the shell. Finally, with one more shudder, the dragon fell out of the egg and onto the blanket. It had survived. I had a *dragon* in front of me, small enough to cup in my two hands. It was perhaps the most beautiful creature I'd seen in my entire life. No one in Ilvera would believe this.

"What do we do now?" Sev said.

"You're the one who stole the egg. Didn't you ask Lilin about how she takes care of the hatchlings?"

At least he had the grace to look somewhat ashamed. He reached out and tried to touch the hatchling, which shied away from him.

The singing was almost unbearable now, not because of its

volume but because of its tone, the way it sounded lost, desperate. It was a newborn baby. It should be with its mother.

I couldn't stand to listen to it. I got to my feet, grabbed a lantern, and walked away. Sev could look after it for now. What was *I* going to do? At least the hatchling had been born healthy, as far as we could tell. But we needed to keep it alive. And soon Sev would be after me about the oils. If I told him the truth about what had happened, would his patrons still think my knowledge worthwhile enough to help me?

After several minutes of pacing in a side passage, I came back to the cavern to see Sev trying to coax the hatchling into biting a piece of dried meat he'd retrieved from his pack.

"Don't do that!" I snatched it away from Sev. "That's too much for a baby. Its teeth need time to develop." I thought. In the old stories the dragons were described as caring for orphaned humans by softening their food until it was palatable to young mouths. I stuffed the meat into my mouth and started to chew.

"What are you doing?"

I held up a hand. It took many minutes of dedicated chewing for the meat to soften into something resembling a paste. Finally I spat it into my hand and held it out to the hatchling.

It sniffed around and under my hand, then chomped down on the meat, nipping my skin in the process. I bit my lip to keep from crying out. Luckily, the hatchling took to the meat and munched happily until it was gone. Yawning, it turned around a few times and flopped onto its belly in the pile of blankets, its song a sleepy burble in my head. I swallowed the lump in my throat. *This* was the fearsome creature

I'd intended to use for my own nefarious purposes?

Sev watched with a peculiar expression on his face. "Where did you learn that?" he whispered.

"I just thought of it. I didn't know if it would work," I said. "But we have to make a plan to take care of it."

"I think our plan has to be to get out of these caves," Sev said. "When we get to Oskiath, my associates will know what to do."

I nodded. "All right. But we can't go back the way we came, and I don't know where these passages lead."

Sev looked around the cavern and up at the ceiling. "The passage we came in through had adornments. Offerings. We could see if the other passages have the same."

I took a lantern and went back down the main passage. There were white candles along the walls, fewer the closer I got to the entrance—though I didn't dare go far enough to see outside.

I turned around and investigated the other three passages. One was adorned primarily with faded silks and fabrics and ended in a cave smaller than the one we were in, which gave me shivers as I stood in it. I left that one quickly.

The other two passages had candles placed similarly to the first, though the candles petered out faster in one than in the other. If these were both passages out of the caves, I could only imagine that one of them was shorter. I relayed this information back to Sev.

"If I'm right, the shorter tunnel would get us out faster. But the longer would get us farther away from the Talons."

Sev lurched upright. "Let's use the longer tunnel." But he was swaying on his feet, and I went to him, putting a shoulder under one arm to keep him up.

"You look hardly well enough to sit, let alone go back on the run with Talons on our tail," I said.

He shook his head. "I'll be fine. Just have to . . . to get used to being on my feet again."

I looked at him, doubts swirling in my head. If he said he could walk, perhaps he could. But he hadn't improved as much as I'd thought he would have given a few days of rest. On the other hand, perhaps that was an argument for moving now. If he worsened, there wasn't a chance I could get the help we needed in time. And besides, the days until midsummer were dwindling.

After some experimentation, we were able to construct a sling out of the blanket that allowed us to carry the dragon while keeping arms free. I took the hatchling first—Sev complained, but he was in no condition to be carrying anything as precious as a baby dragon. We ripped apart one of the tapestries for more bandages and wrapped a length of fabric around his torso, then made another sling for his shoulder.

We'd swaddled the dragon well, hoping that it wouldn't suffer from the lack of its mother's heat. Still, warmth from its body soaked through the blanket and permeated my skin as we walked. By the lantern light I could see that the grayness of the hatchling's skin was fading, giving way to a delicate shade of blue. This dragon didn't smell like anything I recognized, I realized. No acrid stench, nothing that made my nose crinkle in disgust. Maybe dragons didn't smell like that at all. Maybe the smell I'd been associating with dragons all this time was the scent of their fear. Maybe all the things I'd learned about dragons were half-truths, words misshaped by the mouths of their captors.

The tunnel we chose took easily more than two hours to traverse, but finally we arrived at a door. The dragon kit sniffed at it and chirped her approval. I didn't know how I knew she was female, but the moment the thought entered my head, the dragon's presence glowed in my mind. She agreed, it seemed.

"It will be bright," Sev warned as he took the door handle.

He opened the door, and the light blinded me even through my eyelids. When I was able to blink without my eyes watering I saw that it was early morning. Grass surrounded us, a wide open plain. I hunched my shoulders. I didn't like places like this, where there was nowhere to hide. The dragon popped her head out of the sling. Her blue scales shimmered in the sunlight, and a delicate wisp of smoke rose from one nostril as she turned this way and that. I didn't have the heart to push her back down—this was the first time in her life she was in open air.

Sev was looking at me curiously. "What?" I asked.

"Nothing," he said. Still, his eyes followed us as we started across the grass.

We had come out of the ground miles from where we'd entered it, and there was no sign of the Talons here. But still we walked quickly, staying alert.

We had crossed the border from the kingdom of Eronne into Oskiath, Sev was almost certain. Though there was no evidence of a road, we could navigate by the stars at night and the mountains that sprang into view in the far distance by day. Sev pointed at them. "Those are the northern mountains. If we head for those, we'll find our way to Belat eventually."

Belat, the capital city of Oskiath. Where we would finally

meet Sev's mysterious allies. "What happens when we get there?"

Sev looked away.

"Tell me," I said. "Don't I deserve to know after helping you take care of the dragon? And I saved your life back there."

"I *want* to tell you," Sev said. "But . . . well, you know who I am, and my aims. All I know about you is that the Aurati stole something from you. Must have been something exceptional."

I took a deep breath. "*Someone.* Not something. The seers abducted my heartmate from our village."

His brow furrowed. "That doesn't make sense."

"It's true," I said. "I swear it."

The hatchling burbled in its sleep and nestled farther into its blanket.

"So . . . you were just going to walk into Lumina with a dragon and demand they cede your love?"

I grimaced. "I was planning to fly in, actually."

"They must mean a lot to you."

"Her name is Kaia. She's . . . everything," I said simply.

He was quiet for a long time. "You're not really from Oskiath, are you?" he said.

I bit my lip. "What makes you think that?"

He looked at me. "You didn't know about Vir's Passage. You sang in the caves, but you weren't singing in Zefedi. I know songs from all the kingdoms, and I've never heard one that sounds like that. And if you *were* from the empire, you wouldn't mind if your heartmate was claimed, because becoming an Aurat is an honor. So, where are you really from?"

I sized Sev up. He was pale, and his face was clammy. His eyes were bright and feverish, but sharp nonetheless. He might be able to get out his knife, but he would not be able to use it. And I had the dragon. But—none of that mattered anymore. I *did* trust him. All my calculations and considerations of risk—perhaps I'd just wanted a reason to keep him at a distance, despite the way I felt about him. I took a deep breath. "I'm from Ilvera."

He laughed. "That's the secret you've been keeping? It's not like being Verran is a crime in the empire."

"It is if you want to work in the dragon fortress," I shot back. I'd told him the secret that might have gotten me killed, and he'd *laughed.* "And you?"

Sev nodded. "They are . . . a group of people who don't think that the emperor's endless wars are in the best interest of the people. They want peace."

I frowned, stroking the dragon kit's head. Peace. But how, and at what price? "Replacing the emperor will not magically bring peace."

"We know. But neither will maintaining the current course."

"Are your friends the ones in the emperor's prophecy? The shadow prince?"

He stumbled, and I grabbed his arm to keep him upright. "Prophecy—is inexact," he said, his voice strained. "'By the shadow prince's hand the flame will fall.' That was the first prophecy about the prince. But that could mean all manner of things. For example, hand—literal, or metaphoric? Does the prophecy even reference the emperor, or might that be a torch falling? The Aurati adore dispensing prophecies so vague that any outcome can be twisted to fit their words."

"The people we saw in Deletev seemed convinced," I said doubtfully.

"There have been a number of prophecies all referencing the shadow prince of Ruzi," Sev admitted. "Generally, the more a prophecy is repeated the more people accept it as truth."

He shaded his eyes from the sun and looked forward. "I think those trees are the beginning of Belat Forest. Let's see if we can find shelter there for the night."

That night we trapped rabbits and cooked them over a small fire before splitting them between us and the dragon. I still needed to chew the meat first, but she showed a tremendous appetite. She was already noticeably larger than when she had hatched this morning.

"It needs a name," Sev commented. He hadn't eaten much himself. His color was improving as he rested, but that wasn't saying much compared to the way he had looked over the course of the day.

"She," I said.

"How can you tell?"

"I don't know. But I do."

"Talons name their dragons all sorts of things. Zoftar's Revenge, Scibian the Valiant."

I snorted. "Those names are ridiculous." He held out a long piece of grass to the dragon, who nibbled at its end before sneezing. A spark flew out of her nose. "Did you see that?" I exclaimed.

Sev laughed, then coughed. "You sound like a proud parent. So I suppose you have the honor of naming her. Buttercup, perhaps?"

"Definitely not. Anyway, I wonder if she'll name herself when she's older," I said thoughtfully. Since hatching, her song had gotten quieter in my head, but it had never completely disappeared.

"It wasn't an act," Sev said abruptly.

"What?" I looked over at him.

"When I started spending time with you. I wasn't pretending to be your friend just because you were working with Neve." He reached out and took my hand between his.

I stared at him. We'd held hands in the past, but this was different. "Why are you telling me this?" I whispered. "You know I'm with someone." But Kaia, even as we closed in on the north, felt farther and farther away from me.

"Because this might be one of my last chances," Sev said. "Things will change when we get to Belat." He reached out and brushed a stray hair behind my ear. My skin burned where he touched me, and when he leaned toward me, I couldn't help the way my gaze lingered on his lips.

I had to stop this. Not because of Sev, but because of me. I was afraid of what I might do. The lines I might cross.

"I lost the oils," I blurted.

"What?"

I wrenched my hand out of his. The dragon squeaked from where she lay, as if in protest. "I don't know if you remember, but when the Talons came, the only way out was to smash the oils."

"You . . . smashed the oils?"

"Yes! So they're gone. I'm of no help to you now."

Sev went very still. Finally he said, "I'm not sure of that."

"What do you mean?"

"Maren, you sell yourself short. You think yourself ordinary, when you're anything but. You are smart and kind and loyal and brave. Your way with the dragon kit is no less than magic, and your knowledge is valuable—even without the oils. We're in this together."

I felt on the verge of tears. Everything I had told myself, everything I had used to face down the ghosts—he saw it. He saw me, entirely. He *admired* me.

He looked away, leaving me speechless. "Let's get some sleep. We should leave early."

CHAPTER EIGHTEEN

The seer holds a golden goblet in her hands. She takes a sip from it, briefly choking on its contents. "The flame will be extinguished. The dragon will rise," the woman intones.

She shakes off her trance and throws the goblet out of sight. It clangs against the ground.

"Show me the girl, not this poison," she spits out, furious. Three times she has asked for her—three times the same prophecy has come to her lips instead.

I look down upon her. I smile.

The morning dawned bright and clear, but Sev was shivering, and his skin burned to the touch. I bundled him up and wished I had taken more than a torn tapestry from the caves.

"It's—the guardians," Sev croaked as he staggered along. Even leaning on me, he was fading, and we were still only at the beginning of the forest. "They've cursed me for taking Vir's Passage."

"Don't be ridiculous," I said. "It was being thrown against a mountain by a dragon. You need a healer."

"Belat," he said. "We have to get to Belat."

"No, you need help *now*."

He shook his head stubbornly. "Medical district," he said. "Find Melchior. They are the only healer we can trust."

The dragon complained as I shifted her so that I could support Sev's weight more easily. "We'll keep heading toward Belat," I said. "But the second you fall down, I'm getting a healer from the first village we see."

Sev nodded. "I can make it. Let's go."

We came across a grove of wild blackberries later that afternoon, and I ate as we passed through. The dragon sniffed at them but made a displeased noise when she bit into one, and lost interest in them after that. I fed a few to Sev, who managed to keep them down. I was encouraged to see it.

I watched the stars as the evening sky fell away into night. Still heading north. If my reckoning was correct, it had been close to a week since leaving the fortress, leaving only seven days to reach Kaia. Our position was not ideal, and I was exhausted and hadn't covered our tracks as well as I should have. All I could hope for was that, like Sev, the Talons didn't know there were multiple entrances to Vir's Passage.

In the morning I saw a plume of gray smoke rise in the air in the direction from which we had come and wondered whether the Talons had decided to burn us out. I urged Sev to his feet. We kept walking.

We made slow but steady progress. The northern mountains grew in our sights, and toward the end of the day the trees began to thin.

"We should stop here for the night," I said. Sev would have liked to protest, but he was having trouble getting to his feet without my help. "If sleeping will help, then we have to sleep."

He scowled but nodded. I broke out the last of the dried meat. After he had settled into an uneasy rest, I took a torch from the fire and set off into the trees. I was looking for yarrow to bring down the fever. I could only hope to keep him lucid until we could get to a real healer.

The dragon perched on my shoulders. Her skin was darkening as she spent time in the sun, with patches of purple beginning to develop. Her wings were folded neatly along her back at the moment, but when unfurled, I could now see their clear delineation. Somehow she was growing, despite not getting nearly enough to eat. And she had begun to worm her way into my heart—not as a means to an end, but as my own.

Maybe that was wrong. If Sev had been healthy, he might have been more attentive to the dragon. Splitting the duties of caring for her might have split the attachment. But secretly I wasn't so certain. I remembered what Neve had said about the bond between Verrans and their dragons. Perhaps I hadn't been completely foolish to hold the old stories close to my heart.

I found a clump of yarrow growing near a trickling stream and pulled out an entire plant, roots and all. I rinsed the dirt off in the water and turned back to our camp. We didn't have a pot to brew the tea—the small frying pan in Sev's pack would have to do.

Sev took the tea with no complaint aside from a few grimaces. Afterward, I boiled water again and, once it cooled, poured it over the wound in Sev's side. The area around the wound had become an angry, inflamed red, and pus leaked out from where the skin was starting to scab over. Sev hissed in pain as I helped him put on a fresh bandage.

I settled my back against a tree and let the dragon loose to toddle around the camp as I watched. She was inquisitive and had become more vocal, making nonsense sounds that nonetheless sounded familiar. I answered her back in song, and we passed the time entertaining each other until my eyelids grew heavy. Then I bundled the dragon to sleep with me—I would take no chances that she might wander off in the night.

Sev's fever had receded a bit in the morning, but he still moved like a man old before his time. I packed up the camp with care, trying to make our packs as light as possible.

"What happens when we get to Belat?" I asked. "Will there be guards at the gates?"

"Probably," Sev said. "Belat isn't walled like Deletev, though."

I looked down at the dragon. I could still carry her easily, but she was more energetic now and prone to doing inconvenient things. Regardless of whether the gates were guarded, it seemed likely that no one would miss a dragon kit being carted around by two weary travelers. I took the dragon out of the sling and tucked her into the pack on my back instead. "Shhh," I whispered. "It won't be for long." At least I hoped it wouldn't.

I was lucky that she decided to cooperate. We'd been careful to stay in the cover of the forest, but we had to travel faster than our stumbling legs could carry us. We would have to chance the main road.

The road was empty and stayed that way for some time. Finally I heard a telltale creak as a man driving a horse and cart trundled into view. Sev pulled himself upright, but beads of sweat showed on his forehead from the effort.

I bowed as best I could with Sev leaning on me. "Good day. Are you headed to Belat?"

The man looked Sev up and down and shook his head. "Can't risk giving you a ride. I know too many who have died of plague."

"Please," I said. "He doesn't have plague. I swear. There's a healer waiting in the city; I just need to get him there. I can pay."

"Not with him looking the way he does. Best take care of yourself." The man twitched the reins, and the horse walked on.

I sighed and wiped the sweaty hair away from Sev's forehead. "Stay with me," I said. "Just a little while longer now."

He looked slightly green and was holding his injured arm close against his body, but he nodded.

A second cart refused us also, and the third didn't even stop to listen. Belat was so close—and still so far.

"What do I do?" I whispered to myself. Could I bring Melchior to Sev? But that would mean leaving him alone, on the side of the road. I couldn't do that.

But that left me . . . here. Tired and hungry and feet aching. I stopped. Sev stumbled, and I hauled him upright, then lowered him to the ground, where he sat, head braced in one hand. I sat next to him, curling one arm around the pack to keep the dragon kit inside as I pulled out my water skin. I shared the last of it between the three of us. Strange that after fighting off Talons and passing through a cavern of ghosts, it was walking this last leg of the journey that seemed insurmountable.

Whatever it takes. Kaia had promised, and so had I. I didn't want to choose between her and Sev, but I feared that time would force my hand.

The sky was blue and unyielding. My throat was dry, even after the water. And the travelers on the road passed us with little more than a glance. But perhaps there was another way.

I rummaged in my pack and pulled out all but three of my remaining feathers. "I need a cart!" I cried, holding up my hand. There was no point in keeping my head down if it meant Sev's life. "I can pay!"

The first cart passed me by. A few riders on horseback were useless to me—I didn't even try to speak to them. Finally an older Celet woman dressed smartly came around the bend. A young girl sat next to her on the seat, reins held loosely in her grasp. Their covered wagon looked tightly packed.

I stood up, craning my neck. "Do you have a cart I can buy? Any cart will do so long as I can move it myself."

For a moment the wagon kept moving. Then the woman whispered to the girl, who reined in the horse and brought the wagon to a stop.

The woman raised her eyebrows. "Hard times have you, don't they now." She looked over at Sev, concerned.

"He doesn't have the plague," I said hurriedly.

She sniffed. "Do I look like a superstitious fishwife to you? Though he does need a healer."

"Yes," I said. "We're trying to get to a healer named Melchior. They're the only one my friend will accept. He's stubborn. We should have stopped a ways back."

"Long journey?"

"All the way from Gedarin," I lied. "Though he only had the accident a few days ago."

The woman and girl glanced at each other. "I see. Well,

come along, then. The horse won't mind a few skinny things like yourself."

I could have cried. "Thank you. Thank you so much." I passed the woman my coin.

The girl climbed into the back of the wagon and held out a hand to me to help Sev up. I climbed in after him, and we settled on the floor as the wagon started on its way again.

Belat. Father had told me about the city that sat nestled in a valley like a giant's cupped hands in the midst of a series of rolling green hills. Everything he'd said came rushing back to me as the outskirts came into view. Its location had been selected first for its beauty. Only later, after some unrest in the greater empire, had it become the capital of Oskiath. Arts districts and gleaming stone streets and the smell of warm cinnamon that would float through the air in the early mornings, when all the bakers were at work. There was no cinnamon in the air now.

It was a city without a guard wall, but guards stood watch next to the tall stone pillars that passed as gates. I shrank down against the floor as we approached. The wagon cover hid us from outside eyes, but if the guards decided to search the wagon, there would be no escape. The wagon slowed, then stopped. I lay like a statue beside Sev, straining to hear what was happening outside.

"Morning, Janelle," said one of the guards. They knew her by name? "You're a little late today."

The woman laughed. "Had a bit of an accident with a chicken this morning, but here we are."

"Usual cargo?"

"With a few new imports from Ruzi. You'll have to come by the market later."

"I just might. Well, remember to check in with the market clerk."

She hadn't mentioned us. She'd *protected* us. Why? I held my breath—and the wagon rolled forward, between the pillars. We were in.

After a few turns I sat up, looking outside at the city. It was smaller than Deletev, and the streets were clean and well kept, the stones even beneath the wagon wheels. Beside me, Sev lay on his back, breathing shallowly.

By the time Janelle pulled the wagon to a stop, the dragon kit was complaining, trying to wriggle free of my pack. I soothed her absently as I put a hand to the side of Sev's neck. He'd slipped back into the feverish sleep that had worried me for the last several days.

The girl appeared at the back of the wagon and helped me lift Sev out. We settled him on the side of the street, and I looked up at Janelle. "You didn't mention us at the gate," I said.

"The boy needs a healer," Janelle said. "I have no higher calling than to offer my assistance in times such as these. Melchior is well known in Belat—this is their door." She motioned to a building across the street. "Be well, child."

"Thank you," I said. I had no other words to give her.

The girl climbed back up beside Janelle, who clicked her teeth at the horse. The wagon ambled down the street.

I knocked on the door. A harried-looking person with gangly limbs and unusual red hair opened it and looked at me expectantly. "Well?"

I wasn't sure exactly what I could say—how much they

might know, or how much I was meant to keep secret. "I was told to ask for Melchior."

"I'm Melchior," they said. They looked past me, and their face went pale. "*Sev*," they breathed, all pretense of collectedness dropping away. "Come, we need to get him inside at once. What happened?"

Perhaps I was wrong to trust them. But we had come so far, and Sev had said that this was the person I should seek . . . and it had been so, so long since I had come across someone with concern in their eyes for us. For me.

"Thrown against a rocky hill and hurt his shoulder," I said. "There's a gash on his side, maybe internal injuries as well. And"—I lowered my voice—"we stayed for some days in Vir's Passage."

Melchior rolled their eyes. "Superstitious rot," they said. "Here, help me carry him in." They expertly maneuvered Sev's prone body between us, and I stepped in to take some of the weight.

"I know. It's just that Sev was so worried—"

"None of those ghosts would hurt him. They know who he is."

My mind caught their words and filed them away—there was too much else that demanded my attention right now. "He said that we had to come to you."

We turned down a hallway, and Melchior kicked open a door. We laid Sev on the bed, and his head lolled to one side. I couldn't look away. Melchior snapped their fingers in front of my face, and I started.

"Sorry. What?" I said.

"When was he last conscious?"

"Earlier today. But he was having trouble walking. After we got in a wagon, he drifted off quickly. What—what's wrong with him?"

"I don't know yet." Melchior shooed me out of the way. "But he'll be *fine* if you would just let me work," they said. Their face softened. "You carried him from Vir's Passage? You must be exhausted." They pointed to a room across the hall. "Get some rest. I'll tell you when things change, I promise."

Maybe I was more exhausted than I realized, because I took their suggestion without protest. Once in the spare room, I closed and locked the door behind me. There was only a hard cot, but in that moment it was the most comfortable bed in the world. I let the dragon kit out of the pack and collapsed onto the cot, closing my eyes.

The dragon woke me. She was sniffing under the door and singing curiously as I opened my eyes. *Melchior. The dragon. Kaia. Sev.*

I jerked upright. The dragon bounded over to me, and I scooped her up into my arms. The light entering the room from the high window was minimal and useless in gauging how long I'd been asleep.

I had to check on Sev, but I couldn't bring the dragon with me. It would look suspicious if I carried my pack everywhere I went. On the other hand, I couldn't leave her here, where anyone could come in and find her.

A resounding crash from outside the door brought my thoughts on the subject to a halt.

"Shhh," I whispered to the dragon. There was a small closet in the corner of the room. I opened the door and placed her inside. She looked up at me, her song suddenly sounding more like a whine in my head. "Stay here. It's only for a moment," I said. I had to find out what was going on.

I closed the closet door and slipped quietly into the hallway.

It seemed the crash was a one-time occurrence, but there were raised voices coming from the room where Sev was being treated.

"I called you as soon as I could!" That was Melchior's voice.

"Not soon enough. And who is the guttersnipe who dragged him in?" a female voice demanded.

"I don't know."

"You don't *know?*"

"Would you have preferred that I *not* treat your precious golden boy right away? That I spend my time interrogating a girl who clearly saved his life? What's done is done."

My shoulders tightened as the door opened and I found myself face-to-face with one of the most beautiful women I'd ever seen. She was older than me, tall and statuesque with golden brown skin and long hair the color of autumn leaves, worn loose. Perhaps dyed hair was a fashion in Oskiath—Melchior was the only other person I'd seen with such an unusual color. She wore a rich blue dress embroidered with gold thread and expensive-looking boots.

"Who are you?" she said, looking me up and down.

"Maren," I said. "I've been traveling with Sev." I tried to look around her without craning my neck but could only see the corner of Sev's bed.

"Really." Her lip curled in the faintest hint of a sneer.

I lifted my chin. I would not be intimidated. "Really."

"And where did you meet?"

"I don't believe I've had the pleasure of making *your* acquaintance. And I won't answer any questions until I know Sev is all right."

The woman sniffed but opened the door wider. She did not stand aside, forcing me to press past her as I entered the room and went to Sev's side. He was sleeping still, but his color was much improved. I let out a relieved breath.

"Satisfied?" the woman asked.

I crossed my arms. "For the moment."

"Let's get this over with, then. I'm Rowena ben Garret, and you are going to tell me what business you have with Severin."

My stomach sank. I knew that name. Father had told me ben Garret was the name of the royal family of Oskiath. Whether she was a princess or a minor cousin to a princess, she was someone unused to being denied anything. I looked at her closely. If Melchior had called her, she must be involved with Sev's mission.

"It's personal," I said.

"Where did you meet him?"

"I don't see how that's any of your business."

"Severin disappeared without warning! And only now returned to us, gravely injured? It's my business to know where, and how, and why."

She was lying through her teeth. She knew exactly how he'd "disappeared"—she only wanted to know how I fit into the picture. And whether he had succeeded in what he'd set out to accomplish.

I took a deep breath. "I don't know you," I said. "Considering the situation, you'll forgive me if I don't take your word on everything you say."

Rowena's eyebrows shot up, and color rose in her cheeks. "I will not be spoken to in such a manner. Get out."

"I'm not leaving him," I said.

"You are if you don't want to be arrested and interrogated. I can have a guard here faster than you can imagine." She snapped her fingers.

Melchior stood silent in the corner. Our eyes met briefly; then they looked away. I wondered how many of Rowena's threats they had witnessed. How many of them had been brought to fruition.

"Fine," I said. I turned around and returned to my room, closing the door.

I let the dragon kit out of the closet before leaning back against the closed door. The road ahead seemed . . . murky. In the fortress my aims had been clear. While we were traveling, even more so: Don't get caught. But here the dangers were masked. What would Kaia do? What would Sev do? What should I do?

If Rowena was indeed one of Sev's shadowy allies, should I tell her what I knew? I didn't stand a chance of convincing them to help me without Sev's testimony. Would having saved his life buy me enough goodwill? And even if I did tell them everything, would they decide I was too risky a variable to let out into the world?

I needed Sev to wake up. Melchior's words from last night flitted dizzily back into my mind. The ghosts knew him, that's what they'd said. Ghosts who respected the history that seeped into the land. Like an old ruling family. One that stayed true to the earth, and its people. One that a princess of Oskiath would have known. Sev's behavior began to click into place. The way he'd spoken ill of the Talons and the emperor at the fortress. The effortless act he'd put on to impress the Aurati in Deletev. That hadn't been a mask—that was the way he'd been raised. Of the five kingdoms of Zefed, I knew the most about Eronne and Oskiath and had only a passing familiarity with the others— certainly not enough to trust my knowledge of the royal families.

But Sev had mentioned vengeance. And the first kingdom, the first family that came to mind when I considered the question of revenge was—

Ruzi.

By the shadow prince's hand the flame will fall. The rumors. The inheritance razed to the ground. Sev's eyes as he'd spoken about his family. Sev was the missing prince of Ruzi.

My hand went to my mouth. I didn't realize any sound had escaped until the dragon kit appeared at my side, nudging her head against my leg. *The shadow prince of Ruzi.*

Why hadn't he told me? I'd told him *everything*. At least, everything that mattered. My jaw tightened, and my cheeks grew hot. Perhaps my anger was unfair—surely he'd done what he thought he had to do. But the omission still felt like a betrayal. Something broke in me, and a sob escaped my lips. A moment later the dragon tried mimicking the sound.

"That's not a good sound, little one. Best not remember it." I picked her up and tapped her nose with one finger. What was I going to do with her? She was Sev's. But I couldn't hand her over if Sev wasn't even conscious. And I couldn't leave her here, not with predators like Rowena roaming the halls. We could stay in this room until called upon, but there was no guarantee of safety even if I remained with her. And my stomach was rumbling.

I tried to push away my thoughts about Sev's true identity as I washed my face and hands with water from the basin on the table beside the cot. I dug out the last few coins from the pouch at my waist, and then placed the dragon back into my pack and tied the top loosely. She didn't complain, though it was only a matter of time until she began to.

I ran into Melchior as I left the room. "How is he?" I asked.

They smiled. "Better. I expect he'll wake up soon."

I was relieved, and I hated the part of me that still cared, despite how angry I was with him. "Is there somewhere I can go to get a meal?"

"If you go out the doors and take a left, you'll see the market."

"And . . ." There was no way to ask what I needed to know other than to say it. "Will I be allowed back in?"

"Not to worry," Melchior said. "Rowena may run her own circles, but this is not just *any* house. She does not have the final word here."

I refrained from pointing out that this had not sounded like the way of things earlier today. "Thank you," I said. "We've been on the road for some time. Can you tell me how many days there are until midsummer?"

"Five," they replied.

I schooled my features into a pleasant mask and nodded my thanks before following their directions out of the building, even as my heart ached. In five days Kaia might die, if I didn't reach her first.

CHAPTER NINETEEN

For a while I hummed an angry marching song as I walked, one parents in Ilvera taught their children to give them an outlet for their tantrums. I was angry—at Sev, at myself, at the world. He'd *lied* to me. No—he simply hadn't told all the truth. I had to remind myself of that. The right thing to do would be to forgive him. We'd both been in over our heads. But I couldn't, not yet.

It was early afternoon, and there were few people about. Belat had taken little architectural influence from Deletev. Here the buildings were more angular, the stones cut into precise corners that fit perfectly together in the streets. There was a particular order to everything I saw.

The preferred styles of clothing were lighter in color than in Deletev as well, on everyone from the street sweepers to the market vendors to the children playing. It was pleasant. The people were notably unvaried. Most I saw had a mix of Old Zefedi and Celet ancestry. And the city felt small—not like the sprawl I'd always imagined during Father's stories. But perhaps it was my own perception that had changed since I'd left Ilvera.

The dragon kit was behaving herself for the moment. I followed a familiar scent to one of the food carts, where an enormous pot simmered. First I simply inhaled the smell of the peppers I knew from home. My eyes began to water, but not just from the heat. "How much for a bowl?" I asked.

The vendor protested—the food wasn't yet ready. But I didn't want to linger, and I pressed him into selling me some of the stew anyway. It didn't taste exactly like my father's—I could taste that the evelyn peppers hadn't been crisped before being added to the pot—but it was enough to tug on my heart. I found a seat in a quiet alley and ate with abandon. If I closed my eyes, I could imagine I was sitting in our kitchen at home, my parents on either side of me.

After I finished eating, I returned to the market. I'd wandered down two rows of stalls before I realized that someone was watching me. She wore Aurati blue, and she was young. When she saw me staring, she quickly melted into the shadows, and I was left turning in all directions. I checked my pack to make sure it was securely fastened. Inside, the dragon squeaked in annoyance, and I whistled to her softly.

I looked over my shoulder and saw another Aurat. She turned away too fast, inspecting something at a stall across the way, but when I looked in the other direction, I caught the first Aurat walking toward me.

I whirled around to find a third Aurat blocking the way I'd come.

They were hemming me in. I headed toward a stall, pretending I was interested in the sacks of rice. Once I was half-hidden by the stall's curtains, I made a sharp turn and ran.

Indignant shouts rose up as I swerved to avoid the people

in my path, clipping the corners of a few stalls in my haste. I couldn't risk leading them back to Sev. If I did, the healing center would no longer be safe. I had to find somewhere to hide—or get out of the city.

"Stop that girl!"

People around me looked up, startled, but were slow to act. I sprinted past them, grabbing a green scarf off a table as I passed. I glanced over my shoulder—the Aurati were running behind me—and crashed into a cart of cabbages, sending it and myself to the ground. The cabbage vendor yelled, but I couldn't stop. I scrambled to my feet and kept running.

I exited the market, but the route I'd taken led into a residential district. I cursed as I flew past closed doors. I turned a corner, then another, but the streets all looked the same. Nowhere to hide, and no clues for how to get out of this maze.

The dragon kit's complaints were shrill in my ear. "Quiet," I said, my breath coming in pants. I felt nauseated from the stew I'd just eaten, but I couldn't stop.

I pushed myself harder, turned another corner, and folded myself into a doorway slightly deeper than the others. Willing my hands to stop shaking, I smoothed my hair and took off my jacket, then wrapped the scarf around myself and my pack. I took one more deep breath and peeked out of the doorway. There were no Aurati on the street. I whispered once more to the dragon kit in an attempt to soothe her. Then I left the doorway and reentered the street, forcing myself to match the slow pace of those around me.

I would walk until I was sure I wasn't being followed, but I was beginning to rethink my destination. How had the Aurati known to look for me here? If Rowena had called them, I could not assume the healing center was safe. But it seemed unlikely that she would hand me over to them, given what I knew about Sev's quest. Unless the Aurati were involved in this conspiracy as well? Or perhaps the seers had foreseen this, and they had always known where to catch me.

A hand grabbed my wrist, and I turned to see the young Aurat at my side. "She's here!" she shouted. The other two Aurati turned the corner, closing in on me.

I stomped hard on her foot and twisted out of her grasp, then fled in the opposite direction. I'd lost my lead with this gambit—now I turned down streets at random, focusing only on staying in motion. Left. Right. Left. Left. I turned another corner and hit a dead end. *No.*

I turned around to see two Aurati blocking the street.

There was no way out. I drew my knife.

Three tall men suddenly appeared in the street behind the Aurati. "Maren ben Gao," one of them called.

There was only one reason anyone should know that name here. Sev must have woken—and told them.

The men pushed past the Aurati, approaching me slowly. They were dressed in long coats of Oskiath green. The first of them stepped forward and proffered an eloquent bow. They weren't going to arrest me? Were they not associates of the Aurati? I looked past them. The Aurati hung back, looking frustrated.

Perhaps this wasn't the end. I lowered my knife and bowed back, though I didn't dare take my eyes off them. "We haven't been introduced."

"Of course," he said. "My name is Valda ben Garret. We've been sent by my lady Rowena to collect you."

How much did he know? By his attire he looked no more than a captain of the guard, but I wasn't familiar enough with these intricacies to say one way or the other. If he *was* the captain of the guard, the plot to dethrone the emperor must go much deeper than I thought.

I had no reason to disbelieve him, but the sudden turn of events was enough to spin my head. "What about them?" I nodded to the Aurati.

"A misunderstanding, I'm sure," the man said in a pleasant tone. The Aurati frowned but retreated from the street. So the guard ranked higher than the Aurati, at least in Belat.

"All right," I said slowly, seeing no reason to object. "You may lead the way."

The guards escorted me back to the healers' district and through a side door that led into Melchior's house. We went to a room that had clearly been made to serve as an advisory chamber. A large table took up most of the floor, and the majority of seats were already taken. My steps slowed as I realized exactly what I was walking into: a meeting of Sev's allies.

"Maren." My heart leaped at hearing Sev's voice before I remembered that I was angry with him. He was upright now but still pale, seated across the table from me. He'd had the opportunity to wash. His short hair was slicked back and tied with a band, and he was dressed now in clothes befitting, well, a prince.

"You're alive," I said.

"Yes. Thanks to you."

The others in the room looked at me expectantly, but I

couldn't help what I blurted out: "You didn't tell me who you were."

His eyes softened with what appeared to be genuine remorse. "I'm sorry," he said. "More than I can say. I thought it was the only way."

Rowena set down her goblet on the table, cutting the moment short. "Now that you're all here, we can begin. You, sit down." She waved a hand at me. I moved to take one of the few remaining seats.

"The prophecies have begun to affect the emperor—he has the Aurati seers draw new visions and send them every day from Lumina. He's suspicious of his inner circle as well. It is imperative that we tread carefully. That being said, the purpose of this meeting is to discuss the information and resources recently obtained by Severin. As you have heard, he was able to procure a dragon and someone with the knowledge of how to train it." She looked meaningfully in my direction. "Well? Show us the dragon!"

I had no other choice. I had to comply.

The dragon kit burst forth, happy at first just to be free of my pack. It unfurled its wings, lashed its tail, and sneezed. A handful of sparks burst into the air.

"That's it?" a woman said. "It's so . . ."

"Small," interjected an older man in a huff. "Helpless little thing."

"It will grow," Sev said with an air of authority. Grow to be drugged and bound into submission. Grow to be molded into a weapon aimed at the emperor. I folded my arms and scowled.

"But you said that you were unable to procure the necessary

tools for training," Rowena said chidingly. "You have failed to fulfill your mission."

He hadn't told them how the oils had been lost, or they would have been directing their derision at me. He was . . . helping me.

Sev's voice was like ice. "As I told you, there were complications. Maren worked as the Aromatory's apprentice. She knows what is required. She can direct the training effort."

The dragon seemed to be catching the timbre of the conversation. She ran back toward me and jumped into the safety of my arms.

"Assuming that Maren will perform. What do you even know of her?" This from the captain of Rowena's guard, as though I were not sitting directly in front of him.

Sev glanced at me. "She can be trusted with this. I swear it."

A tall, thin man standing in the corner stepped forward. "If everything you said is true, perhaps we're wasting our time on an untried apprentice. I've been spending some time with the Talons. Dolok is a promising lead. We might convince him to join the Dragons' cause."

I couldn't stop myself from snorting in angry laughter. "You call yourselves the Dragons?"

The man with the clipped beard looked at me for the first time since we had sat down. "Do you think this is funny?"

I let out another laugh. Perhaps I was succumbing to hysteria. "You're an organization of sitters. Talkers. You're no dragons."

Rowena leveled a glare at me. "Our name honors the power of the dragons, currently shackled by an unwise leader. When the time comes, we will rise."

"On power that is not yours."

"There are things at work that you cannot possibly understand."

I stood up, placing the dragon on my seat. "I understand that you want change on the backs of the beings you claim to want to free. You're all hypocrites."

I turned to Sev, but he was studiously looking away from me. "Sit down, Maren," he said.

"What?" He'd said much the same things to me, and others, even in the fortress.

"These are not things we can *afford* to think of now. There is a time and a place."

My stomach twisted. He'd made a similar argument during our travels, but I had thought—hoped—he might have changed his mind after all we'd been through with the dragon kit. "When? After you've managed to kill the Flame of the West and take over the Talons? Am I to believe you'll release the dragons from captivity then?" He pressed his lips together and did not respond. It pained me dearly to look at him and see someone dressed in all the raiment of a prince, not the person I'd thought I'd come to know. The person I'd almost kissed—

No, I would not think of that.

"What an emperor you'll be," I said quietly.

"That's enough," Rowena said. "Since you're clearly not going to be helpful, you are excused from this meeting. Valda, escort her to her room."

I pushed back from the table. "Fine." The dragon kit wrapped around my leg.

Rowena raised her hand. "The dragon stays here. Severin?"

Sev's expression was stony as he stood and walked over to my seat.

"Don't do this," I said, clutching the dragon kit tighter against me. But he was already grabbing her around the belly, pulling her away. The kit cried out in dismay as the captain of the guard hauled me upright, breaking my hold on her.

This pain was too familiar—the agony of being wrenched away from the one I loved. I desperately wanted to go and comfort the kit, but I was so tired of struggling. I was so tired of everything.

"You're going to end up just like *him*," I said, glaring at Sev as I was taken out of the room. The conversation picked back up again even before the door closed. The kit's furious cries rang in my head long after I had been locked in my room. I cried and didn't bother to wipe away the tears.

When the knock came later, I expected Sev's contrite face to greet me. If not him, then perhaps Melchior. But it was Rowena who actually stood in the doorway after the lock clicked open.

"What do you want?" I said.

For once she did not look insufferably superior. She bowed—a slight bow, but a real one. "May I come in?"

No, I thought. But I stepped away from the door and allowed her to enter. She crossed her arms, then uncrossed them. Was the woman actually nervous? About speaking to me?

Finally Rowena cleared her throat. "You must understand, Maren. The duty of our council is to the future of Zefed. That duty is much greater than the sentimental attachments of one person."

She was talking about me—and perhaps the Sev I'd thought I'd known. The worst part of it all was that not too long ago I would have agreed with her. When I had started this journey, I had one objective only: to free Kaia. Anyone else—anything else—was immaterial. But the longer I'd been in Sev's company, and the more time I'd had with the dragon kit . . . my feelings had changed.

"I understand that you believe that. But I don't know why you're trying so hard to convince me. I'm no one."

She pinched the bridge of her nose, frustrated. "Severin spoke for you most compellingly. We need someone to help us train the dragon, and we want you."

They still wanted me after everything I'd said? That couldn't be right. Several people in the meeting would have objected, and didn't they have another option in that corruptible Talon? There had to be something more at play. Perhaps they thought I had more information to share.

"I don't have the resources," I said after a moment.

"Money is not an issue. We can create a workshop to equal the one you had at the dragon fortress."

I pretended to think this over. If I were truly going to help them I would have to tell them that without mirth wood oil, they had no hope of bringing their plan to fruition. "Sev and I made a bargain. Did he tell you what he promised me?" I said.

"Of course," Rowena said smoothly. "It won't be a problem."

She had to be lying. After the meeting, it was impossible to believe any of the council members would risk losing me or their allies in what I'm sure they considered to be a mission guaranteed to fail.

If I refused Rowena now, they would still detain me. I was certain of it. And I could give up any chance of reaching Kaia in time.

"All right," I said. "I'll do it."

Once Rowena had left, I began preparing for my escape.

I upended my pack and spilled its contents onto the bed, then swept my fingers around the sides and bottom to make sure it was completely empty before repacking. If nothing else, I would do this right. My fingers touched glass, and I recoiled in surprise. I reached out again and closed my fingers around—

A vial.

One vial, that had somehow been caught in the seam.

I sat down, turning it over between my fingers. Its contents were secure. I opened it and took a quick sniff: fire root.

I laughed. What a useless thing. Better lavender or gray ivory, or absolutely anything that was not guaranteed to make any dragon that smelled it explode into a massive inferno of rage. But still I pocketed the vial as I packed my things. It was somehow comforting to know it was there.

I picked up Kaia's dragon figurine next, turning it over in my hands. If I could get out of Oskiath, I could go home. Cut my hair and buy new clothes, take the back roads to Ilvera. I could forget I had ever done this. I could be free of all this weight. Nurse my wounds and my losses. Mourn Kaia the way I'd planned when she was first taken—alone, in my dark room.

But I immediately dismissed the thought. I could never abandon Kaia. And I was surprised to realize I also couldn't go back because of *me*. I had changed, stretched and grown over this journey. Running and hiding was no longer an option, and not because of anyone else's expectations. I had set myself to a task, and I would see it through.

Whatever it takes.

I'd played the part of resigned accomplice well enough that my door had not been locked after supper, though I hadn't seen either Sev or the dragon kit since the meeting. I lay on the cot fully clothed, timing the patrols that passed my door. After about an hour, I was confident I knew the pattern. It was time.

I shouldered my pack, picked up my boots, and walked to the door. I had counted on being quick about my exit—I hadn't accounted for the sudden shriek that reverberated in my head. The dragon kit was somewhere near me, and she knew I was leaving.

I pressed my forehead to the door. *Please. Don't be upset. I'll come back for you.*

I couldn't take her with me, not to Lumina. She was too small. I didn't know what I was walking into. I didn't even know if I would return. I didn't want to admit it, but she would be safer here while I was gone. And I could at least still trust that Sev would care for her to the best of his abilities.

None of these points reassured either of us as the keening in my head grew louder.

I'm sorry. I had to leave now, or be tempted to stay simply to soothe her fears. I did my best to ignore her cries as I crept out of my room.

I evaded the guard and made it to the front door of Melchior's house without trouble. I closed the door quietly behind me and knelt to put on my boots. I'd taken care to dress differently than I had during the day, and to tuck my hair underneath a scarf, in case the Aurati were observing the healing center. I looked around but didn't see anything out of the ordinary. I headed toward the city limits.

I was past Belat's gates by the time there was a hint of blue in the sky. I let my boots point for one long breath in the direction of home. Toward Ilvera. Then I turned north and began to walk.

It was different, traveling alone. Before all this had started, it had been Kaia and me without fail. Then I had become accustomed to having Sev at my side instead. But I found that I didn't mind being alone. Although I did miss the feel of the dragon kit perched on my shoulder.

That night I slept a dreamless sleep, but I still woke up afraid. Kaia was running out of time. By my reckoning I had three days left. Three days to get to Lumina, come up with a plan, and execute it. I no longer carried anything that was likely to raise suspicions, but neither did I have anything that would be useful in tricking my way inside the stronghold. The best I could come up with was to pretend I wanted to join their ranks, and even that was doubtful. All of Lumina would be preparing for the midsummer initiate trials. Perhaps the confusion would afford me a larger window to slip inside, but surely the initiates would be kept under lock and key if the failures were to be disposed of.

Such were the thoughts occupying me on my way through the forest of Belat when I heard a twig snap—and then a whinny. I pulled my knife from my belt and ducked behind a tree, waiting for the rider to round the bend.

Two horses came into view, but there was only one rider. *Sev.*

I reacted without thought, stepping out into the road. He swung down from his horse and ran to me, his expression full of worry. He crossed the distance in a few long strides and wrapped his arms around me in a tight embrace.

"What are you doing here?" I asked. It was the only sentence I could string together into any sort of sense.

"I brought you something." As if on cue, the dragon launched herself out of his pack and off his shoulder, catching a moment of wind before tumbling down on top of me in a tangle of limbs. I was crying and I couldn't stop. She was here. With me.

"How?" I said. "How did you do this?"

Sev let me go, suddenly looking shamefaced. "There's been an uproar since you ran off—the council can't decide whether to come after you or not. Anyway, she wouldn't stop crying so I said I would take her for a walk."

I was close to speechless. "That worked?"

"Apparently she wasn't eating. Not to mention the noise. They trusted me with her. Also, people don't argue with you when you've been ill—they worry it might delay the recovery process."

"Clearly," I said. The dragon wrapped her tail around my neck, and I gently loosened her grip and set her down on the ground.

"So I've been thinking," Sev said. He held up a hand, stopping me from interrupting. "What you share with this dragon is unlike anything I've ever witnessed." There was a note of sadness in his words, and resignation. "There isn't a lot of certainty in my world right now," he continued. "I don't have a lot of *choice* except for what to believe in. And I believe in change—and in you. The dragon is yours. She's bonded to you in a way I couldn't possibly hope to replicate. The dragon belongs with you. And if you'll have me along, I want to help you."

The dragon kit nestled up against my leg, contented mews spiraling in the air.

"But what about all that you said during the meeting? Was it all a lie?"

He looked down. "No. Not all of it. But I've thought a lot about us these last few days, and the dragon. I still intend to kill the emperor. I'm not sure what will happen after that, but I swear to you—I will do everything in my power to free the dragons."

I could feel a bubble of emotion building in my chest, and I couldn't stop myself from smiling.

Sev went on. "Besides, I'm not sure how you're going to manage to get into Lumina without me."

"I managed just fine with the fortress," I retorted.

"With no escape route or supplies. Need I go on?" But there was no barb in his words, only a hint of humor.

"I suppose you have a better plan?"

He nodded to the horses. "We're messengers from Oskiath. Official diplomatic business, not uncommon in these parts. I brought a uniform for you. We'll get in and cause a distraction in the kitchens on the way out. Then you'll have the opportunity to search for Kaia."

I had to admit it was better than anything I'd come up with.

"Are you sure you want to do this?" I said. "If we make it out alive, the council may turn on you and try to reclaim the dragon. You'd be giving up so much." *For me.*

"I told the truth that day at the camp. We're in this together."

The dragon nibbled at my boots. I wanted so much to accept his offer, to trust him again. But there was one question still eating at me.

"Why didn't you tell me who you were?" I asked. "I told you—everything. And you were the prince of Ruzi that whole time!"

Sev's face grew sober. "It's a secret I've kept for a very long time. My brother was executed for treason—he wanted to free Ruzi from the empire. My mother was hunted down. I'd been in hiding for years before the council found me." He let out his breath in exasperation. "I tried not to be a prince. I never needed a kingdom, not like my brother. But after my mother—I could not let her death go unavenged.

"When I was with you, though, I was able to forget my past, my title," he continued. "And Maren, I swear I wanted to tell you. But when you told me about Kaia, I knew the truth would come out on its own, and we'd have to part ways eventually. So I decided to wait. To pretend I wasn't . . . who I am. That we weren't—"

"Who we are," I finished.

"Yes."

"I understand," I said softly.

"Forgive me?" Sev offered me a smile.

"I do." And I did, truly.

"Then let's ride."

We reached the Aurati stronghold early the next afternoon.

Lumina was a tower of white stone carved from a mountainside, so that from a distance it was almost invisible, and looked out across the land with farseeing eyes. It was taller than the dragon fortress and no less imposing. I hated it on sight.

We stopped amid some trees to change into the Oskiath livery Sev had brought—short coats and trimmed trousers, all in shades of green.

"What now?" I whispered as Sev and I looked out at Lumina. The occasion seemed to warrant whispering, and the dragon seemed to agree. She had spent most of the ride on my shoulder with her wings extended, almost like she was flying. Now she curled in around herself again, digging her claws into my clothing.

"Follow my lead," Sev said. "They won't question us if we have messages too urgent to entrust to the usual Aurati scribes. After we've delivered them, they'll send us out through the kitchens. I'll cause a distraction, and you can find Kaia."

"How will you get out?" For that matter, how would *we* get out? I had to hope that Kaia had learned something useful during her time here.

He grinned. "I'll think of something. It'll help that the trials are just around the corner—the place will be busy. If all else fails, I can tell them that I'm the lost prince of Ruzi. That ought to cause a kerfuffle."

I smiled back at him, and we held each other's gaze a moment too long. A twig snapped in the brush behind us, and suddenly one of my arms was being twisted behind my back, the pain driving me to my knees. The dragon kit fell from my shoulder and launched herself in a rage before being batted to the ground and stuffed into a sack.

I cried out, and Sev shouted, drawing his sword—but he

froze just as I felt the cool kiss of a blade against my throat.

A woman spoke from behind me. "Drop your sword, traveler."

Sev met my eyes. I shook my head minutely, helplessly. Slowly he lowered his sword to the ground.

"On your knees."

Sev complied, and the Aurati quickly bound our hands behind our backs.

There were six of them—three on foot, blades drawn, and the rest on horseback. How had they found us? No one had known where we were going, and we were too far away from Lumina for this to be a normal patrol.

The Aurati pulled us to our feet and pushed us forward, marching us toward the stronghold ahead of their horses. Sev walked in front of me. I couldn't see his face, but at least his steps were steady. I couldn't see the dragon.

"Right where the Prophet said they would be. Easiest catch this year," one of them said. The comment seemed strange. From their robes, I knew our captors were seers. But if all seers had access to these divine prophecies, why would they need to depend on a special prophet?

A dream swam back to the surface of my mind—the inscrutable woman kneeling before the fire, the prophecies that flowed from her lips. I hadn't understood it at the time, but now, too late, it was coming into focus. What if not all seers had the gift of prophecy? What if only a few—or only one—had it? My lips parted in surprise. One question had haunted me ever since Kaia had been taken: Why had the seers taken her when there were so many willing girls in the empire?

Because they needed *her*. She was meant to be the next prophet.

The revelation rang through my mind, and I began to cry. If Kaia was a prophet, the Aurati would never let her go. My quest was all for nothing. I might as well scream for the stars to realign.

My body was numb and my vision hazy as the seers drove us down the hill. Lumina's heavy wooden doors opened, and we entered the stronghold. Though the outer architecture was stone, the inner supports were intricately carved wood. The Aurati marched us to a holding cell near the entrance and locked us in. I watched them walk away with the dragon, ignoring her thrashing from inside the bag. Her cries still echoed in my head after the Aurati's footsteps faded away.

"No!" I went to the door and kicked it. It didn't budge, not that I really expected it to.

Sev let out a harsh, enraged cry. I felt the same.

What would happen to the kit? I was having trouble breathing even thinking about it. It would probably be sent back to the fortress. And Sev—Sev would be turned over too, and all because he had tried to help me.

Time passed. I assumed it did. There was no light in this cell except through the slats in the door, and no movement from the outside. In the darkness Sev's hand found mine, and I held it tightly.

"Sev—" I didn't know what to say.

"It's all right," he said quietly. "It will be all right."

He could not know that.

The dragon kit sang in my head. She was still angry, but no

longer struggling in the same way. Someone had taken her out of the bag. The kit's song grew louder—closer.

"Someone's coming," I said.

The door swung open at last, clanging against the wall. An older Aurat wearing an ornate headdress entered the room. She was carrying the dragon kit.

I stood up, fighting the urge to rush at her—it would only make matters worse. It was difficult to look away from the dragon, as she was squirming in distress, even though the woman was handling her gently. But I raised my head, looking the Aurat in the face—and gasped. I'd seen her features before. She had been in my dreams, speaking prophecies. She was the true seer.

"Leave us," she said. The guards behind her glanced at each other but left the room.

The Aurat stood for a long time in silence.

"You," she said finally, nodding at me. "You're from Ilvera."

There seemed no point in lying anymore. I nodded.

She raised a knife and cut through the bindings around my wrists, freeing my hands. "Come with me," she said, lifting her chin imperiously.

I didn't want to leave Sev. "What about my companion? And the dragon?"

She looked down at the dragon in her arms almost as though she'd forgotten she was holding it. "The dragon will come with us, if you cooperate. And your prince will be here when you return."

The prince. They knew who he was.

"Why should I trust you?" I said.

The Aurat made an impatient sound. "Do you think you truly have a choice in the matter?"

I had a choice. I could refuse, until they threatened Sev or the dragon. But she was right—I wouldn't choose to see them hurt. I moved reluctantly. The Aurat rapped smartly on the door, which opened before us. Sev watching after me desolately was the last thing I saw before the door swung shut again. We walked into Lumina's depths, through hallways and down staircases until I had no hope of finding a way out without help. After what seemed like forever, we stopped at another room.

I held my breath, bracing myself as the Aurat opened the door.

CHAPTER TWENTY

Kaia.

Kaia in initiate's robes. Kaia thinner than I remembered. The tumult of thoughts in my head was dizzying, but there she was, before me—the same as ever, and not the same at all. She looked up, flew across the room, flung herself into my arms. Our lips met in a passionate kiss, and for one precious moment everything stood still and I was home.

The world crept slowly back into my consciousness. I pulled back reluctantly, raising my hand to touch her cheek. Holding her was exactly as I remembered, and we were both crying as we embraced. "Are you all right?" I said, slipping into Verran. "I've been so worried!"

She shook off my concerns. "I'm fine, but you! I thought you would never leave the mountain! How did you get a *dragon?*" To that there was no good answer, not in this room. I only buried my face in her hair once more, highly aware that I didn't smell anywhere near as good as she did. Only a cough from the Aurat returned us to our senses.

"I brought you here because I need your help," the Aurat said.

Kaia stepped back from me, but held my hand. "Listen to her," she whispered.

I tried to make my shoulders relax, though my first impulse was to snatch the dragon from the Aurat's arms and strike her.

The Aurat set the dragon down on the floor. She ran to me and curled herself around my leg, and I picked her up, cuddling her against me. She was shaking, terrified. So was I, though holding her restored a fraction of my balance.

The Aurat then took off her headdress. Underneath it her hair was thin and gray, despite the fact that she couldn't have been much older than my own mother. "I am the Prophet," she said. "Every Aurati prophecy passes through me."

I looked at Kaia. "Is that true?"

Kaia squeezed my hand. "Yes. I've seen it."

The world was shifting under my feet, and I didn't know how it would settle. I'd had an inkling—a revelation—but that was nowhere near the same as having it confirmed. I was face-to-face with the Aurati Prophet. The only one.

I looked back at the Aurat. "What about the seers who make the pilgrimages?"

She waved off my question. "They get the prophecies from me. Besides, do you really think every one of those prophecies is true?"

I thought of my own prophecy: fire. Had it even been true? Or had they just told me something that would be easy to claim had been fulfilled?

The Prophet continued. "My time is waning. I've been dreaming for years of my successor. A girl from Ilvera. When the seers came to your village, they thought that Kaia was the one. But she has been found . . . incompatible. As time went on, I realized I saw someone else passing through my visions. You."

"*What?*" I was flabbergasted. Both that Kaia could have been found wanting in any way—something I found almost unimaginable—and that they would want *me* for anything. "You're wrong."

The Prophet put her fingers to her temples, rubbing in small circles. "I assure you there has been no mistake. You have the ancient gift of dragon dreams. I've been waiting for someone like you to appear for many years."

Me. The sheer magnitude of what she was saying was only just beginning to sink in. In a flash I saw what might have been— me ripped from my parents' arms, escorted down the mountain, brought here, to this stone tower, and . . . I didn't know what. I would never have met Sev. Or Neve. Or the dragon. "Why didn't you see this from the beginning?" I said artlessly, not quite expecting a reply. "If it was me, why didn't you know?"

"Perhaps when I first had the vision, it wasn't you in it. Perhaps you were not ready. People's fates are constantly shifting. You'll learn that here. But you have been called now."

There was a strange, slanted way in which that made sense. The person I had been in Ilvera was so different from who I was now.

"And you want me to be . . . the next prophet?"

She nodded. "It's necessary."

I hated the way she said it. The dragon's claws pricked my skin, sparking courage.

"Necessary for who? You stole Kaia from me. And now you want me as well?" I didn't want to be an Aurati seer. I had grown up despising everything about them. They were the emperor's minions, and to be forced to join them now, after everything I had seen and done . . . The thought repulsed me.

The Prophet looked at me, a sad, pitying expression on her face. "You came to Lumina to get your heartmate back. There is no reason why you cannot complete your quest. Submit, and both your companions and the dragon will be released."

Kaia and Sev free. The dragon kit safe. In exchange for my life. "Why should I trust a word you say?"

"The Prophet never lies," Kaia said. "She can't. It's tied to her power."

Kaia's words didn't sit well with me. Was she actually suggesting that I take the Prophet's offer, even if it meant we would be separated again? I didn't know if I could bear it.

"I want to talk to Kaia," I said. "If this is as important as you say, you'll leave us be."

The Prophet looked long at us, considering. "Fine," she said. "But soon this offer will expire. I will not make it again."

She swept out of the room, closing the door behind her. I didn't need to hear the lock click to know I wasn't leaving unescorted.

I turned to Kaia. "Are you well?"

Kaia's eyes rested on the dragon. "Yes, I . . . They've treated me well."

"But I had dreams about you," I said. "They were hurting you."

She bit her lip and looked away. "They were trying to make the power come," she said. So they had hurt her here. I would destroy every single person who'd had a hand in it.

She suddenly held her own hand out. "Can I touch it?"

"The dragon?" I smiled. "Of course." The kit was still clinging to me, but she made no objection as Kaia tentatively brushed her fingers along the ridge of her spine.

"She's a girl," I said. It was so good to speak Verran again—I'd forgotten how much smoother the words felt on my tongue.

"And you," she said. "What happened to you?"

"I came to rescue you," I said helplessly.

Unexpectedly, her eyes filled with tears. "You really came here for me?"

"Kaia, how could I not?"

She leaned over and pressed her forehead to mine, and I could feel the tremor that ran through her. She wasn't well, no matter what she said.

"Tell me the truth. What will happen if I refuse?"

She closed her eyes. "They've told me that a true prophet is rare. If you are one, they'll never let you leave. They'll force it on you even if you refuse. They might kill me to punish you, or . . . torture me to make you comply."

I took a deep, shuddering breath. "What about if I agree? Will they let you leave?"

She nodded without hesitation. "The Prophet never lies," she said. "That's true. But Maren—I can't leave."

"What do you mean?" I asked.

Indecision flickered over her face and was gone. "I mean, I can't leave you. You are here because of me. I can't let you face *that* alone."

"Kaia, if I do this, you *have* to get out. I can't take the chance they'll change their mind later. I've heard what they do to initiates who aren't deemed suitable."

Kaia shook her head.

Tangled webs upon tangled webs. I sat down, letting my head fall against my hands. I had come to Lumina to rescue Kaia. In all my imaginings I had never thought that *I* would have something the Aurati would value . . . something that Kaia lacked.

I looked up. She had sat down next to me, her long hair braided severely. She was staring down at the dragon, an unfamiliar expression on her face—longing?

"What happened when they brought you here?" I said.

"There's not nearly enough time for that story now."

"Did you try to escape?"

She looked away from me. "Yes," she said softly. But it was tentative, qualified by something she wasn't telling me.

I hesitated a moment before I took her hand in mine. Strange that I had spent so long with her as my guiding coordinate only to be afraid to finally touch her. "Kaia. What happened?"

"I tried to escape. I did," Kaia said, her voice quivering. "But maybe I gave up too easily. Try to understand, Maren. They said I was *special*, and I was. At least, I thought I was. And then you came all this way; you—you're the prophesied one, a *hero*—"

"I'm not much of a hero," I said bitterly. "I made a mess of so many things. You have no idea."

"But you must have done so many things to make it here with a dragon. Things I could only imagine." There was an unfamiliar tone in her voice. Was it surprise? Admiration? "They're different than we thought, you know," she continued. "The Aurati are powerful, but they're not monsters. They do important work. Lumina is a sanctuary for any girl in the empire who desires to come here—girls with no other opportunity to reach so high!"

"How can you say that?" I asked. "This is no sanctuary. They *kill* the girls who don't pass their tests. They're spies for the tyrant. They terrorize our people."

"They *are* our people!" Kaia cried. "Some of them, anyway. Not everything is so simple, Maren."

My voice trembled. "They ripped you out of my arms. Are you saying you would stay with *them?*"

"I don't know what else to tell you. As an Aurat, I could have the life I always dreamed of. I could see the empire. I could take care of my mothers!"

I felt sick. What had happened to her here? As much as Zefed had changed me over my journey, Lumina had changed her. Dimmed her light to a pale echo of what it once had been. The Aurati had bruised her, beaten her down—there was no other explanation for what I was hearing. And I wanted to burn them all for it.

There was a knock on the door. The Prophet reentered the room. "Well?"

I stood up, not looking at Kaia. "I'll do it. On condition that they go free. *All* of them."

"Don't do this," Kaia said. "You don't know what you're promising. I'll be fine."

"And you don't know what you're saying," I replied sharply. "You cannot stay here, after what they've done. I came here to free you, and I will. Whatever it takes, don't you remember?"

"But—"

"Be quiet," the Prophet said. Then she turned to me. "You agree to become the next Aurati Prophet, in exchange for the lives of your heartmates?"

Heartmates? I could not ponder this now. "I do," I said firmly.

"So it shall be."

I took a deep breath. "I want a guarantee."

"By all the power given me, I swear."

That wasn't nearly good enough. But that was all I had.

"Come," the Prophet said. "We have more to do."

I looked at Kaia, who shook her head. "Where you're going, I may not follow. I'm . . . unsuitable."

It was the hardest thing I ever did, peeling the dragon kit from my body and passing her to Kaia, who held her awkwardly as she squirmed. I touched my fingertips to the kit's forehead. *Go with Kaia. She will take care of you.*

I straightened, locking the dragon kit's howls out of my mind. "The boy I came with is named Sev. Make sure the dragon goes to him and no other."

She nodded, tears in her eyes once again. Then she reached out her hand and clasped mine, passing something thin and inflexible between us. When she let go, I opened my hand to find a small silver hair clasp—my own. I'd given it to her the night of the Telling, and she'd kept it. Through everything, she'd kept it.

"Kaia," I whispered, a lump in my throat. "I love you."

Then the Prophet's hand was on my arm, guiding me out of the cell. I slipped the clasp into my pocket. I couldn't bear to look back as the door shut and I left them behind.

"Where are we going?" I said.

"An initiation."

"You can convene the seers so quickly?" Now that I was

committed to this, I couldn't see a reason not to ask the questions that came into my head. It wasn't as though they could do worse to me than what they were already doing.

The Prophet shook her head. "Seer business is the most sacred art of the Aurati, and there is no person in this stronghold more sacred than me." A trace of bitterness crept into her voice. "Secrets must be kept."

"But you're the Prophet. Surely there are junior seers to handle this." Walking the hallways with unwilling initiates seemed a thankless task to me.

"No. This I, alone, must do. Especially considering ... recent events." She was referring, I supposed, to the fact that Kaia had been brought all the way here by the Aurati seers and then been found wanting. Considering that, it made sense that she would not let me out of her sight until the initiation was complete.

We continued to walk. "Why can't any Aurat be the Prophet?" I asked.

She looked at me sideways, considering. "The Prophet must always be a daughter of Ilvera," she said in Verran.

"You were one of the stolen girls?" I couldn't hold back the horror in my voice.

"Yes. All the past Prophets were."

"Then how *could* you? You know Ilvera, our people. How could you aid in the abduction of one of us?"

The Prophet turned her face away from me. "The role of the Prophet is an essential one. The rest of the Aurati will listen to your words and interpret them for the good of the people."

"I thought you couldn't lie," I said, challenging her words.

She paused. "For the good of *some* people," she amended.

"For the good of the empire. And the empire is the people."

"You're Verran. You should know better."

"You're young," the Prophet said. "When you're older, you'll see. Things are not so easy."

Her words—an echo of what Kaia had said—chilled me to the core.

We descended a staircase that spiraled down into the earth. It was as though we were entering another realm as the darkness enveloped us. The Prophet carried no lantern but walked with confidence. I stumbled behind her, edging gingerly down the stairs.

An orange glow emanated from below us, growing brighter as we continued farther down. We finally came to a landing that was solid rock, and I saw that the light was coming through the guard hole in an enormous door that was easily twice my height and longer across. The Prophet withdrew a key from her pocket and unlocked the door, ushering me inside.

We entered a cavern so large the sounds of our footsteps echoed. The walls were high and lit by a fire that burned in a pit in the center of the room, clouding the air with an acrid stench. My nose twitched, and I sneezed. The Prophet said nothing as I took in the tapestries hanging on the walls, the smooth stone floor . . . and on the other side of the cavern, the dark mass that bled shadows over the ground. A dragon.

My jaw dropped. She was enormous, taking up almost half the room, scales so black her body seemed like the absence of something, rather than a presence. My mother's words came flooding back—that sometimes dragon dreams told the future. The prophecies that the Aurati spread must all come from this dragon. *That* was why the prophet had to be a Verran girl. Only Verrans could receive dragon dreams.

The dragon was asleep, but it was restless—her claws trembling, tail twitching. The air was heavy with mirth wood oil tempered with lavender. The trainers in Deletev had used the scent to end the pit fight, and it seemed the Aurati used it for a similar purpose here: to keep her asleep.

"How is this possible?" I breathed.

"It is not for you to ask questions, but to obey," the Prophet said. "You must now bond with the dragon in order to control it and share its dreams."

I shook my head. "You asked me to be the Prophet, not—not to participate in doing harm to a dragon."

"This is what being the Prophet means. And if you do not obey, I will bring the full weight of the Aurati down. Not just on Kaia, or your prince, but on Ilvera, too. Now, stand here." She indicated a platform at the center of the room that stood next to the fire, over which was suspended a small shallow bowl.

I took a step back. I *knew* this place. I turned, trying to imagine what this cavern would look like from different perspectives. In my dream, I had been the *dragon*.

"Come, come," the Prophet said. She nudged me along, and I followed, at a loss for what else to do. In the dream there had been ceremonial words, but that didn't seem to matter to the Prophet, who was moving quickly. There was a cup sitting on top of a plate on the ground. She picked it up and dipped it into the bowl, filling it with a dark, viscous liquid. My eyes were watering from the smoke of the fire. The Prophet handed me the cup. "Drink," she said. "The dragon is old and resistant to more traditional bonding techniques. The bond must be opened with blood."

I stared into the cup. The liquid was hot and smelled a little like metal. I looked again at the dragon, which shifted and sighed in its sleep. Then I brought the cup to my lips and drank.

The hot taste of blood burst over my tongue, and I choked. The Prophet put her hand over my mouth, forcing my lips closed as I tried to spit it out. "*Drink*," she said.

I couldn't I couldn't I couldn't. The blood—dragon blood?—was congealing in my throat, forcing its way up my nose, anywhere but down, and the Prophet's other hand covered my nose. I couldn't speak, couldn't breathe except to swallow and cough—pain across my arm—the Prophet had cut me. My own blood dripped into the fire, and my legs weakened.

The earth shifted beneath my feet, and the world fell away from me.

It was as though I saw the room from a great height. My body was lying prone on the floor, and there was someone standing beside me, looking down. No, not someone—the dragon herself. She lowered her huge head and sniffed at the Prophet, who seemed to be frozen in place, and at my body, and then, surprisingly, she seemed to look right at me—and I fell again into someplace that was completely outside of time. A dream. A memory.

She never knew how the enemy had gotten past the guard. When she woke, it was too late. The men had clouded the air with their overpowering scents. Her limbs and thoughts grew sluggish, and she could not fight or breathe fire—she only waited, weighted down, while they stole her away. Chains over her wings and a rickety wagon—she launched into the air a few times, the wagon bouncing along below her, until she exhausted herself. By the time they reached this infernal place of wood and stone, she had stopped trying to free herself. They broke her, drugged her, until all that was left were the dreams.

Had this dragon *been there*, when the first Flame of the West came to the mountain?

I raised my head to find that we were back in the cavern, everything still frozen around us. The dragon watched me patiently.

A deep, gravelly voice suddenly spoke in my mind. With awe, I realized the dragon was speaking to me. *Now you see. Somehow they knew that without a mother, the other dragons would be lost. They trapped me like this, and I waited a very long time. For you.*

Dragon dreams, Mother had said. And she'd been right. The dragon had called to me the day I'd wept in the ruins, and I'd let her in. We had been intertwined ever since. She was the reason I had heard the dragon songs and experienced those dreams. She had been guiding me the entire time.

Maybe the Prophet had been right too. When the seers came to the mountain, I hadn't been the person they wanted. The person the dragon had needed. But perhaps I was now.

The dragon arched her back and flicked her tail. *You have done well, daughter of dragons. But I am tired. They have kept me like this for so long. My body is old. My head is low.*

"But we need you," I said. "Ilvera needs you. The other dragons need you. You have to wake up."

The dragon blinked slowly. *I am tired,* she repeated.

"I will help you wake, and when the dragons are free, you can sleep."

If I wake, I may burn them all.

Through her, I sensed a river of bubbling fire below the tower of Lumina. Perhaps it had been called from the earth by the dragon when they entombed her here—perhaps it had always been here.

A lifetime ago I had been given a prophecy. The Aurat had looked into my eyes and said one word: fire.

I swallowed. "Then let them burn."

Abruptly I came back into myself.

My throat was scratchy and sore, and I was splayed limply on the ground. My head ached as I pushed myself slowly up into a sitting position. The cavern throbbed with heat, though I couldn't tell whether it was from the fire or the dragon blood I'd been made to swallow.

The Prophet watched me intently. "What did you see?" she said.

I wondered briefly what had happened to her the first time she was brought to this chamber. How much she had struggled. What the dragon had shared with her—and what she had done with that information.

I couldn't tell her what I'd seen.

I had to wake the dragon.

"I . . . it was a little unclear," I said, stalling as I scanned the room. The fire was stoked with wood soaked in mirth wood oil, so the fire had to be put out. There was no water in the cavern, but perhaps I could use the tapestries on the walls. "There was a dragon."

The Prophet frowned. "Did it say anything?"

I had to get to the hangings. I pretended to struggle to my feet, trying to make myself seem more disoriented than I was. I put my hands to my head to mask my roaming gaze.

"She said she's been here a very long time," I said.

The hangings were depictions of the Aurati throughout history, their feats illustrated for posterity. It puzzled me to see them here. Such a display seemed more appropriate for the halls upstairs, where they would be seen every day.

I didn't think the Prophet had a weapon, but neither did I.

I coughed, bending over at the waist. The Prophet moved toward me as though to offer support, and I barreled into her, pushing her against the wall. Then I ran to the far side of the cavern and ripped down the first tapestry, grunting with the effort. I moved on to the next tapestry, and the next.

The Prophet staggered to her feet and ran for the door, where she pulled on a rope I hadn't noticed before. It rang a deep bell so loud that it reverberated through my bones. Then she turned back to me, drawing a long knife, and we faced each other across the fire. "That was a mistake," she said.

"That was the first good thing that's ever been done in this chamber," I replied.

She darted at me. I snatched the heavy plate off the platform and blocked the Prophet's knife jab. Lavender oil ran down my wrist. I twisted away from her second attack, but the blade caught my injured arm, and I yelled in pain.

The Prophet moved toward me, and I grabbed the goblet,

forgotten on the ground, and threw it at her. As she ducked, I hefted the plate in my remaining good hand, then swung it at the side of her head. She staggered on impact—I hit her again, and she dropped to the floor. I spat blood and kicked her in the stomach. My heart was beating fast but not from fear. I had met the mother of dragons, had shared her dreams, and I was strong.

"You wanted me to carry out the dragon's dream. And so I shall." My voice was harsh, full of blood and smoke. "I am waking her."

She coughed and groaned. "You fool! Don't you realize what you are doing?"

"Only what you should have done long ago," I said.

"The empire will suffer for this. The *people* will suffer." But her voice was small and shrill. Everything that had made her intimidating was melting before my eyes. She had meant to make me take her place. Perhaps I still would. Perhaps the power she'd gained from decades of dreaming was now passing to me, for in this moment, I felt invincible.

I leaned over her, speaking softly. "You cannot stop me. If you try, I will kill you." I smashed the bowl down on her dominant arm, and I heard a sickening snap. The Prophet screamed. I bent over and took the knife from her, then tucked it into my belt.

I didn't like turning my back on her, but I had no other choice. I ran from tapestry to tapestry, ripping them from the walls and throwing them on the fire. One tapestry would probably be consumed by the flames, but many might help smother the fire.

The air filled with even more smoke and the scent of mirth

wood and heat and dust. I retreated to the corner of the room farthest from the fire and crouched low to the floor, where the smoke was thinner, my eyes stinging.

I heard footsteps pounding above me. The Aurati guards were coming, and still the dragon slept.

My stomach twisted. I had been so sure that this was the answer. What else could be keeping her asleep besides the remnants of the lavender oil?

The oil. I drew the last vial from my pocket and held it out in the light. Fire root.

The dragon stirred but did not wake as I hurried over to her.

Just as I reached the dragon, the door burst open, and a group of Aurati guards streamed into the cavern.

"There!" shrieked the Prophet from the ground. "Arrest that girl!"

But the guards paused—stopped in their tracks by the sight of the dragon. Not all Aurati knew the secret of the prophecies, it seemed.

Taking advantage of their confusion, I unstoppered the vial and threw it on the stone before the dragon.

Fire and brimstone overwhelmed my senses, and I darted back. If this did not wake the dragon, I feared nothing could.

She moved.

She moved, and it was like a mountain moving, shaking off slumber. Her eyes opened, foggy at first, then brighter and sharper.

She moved, and I had thought I knew how large she was, but now she filled the room like a storm cloud, threatening pandemonium.

"Well met," I whispered.

Behind me, there were more than a few muttered curses.

The dragon blinked and bowed her head to me. *I am in your debt.* She dug her claws into the stone, and it cracked. She tried unfurling her wings, but there wasn't enough room in this cavern for that. She arched her back and stretched and opened her mouth, and when she smiled, it was with deadly fangs.

Come.

I climbed on her back and settled in the groove of her neck, just above her wings. She felt as warm as a furnace.

"Run!" I shouted in Zefedi, knowing that some of the guards might be innocent, misguided initiates. "Get out of here!"

The dragon punctuated my words with a roar of flame, and the guards fled. The entire cavern shook as the dragon stamped her feet, and cracks bloomed up the walls. She raised herself, and I flattened myself as best as I could as I realized what she was about to do.

The dragon lowered her head and aimed a jet of fire at the cavern's massive door, then charged. The heat was all consuming, as though the belly of the earth were splitting open. Rocks broke against our bodies, and the walls shook again, setting off multiple tremors as we climbed the staircase out of the depths of Lumina.

Screams echoed through the halls as we rose. I craned my neck as we passed hallways, trying to count the levels. Which way to Kaia? Which way to Sev? The cell in which they'd held us had been on the first floor, to the right of the gate as we'd entered.

We burst into a grand hall, and I slid off the dragon's

back. She reared up, and my breath caught in my chest. She was nothing short of magnificent. Her armored chest was as wide across as a small house, her scales black as night, and her enormous wings were well muscled and solid, the membranes stretched tight as they unfurled completely. She flapped her wings, creating gusts of wind that nearly knocked me over. She breathed fire, and flames began engulfing the tapestries and walls of the hall.

I turned and ran. I was on the right floor—I was sure. But there were so many halls and so many rooms.

"Kaia!"

The ground shook and I fell. I quickly got up again.

"Maren!"

The heat was building beneath my feet. I turned and dashed back the way I'd come, toward the sounds of Kaia's voice and the dragon kit's panicked song cutting into my mind. The halls were crowded now, Aurati pushing against one another in an attempt to flee the stronghold. I fought past them. I had heard her. I was sure of it. And then—there she was, the dragon kit squirming in her arms.

The dragon leaped into my arms and nestled against me, sneezing as she inhaled the smoke on my clothes.

"How did you get out?"

"The cell wall collapsed," Kaia shouted. "What have you done?"

"I'm getting us out of here!" I shouted back. "Where's Sev?"

Her face fell. "They took him!"

"Who did?"

The ground rumbled beneath our feet, and the dragon kit

shrieked in alarm. I grabbed Kaia's hand. There was no time to explain, no time for anything but to run with her as fast as we could, fighting through the streams of Aurati in the halls.

We burst out of Lumina and through the courtyard. We sprinted until we were in the fields beyond, and only then did we stop and turn. Behind us the stronghold was trembling, on the verge of collapse. Then, without warning, the mother dragon burst through the top of the tower, shattering the sky with splintered wood, stone, and fire.

CHAPTER TWENTY-ONE

W hat is *that?*"
I turned around to see Rowena ben Garret standing
behind me, flanked by a troop of soldiers wearing Oskiath green.

"*That* is a furious dragon," I said. I craned my neck, looking
around her. "Is Sev with you?"

Her gaze fell on me and sharpened. "No—he's not with you?"

Cold tendrils of fear wound around my chest. If Rowena
hadn't taken him—had he been trapped in Lumina? I turned
back to the burning wreckage, searching.

"No," Kaia said. "There were other soldiers here before the
destruction began. They wore Gedarin colors."

So he was alive. I breathed a sigh of relief, but Rowena
cursed.

"Where would they have taken him?" I asked.

"Straight to the emperor," she replied. "The Flame has been
hunting him for years."

An involuntary cry escaped me. It was not difficult to imagine what the emperor would do to the shadow prince of Ruzi.

Rowena had turned back to Lumina. "Maren. Is this what
you came to Lumina to do?"

"More or less," I said. Kaia was gripping my hand tightly, and I was trying to feel comforted by it. But I'd still lost Sev. "But what are you doing here?"

"We came after you and the dragon. We agreed that despite the inconvenience, you were too valuable to let the Aurati keep. Of course, we hoped to get to you before—" She waved a hand vaguely, indicating the ongoing destruction.

"Will you help me now?" I asked. "They can't have gotten far with him."

Rowena looked down. "He's too important for mere soldiers to handle. Once his identity was confirmed, a Talon would have been summoned. He's long gone by now."

"But . . ." I wanted to throw something, to scream until my voice was gone. He couldn't be beyond my reach. He couldn't be *gone*.

Lumina's white walls were crumbling, but that didn't seem to be enough for the mother dragon, who was hovering next to the stronghold and blanketing it in flame. I closed my eyes, reaching out. *I need your help.*

I wasn't sure she would hear me, but after a moment she peeled away from Lumina and flew toward us. The soldiers scattered, and I was left standing alone as the dragon descended and landed, shaking the earth. I didn't blame them. She was a creature to be reckoned with.

She sniffed as she peered down at the dragon kit, who looked up at her without a hint of fear, and something suddenly occurred to me.

"Forgive me, great one," I said. "I should have asked before. What name may I call you by?"

A wisp of smoke escaped the dragon's mouth, and she made a satisfied sound. *Your kind may call me Naava.*

"Naava." I swallowed, well aware of our audience. "One of my own was taken today. Will you help me find him?"

Yes, she said. *To repay the debt I owe you, I will help you find your companion.*

She bowed her head, allowing me to scramble onto her back once more. I positioned the dragon kit in front of me so that I could keep a hand on her—I could not allow her to fall.

I held out a hand to Kaia. "Come with me," I said.

She took a step back, shaking her head. There was a shadow over her, the girl I'd first fallen in love with. "I'll wait for you here."

"Kaia. Take my hand." This time my words were firm, leaving no room for argument.

She moved reluctantly, but she came, perching timidly behind me and wrapping her arms around my waist.

"We'll send word once we find him, so you can meet us," I called to Rowena. Before she could argue, Naava bent her legs and launched off the ground, and we were in the air.

Flying was an entirely different sensation from the dash we'd had in the bowels of Lumina. Flying was the rush of wind around us, the feeling of weightlessness. Flying was the sun on my face and the open sky ahead and the sensation of falling without fear of the ground. Flying was freedom. Kaia's grip tightened around me.

The land receded below us, and I looked around. Lumina was completely destroyed, its white stone tarnished. Some Aurati had gotten out—but not all. There was no hiding this. The emperor would consider this an act of war.

I'd only sought to rescue Kaia. But what I'd uncovered and done was so much greater. Naava was awake, and free. But what would happen once she returned to Ilvera? She had spoken of her weariness, her age. Was she like Neve and the Prophet—unable to die without a successor to take her place?

The dragon kit mewled plaintively, and I tucked my chin over her head. "Not yet," I told her. She wasn't ready to fly, not at this height.

I searched the roads as we flew, looking for any sign of a military party. Whenever panic began to rise in my chest, I reminded myself that Sev wasn't dead. The emperor would want him alive first, to bleed out of him all the schemes and information to which he was privy. I had found Kaia in time. I had to believe that we would find him, too.

Naava climbed higher, and as I turned to look over my shoulder, I saw movement in the distant sky. Two Talons were streaking toward us.

Kaia must have seen them too, because she stiffened against me. But I just smiled.

I was Maren ben Gao Vilna, daughter of Ilvera and of dragons. Fire was in my blood, and I would not rest until the dragons and those I loved were free of the tyrant. Let them try to stop me—I was ready.

ACKNOWLEDGMENTS

It is impossible to name everyone who had a hand in this book, so I apologize in advance for the inadequate nature of the following.

Thank you to my agent, Rebecca Podos, who said, "Why don't we make it official?" on our first Skype call and kicked off the start of a wonderful partnership. You are exceptional.

To Catherine Laudone, whose keen editorial eye made this book much better than I thought it would be. Thank you to the entire Simon & Schuster BFYR team, including Justin Chanda, Milena Giunco, Lili Feinberg, Katrina Groover, Emily Hutton, Chloë Foglia and cover artist Olivier Ponsonnet, whose work first made me sit back and think, *Wow, that's going to be a book.* An author may be the public face of a book, but its existence is the culmination of the efforts of so many.

To the early readers of *Shatter the Sky*, who helped it grow from nothing into a vaguely book-shaped thing: Greg Batcheler, Heather Goss, Clarissa Hadge, and Kate Mikell. Thank you to Mackenzi Lee, for fielding every panicked question I have without telling me I'm ridiculous.

To everyone at the Madcap Creating Worlds retreat, especially Natalie C. Parker, Tessa Gratton, Roshani Chokshi, Dhonielle Clayton, Julie Murphy, and Tara Hudson. Your wisdom is infinite and you shared it so generously. This book might not have been a book without you.

Thank you to my family—we are weird, just as we should be. To Koda, who will always be the very best.

And to Martin—you told me that one day you would be drinking a cup of coffee at the back of a bookstore while I launched my first book. You were right.

Turn the page for a sneak peek at
Storm the Earth,
the epic conclusion to Maren's story.

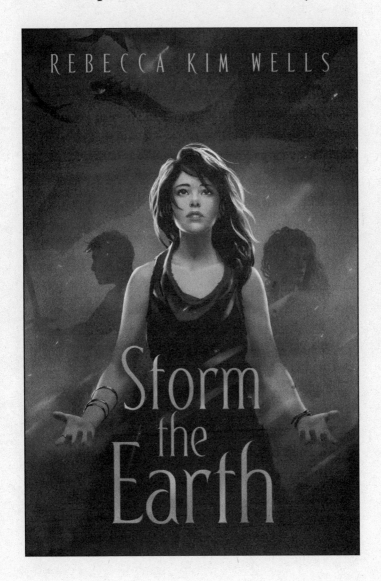

MAREN

Naava roared, her cry reverberating through my entire body. I turned my head just enough to see the sky we'd left behind. The Talons were gaining on us.

"Can you outfly them?" I called to Naava. I'd hoped these Talons would land to investigate the wreckage of Lumina—instead they had bypassed the ruins entirely once they had seen us flying in the distance. And for all my bravado, I did not know how to confront a battle-ready Talon or their dragon. It had been mostly luck that I'd escaped those I *had* encountered.

Naava extended her wings to their full span, taking in an enormous breath. *You must hold on. I haven't carried your kind in some time.*

Hold on? I wrapped my arms as far around her neck as I could, hunching forward to keep the dragon kit tucked between our bodies. She squeaked in protest, digging her claws into my shirt. I called to Kaia, "She says to hold on!"

Whatever reply Kaia might have given was lost to the wind, but her arms tightened around me—just in time, as Naava swooped low, and my stomach lurched. The height that had seemed glorious only minutes before turned terrifying. If I lost my grip—I didn't even want to think about it.

Glancing back, I saw that the two Talons had halted their approach, their dragons' wings beating just enough to keep them aloft. The wind shifted, and I caught a whiff of fire root . . . and saltwater pearl. The Talons had instructed the dragons to wait. But why?

Instead of taking the opportunity to flee, Naava made a sharp turn—and shot directly toward them!

Kaia gasped, and I grabbed the kit just as she started to slide off Naava's neck. *What are you doing?* I cried.

Naava ignored me, and I tried to control my growing panic as we drew closer to the Talons. The only thing keeping my breathing steady was that despite our approach, the dragons made no move to attack. It suddenly occurred to me—the Talons were accustomed to hunting creatures on land. There were few things that could threaten a dragon, and none that could take to the air. And with all dragons in Zefed under the emperor's control, these Talons had never fought against one of their own before. They didn't know what to do any more than I did.

Naava pulled up just a few feet from the Talons' dragons, her great wings flapping. The Talons were dressed in identical black uniforms with leather armor and helmets, bandoliers strapped diagonally across their torsos. We were close enough that I could see the confusion on their faces. These Talons must have been told to investigate the disturbance at Lumina, but it was clear no one had warned them about an enormous dragon wreaking havoc upon the land.

I glanced at the dragons. They both had dark green scales, though one had a longer tail than the other. On the ground, they would have been at least twice my height. But compared to Naava, they seemed small. Neither of them carried cargo large enough to be human. My heart plummeted. Sev must be long gone, then.

One of the Talons raised an arm and shouted across the sky. "You have stolen the property of His Beloved Grace, the Flame of the West. Surrender the dragon!"

Naava roared in anger, and I almost laughed. How could they possibly think that *I* was the one in control? Of course, a Talon would have no other way to understand what they saw— the concept of a free dragon was entirely foreign to them.

"Dragons are not property!" I shouted back in Zefedi. "And those dragons have been held in captivity for long enough!"

I nudged Naava with a thought. *They don't have Sev. We should leave while we still can.*

No, she replied. *They smell wrong. They are all—wrong.*

She roared again, letting out a furious jet of fire, and the other dragons finally retaliated, their flames cutting so close I felt the heat against my neck as Naava flapped her wings, taking us high and out of their reach. I barely had time to flatten myself against Naava's back before she folded her wings and entered a steep dive toward the Talons. The scent of fire root was strong around us, but as Naava spun through the air, I saw the dragons hesitate.

Kaia screamed as we cut through the space between the Talons, and then we were behind them. Naava banked in a tight turn as the dragons wheeled to face us. She was faster than them, and nimbler, too. The Talons fumbled with their bandoliers, reaching for new vials of oil.

My children! Naava roared.

The dragons' heads snapped toward us. And then Naava sang.

The kits at the fortress had sung in quiet, burbling tones

that could be explained away as an uncanny wind by those who worked at the fortress. Even the yearlings had sung in their sleep, their soft voices ringing only in my ears. But Naava's song now was furious, an elemental shriek that crashed through the air. To most humans, I imagined that her song must sound painful—a ferocious battle cry. But I could hear the melody, and the sorrow and urgency layered throughout. There was no Verran equivalent of this song, but I understood what she was doing. She was pleading with the other dragons.

Their gazes followed Naava as she dipped in the air and brought us nearer. I was close enough to see the Talons' shocked faces below their helmets—and then I watched as the dragons' heads tipped curiously to one side. The Talons reared back, yanking at their reins, and the dragons bucked in midair and refocused, baring their fangs and spitting fire. Naava snapped her wings closed and dove as a plume of fire rushed into the piece of sky we had just occupied. She pulled out of the dive so quickly my breath caught in my chest. My arms were burning with the strain of holding on as Naava burst upward again, arrowing straight back toward the Talons.

They split in opposite directions this time, and Naava tore after the dragon with the shorter tail. The dragon kit was pressed rigidly against my chest. Kaia's arms squeezed viselike around my waist, forcing my breath higher and shallower.

We pulled up next to the dragon. The Talon's eyes widened in fear as Naava whipped her tail to the side, striking the Talon across the chest.

She tumbled from the saddle, but her arm tangled in the dragon's reins as she fell, yanking her body to a halt. She cried out in pain as she dangled. The dragon roared and swerved, its head dragged down by the weight. Naava beat her wings, and we rose higher in the air. She was preparing for another dive.

A movement caught my eye, and I turned my head just as the second dragon slammed into us, striking at Naava with its claws.

The sky went sideways. For a moment we hung in the air, weightless—and then we were falling.

I clung to Naava as my head filled with the dizzying image of the ground rising up to meet us. Kaia screamed, and I closed my eyes. For one—two—three breaths we tumbled. Then Naava's wings spread, catching a gust of wind and sending us into a glide.

My hands were shaking with cold and adrenaline, but my relief was cut short by the warm, metallic scent of blood. I looked down—the dragon kit was all right. Her blue scales had grayed around the edges, but she wasn't crying. Kaia's arms remained locked around my waist. I turned, trying to see her face.

"Are you hurt?" I asked.

"No," she said, pressing her cheek into my shoulder.

That was good. But Naava was flying unevenly, her left wing less than fully extended. It was difficult to see against her black scales, but there was a gash above her elbow joint and blood welling up from the wound.

We had to get to the ground. I looked around. The Talon was busy attempting to help her comrade back into her saddle, which bought us some time. But soon they would recover, and I did not want to contemplate our chances against them now that Naava was hurt.

Naava seemed to disagree. Despite her unsteady wings, she circled us back toward the Talons. She drew in a deep breath, and I could feel her body expanding. Then she opened her mouth and let out a column of flame so large that it engulfed the dragons and their Talons.

Human screams and the scent of burning flesh filled the air. The dragons dove down, taking the Talons with them. I expected Naava to follow, but it seemed that she had used most of her strength with this attack. Her breathing was hitched and shallow, the flap of her wings increasingly erratic. Instead of swooping after the Talons to finish what she had started, she turned carefully in the air and kept us at a good distance. The Talons were badly burned, but the dragons' injuries looked minor—it seemed that dragons weren't so sensitive to fire.

You have been held by human hands too long, she called to the dragons. *Come with me!*

The dragons startled. It was as though they had never heard one of their own speak before. Perhaps they hadn't. Before Naava, I'd only ever heard a dragon sing.

Despite her exhaustion, Naava was entreating them to join her. There was nothing holding them back now—the wounded Talons were too weak to control them. All the dragons had to do was throw off their riders and follow. But when Naava turned in wobbly circles, looking over her shoulder, the dragons did not come. They simply watched her, as if entranced.

The dragon kit shivered. I suddenly realized that the air around us had cooled, and clouds were rolling in. We were losing height, despite Naava's determination. She would not be able to fly for much longer, no matter what else came our way.

"We have to go!" I shouted aloud.

No! Naava snapped. *I will not leave them.*

But she was done—I knew it as she let out another flame

that was more spark than fire. She gave a long, mournful cry.

You're losing strength. We have to get to safety! I pleaded with her.

At first I thought she would refuse to leave. But at last she turned away, leaving the Talons injured and the dragons in a haze as we fled.

The clouds quickly obscured the sky behind us as Naava flew low over Belat Forest. Landing in the forest would be ideal, as the trees would provide shelter and disguise our presence. I cast my gaze to the ground, searching for a safe spot. Naava was listing lower and lower.

"There!" I pointed to a small clearing carved out of the trees. Man-made or natural, I saw no other option. Naava took my direction without hesitation.

We swooped down, narrowly avoiding the trees that hemmed in the clearing. Naava landed heavily, and the impact jarred me to my bones. The dragon kit leaped to the ground. I followed, folding into a graceless heap as my legs collapsed. Kaia slid down last. She staggered toward us and dropped down next to me, resting her head on my shoulder. Relieved of her passengers, Naava folded her wings and settled down into a mountainous coil, closing her eyes and letting out a gusty sigh.

The dragon kit nestled into my free side, and I looked up. My view of the sky was ringed by the towering pine trees that surrounded us. There was not a sound in the forest beside our labored breathing. We had survived. My arms were too heavy to lift and my legs were shaking and my back ached with the strain of having lain across Naava's body, but we had survived.

My vision blurred and I closed my eyes, giving in to my exhaustion and the waiting darkness.

SEV

I woke suddenly, surfacing from a pool of murky, dreamless sleep into—darkness.

I was lying on a cold stone floor. What little light there was fell in through a sliver of a window high up the wall and gave no hint as to the time of day. It was deadly quiet. I tried to remain calm as I took stock of the situation, but my heart was racing. I was alive and mostly uninjured, though there was a sharp pain in the back of my head as I shifted. I reached up gingerly to touch the area, and my fingers came away sticky.

What—? Memory flooded me. Maren. Lumina. The Aurati handing me over to the soldiers, who had called down Talons to transport me to—

Gedarin. The heart of the empire.

This dungeon had no identifying features, but the emperor would not chance losing me now that he had me in his grasp. And the emperor almost never left his court in Irrad these days. Which meant that he must be there now, and, therefore, so was I.

I forced my breathing into a controlled rhythm. Irrad, the capital of Gedarin. I'd been here once, a long time ago—before my father's death, my brother's treason against the emperor, my mother—I shook off those thoughts. I'd been a child, but there were still details stamped into my memories. The way footsteps echoed on the glass floor of the receiving chamber. The endless hallways of burnt black stone, the eerily white walls. The smell of the Flame's coffee in the morning, dark, bitter. I'd hated the place even then. And it would likely be the last city I ever set foot in.

I pushed myself to a sitting position and then slowly got to my feet, grimacing as aches and bruises made themselves known. I stretched slowly, trying to ignore the pounding in my head. There was a mat against the wall that stank of decay, and a bucket in the corner for relieving myself. I should have counted myself lucky. Prisoners enjoying the emperor's hospitality weren't even guaranteed a room free of carnivorous beasts, and at least I had that luxury.

I turned and saw that the front of the cell was a wall of iron bars, through which I could see the hallway and into the cells opposite mine. Every last one was empty.

It couldn't be a coincidence that there was no one else here. The emperor of Zefed was a vengeful tyrant. There was no world in which his dungeons were unpopulated—unless he had moved his prisoners to keep me solitary . . . or executed them.

It was disheartening that both scenarios seemed equally likely. So there was no one here, and nothing to do but wait.

I sat down on the mat and quickly concluded that the floor was a better option, despite the damp. I lay on my back and began to count the stones in the ceiling. Somewhere above me was the sky, the sun, the world. I thought of Maren. Had she succeeded in her quest to save Kaia? She'd looked so frightened the last time I'd seen her, following the Aurati Prophet, but so resolute. And me? I had fallen directly into the trap that had been set for me. I shouldn't have—

Shouldn't have what? Trusted Maren? Following her lead

was what had brought me here, but what else could I have done? What other path could I possibly have taken, from the moment I had grasped her hand and run through the streets of Deletev? What other choice could I have made from the moment I had seen her with the dragon kit, from the moment she had smiled at me for the first time, sunlight filtering through her hair?

My breath hitched, and I tried to think of something—anything—else. Dwelling on my past actions would accomplish nothing. Besides, my head was starting to throb with pain, and despite my best efforts, my eyes drifted closed.

When I woke again, I found that a bowl had been pushed through the bars while I slept. Though it was disappointing not to have seen the guard, my stomach rumbled at the prospect of food. I picked up the bowl—watery rice, a scoop of unseasoned vegetables floating on top of the broth. The thought of poison flickered through my mind, though I dismissed it quickly. The Flame of the West wouldn't kill me quietly, poisoning me somewhere deep in the bowels of his empire. He had captured the shadow prince of Ruzi, the bane of his existence. He would put my execution on display. The only question was *when*.

So I ate, and then I slept some more, on and off. I saw the guard who delivered my next meal, a tall man who had doubtless been chosen for his uncanny impersonation of a stone statue. I didn't even attempt to talk to him.

My legs cramped if I sat too long in one position, so I stretched them out one at a time. I traced the grooves between the stones with my fingertips. A strange, numbing calmness settled over me like a mantle, shielding me from the fear I knew was waiting. Now what I felt most was regret. I was beyond the reach of anyone who could possibly help me. I would never avenge my mother. I would never tell Maren the depth of my feelings for her, or see the dragon kit grow. The Flame of the West had me now, and I could see nothing in my future but death.

What a pathetic waste.

The next time I woke, the emperor was standing on the other side of the bars.

There was nothing to be gained in feigning sleep—he'd only kick me awake. I sat up. For a moment we stared at each other, the torchlight from the hall illuminating our faces. He was about my height but more solidly built, his black hair hanging in a straight curtain down his back. He was a few years older than my brother Callum, which put him in his midthirties. Rafael, emperor of Zefed, Flame of the West. The last time I'd seen him, he had newly inherited the throne, and my family had been just another of the other four royal families of Zefed.

He wasn't dressed in court attire—the only signs of his position were the circlet of gold he wore and the three guards flanking him. I longed to rip that circlet from his head, to squeeze his throat until his face mottled purple and his legs gave out. To take the sword from his belt and—

"Vesper Severin Avidal. The shadow prince of Ruzi, before me at last." His voice was rich and melodious. A deception, like the rest of him.

I flinched at the sound of my full royal name. I hadn't used it since leaving Ruzi, and hearing the emperor speak it was almost unbearable.

I rose to my feet, my limbs shaking as I approached the bars.

For the last ten years this day had haunted me, no matter the lengths I'd gone to escape it. I had dreamed of every scenario, imagined the weight of the sword in my hand, the dragon I would ride, the look on his face as I cut him down—but now the day was here, and I was no avenger, alight with fury. It was over.

Still, I would not give him the satisfaction of seeing me cower.

"Come to kill me?" I said.

"You've been a thorn in my side for too long," he said, his gaze cold. "The little prince of Ruzi. The rest of your family was so easy to dispose of, but you've managed to elude me for years. So you can imagine my surprise when I learned that you'd gone to Lumina. Were you *trying* to get yourself captured?"

When I didn't answer, he continued. "I should kill you, but I find myself curious. You see, I know you've been running around my empire with the Dragons—such a grandiose name for such a pitiful band of traitors. Still, there are a few details I believe you could provide."

The emperor nodded to the guards, who unlocked the bars and entered the cell. Two of them grabbed me by the arms, pinning me between them as the emperor came to stand over me.

"What makes you think I'll tell you anything?" I spat.

Rafael grinned, his teeth glinting in the dim light. "You may be the shadow prince of Ruzi, but that title means nothing within these walls."

He raised his hand, beckoning to someone behind him in the hall. I hadn't noticed her before—a woman wearing healer's robes.

Oh no.

"I'll make this easy for you," Rafael said. "I'm going to ask you questions. If you lie to me, I will break your fingers, one by one. After that, we'll start cutting them off. If you tell the truth, you get to keep them. Do we have an understanding?"

What an enticing offer. I managed to shrug under the weight of the guards' hands on my shoulders. "Seems like I don't have much of a choice."

The healer handed an open vial to the emperor, who passed it to the third guard. I smelled the metallic slick of Brika's kiss, the truth serum used for interrogation back at the dragon fortress. My pulse quickened. I had practiced counteracting Brika's kiss, but that had been droplets in water, not an entire vial of it.

The guard pinched my nostrils shut with one gloved hand and pushed the vial against my lips with the other. I considered resisting, but to what end? They would break my fingers and drug me anyway. Resigned, I opened my mouth and drank. The viscous liquid slid slowly down my throat, and I shuddered as I swallowed, my vision immediately swimming.

My head lolled back, and I sank to my knees. With my eyes closed, the world sounded like I was listening to it from underwater. The healer's voice drifted by, out of focus.

Fingers snapped in front of my face. "Open your eyes."

I slowly opened my eyes. The light was glaring at first, but it dimmed as I blinked. They were still here, around me. I could feel the guards' hands pushing me down. My fingers were tingling, my breathing echoing in my head.

"Vesper. Who is the girl who traveled with you to Lumina?"

Maren. So easy to let the name slip, but there was something holding me back. Relief, perhaps. If he was asking me that, perhaps he didn't know about the kit, or Maren's abilities.

"No one," I said, the words muffled to my ears. "Picked her up on the road in Eronne." I ground out the lie, every word so heavy it required extraordinary effort to push past my lips.

The emperor snorted and looked to one of the guards. There was a snapping sound and my hand was on fire—I cried out, my vision blurring as I fell forward before the guards pulled me back upright. I didn't want to look but couldn't stop my head from turning. My finger was still attached, but it was bent back at an unnatural angle. Tera's bones, the guard had *broken my finger*. I swallowed hard, trying to focus. "Losing your nerve?" I taunted, hoping to sound braver than I felt.

Rafael just laughed. "Don't test me again, Vesper. Now tell me, what's the girl's name?"

I breathed out slowly, pretended to weigh the punishment in my head. Sweat beaded on my forehead as I opened my mouth, preparing to lie. "Senna," I said, managing not to choke on the name.

"What do you know of her?"

Sweat was dripping into my eyes now, trickling down my chest, despite the damp, cold air of the cell. "Barely anything." My heart was beating faster, faster, faster—how much longer could I withstand the serum?

"You're lying," he said. "You two were spotted together outside of Deletev. I know all about the girl Maren—how she arrived at the dragon fortress *and* how she left."

No. The pain in my hand intensified, and my ears started ringing. He knew about Maren, and if he knew that, he must know where she came from. Ilvera wasn't safe—did Maren know?

I swallowed down the bile coming up in my throat. "I don't understand. Why are you asking me questions to which you know the answers?"

Rafael brushed the question aside. "Was she working with you from the beginning?"

He knew I had lied already, so what answer would be safest?

"She was my partner." The words flowed without hesitation—technically, it wasn't a lie. We had indeed been partners . . . after escaping the dragon fortress. And if he thought that Maren had only been my accomplice, then perhaps he wouldn't look further at what she had been doing.

Maren. Her hands on my skin. The fierceness of her expression as she faced down the Talons. The tenderness she had shown when she spoke about Kaia. The way she laughed when she gave herself permission to.

Rafael loomed over me. "Is she an Aurat?"

"No. I don't think so," I said.

"Then who told you about the dragon?"

My eyebrows furrowed in unfeigned confusion. "What dragon?"

He couldn't be asking about the kit. The source of the dragon egg was obvious.

Another lance of fire—another broken finger. I shouted in pain. Rafael grabbed my face in one hand and forced my head up. "Look at me," he snapped. "How did you know about the dragon?"

"I don't know what dragon you're talking about," I said wearily.

It was the unvarnished truth, and the words came so easily that he must have believed me. He stepped back and nodded to the guards. They dropped me, and I hissed in pain as I fell forward onto my injured hand.

The emperor crouched before me and yanked me up by my shirt so that I could see nothing else but his face, which was twisted with rage. "You are only as valuable to me as the information you provide. If you expect to stay alive, you'll cooperate when next we meet."

Then he was gone. The healer knelt by my side. "This will hurt. Here—bite down." She handed me a leather strap.

I wanted to joke but couldn't catch my breath. Instead I put the strap between my teeth and bit as she took my injured hand and did something that sent white pain searing across my brain—

The healer was the only person left in the cell when I came to my senses again. She had set my fingers and splinted them against the others while I was insensible. She must have done something else, too—given me medicine, or performed an incantation—because the pain had lessened somewhat, though I expected it would soon return in full force. Now she was occupied packing away her supplies.

"What dragon is he talking about?" I asked, my voice sounding hoarse. I pushed myself into a seated position with some difficulty.

She barely looked at me. "Try and get some rest."

"But—"

"Take care of those fingers," she said firmly, cutting me off. "You'll need your strength."

How ridiculous, that she was advising me on best healing practices *here*, in the emperor's dungeon. I laughed mirthlessly as she left the cell, then leaned back against the wall, reviewing the interrogation in my mind. Something had happened with a dragon, or *to* a dragon—that much was clear. And there had been a strange, desperate undertone to his questions. *Fear*, I realized. The Flame of the West was afraid.

I smiled. Perhaps there was something to hope for after all.